NO TIME *for*
DUPLICITY

A Psychological Thriller

D.J. Ciccarello

ISBN: 979-8-9898435-6-5 (E-Book)

ISBN: 979-8-9898435-7-2 (Paperback)

ISBN: 979-8-9898435-8-9 (Hardcover)

Library of Congress Control Number: 2025900261

This book is a work of fiction. Names, characters, businesses, places, events, locales, organizations, and incidents are either products of the author's imagination or used in a fictitious manner. Any resemblance to actual persons, living or dead, is entirely coincidental.

For more information contact: https://www.djciccarello.com

Published by D.J. Ciccarello
Atlanta, GA, USA

Also by D.J. Ciccarello

Boys Like Kevin

The Lucky Chip

No Time for Duplicity

To the truth hidden within us all.

"Each of us is born with a box of matches inside us but we can't strike them all by ourselves."

— Laura Esqivel

Preface

du.plic.i.ty

1. The contradictory doubleness of thought, speech, or action.
2. The quality or state of being double or twofold.

Duplicity comes from the Latin word "double" or "twofold." Its original meaning in English is a deception in which one intentionally hides true feelings or intentions behind false words or actions. If one is being duplicitous, there are two of them: the falsehood showing and the truth hidden. The key to the idea of duplicity is one hides in order to make people believe something that is not true.

1

ABSOLUTION

(Tuesday the 10th)

Parker Grant scanned the sprawling cityscape, the past week's chaos finally settling into something manageable. Twenty-six floors below, Midtown stretched out like a meticulously arranged chessboard—streets precise, avenues intersecting in clean, deliberate lines. The rigid order of it all steadied him. Yet beneath the city's orderly surface, a quiet dissonance lingered—elusive, but impossible to ignore.

The morning light streamed through the high-rise windows, carving sharp angles of gold against the pristine white walls. It bathed Parker in warmth as he sipped his coffee. He drew a deep breath and exhaled slowly, soaking in and savoring the serenity after a week of madness.

With a final glance at the city below, Parker stepped away from the floor-to-ceiling glass, his movements as precise as the lines of the sleek modern furniture that filled his condo. He passed the thick crystal Baccarat bowl on the kitchen's long, gray-veined marble island. Nearly everything was in its place, evidence of the incident irrefutably absent—as if it never happened. Parker had done what was necessary, but the reckoning clung to him like a stain he couldn't scrub away.

The thirty-one-year-old paused in the hallway to tighten the knot in his tie, precise and deliberate. The mirror caught the morning light, a faint glint drawing his attention before he straightened his collar. The image radiated confidence beyond his years—every inch of his 6'1" frame, from his polished shoes to his perfectly tousled dark hair, represented routine and structure. But as he leaned closer to the glass, his green eyes betrayed a flicker of uncertainty, a hint of unease. Still, he slipped on the round, wire-rim glasses, giving him that final touch of composure. Running a hand through his hair gave the dark brown waves a deliberate ruffle, maintaining its purposefully disheveled appearance. A grin tugged at the corners of his mouth—he had been tested, pushed to his limits, and prevailed.

Parker glanced back into the kitchen and living room, the morning light bathing the space with absolution. Still, an unshakable discomfort tugged at the edge of his thoughts, like a shadow in the corner of his vision, until he suppressed it beneath layers of practiced composure and conviction. As the door clicked shut and locked behind him, the weight of the past week's turmoil finally lifted from his shoulders. Today, Parker would reclaim control of his carefully curated life.

Dr. Warren's small practice occupied a restored 1920s Craftsman-style home in the prestigious Ansley Park neighborhood. As Parker stepped inside, his dress shoes tapped a steady rhythm against the polished hardwood—orderly, precise, purposeful. The walk to his office was familiar, almost ritualistic, a return to his routine.

"Good morning, Parker," Olivia greeted from behind the

reception desk. Her warmth was effortless, her mahogany skin and shoulder-length braids framing a face that could soften even the most guarded clients. In her late forties, she was a favorite among colleagues—wise, perceptive, and quick, with a knowing smile that put people at ease.

"Did Stephanie take good care of you this weekend?"

His grip tightened on his vintage leather satchel, hesitation catching in his throat—just as when his mother or the nosy neighbor in 2608 pried about Stephanie. "No," he said. "We're not seeing much of each other these days."

Olivia shifted her attention away from the screen and toward him. Her head tilted as her expressive brown eyes narrowed in a knowing, disapproving nod. "You know, Parker, at some point, you'll have to stop finding fault in everyone you date."

A dry chuckle escaped him. "So you have spoken with my mother again." He fumbled through his satchel, avoiding eye contact with her.

"Hey, before I forget," Olivia added, "there's a package for you on your desk. It was outside the front door this morning when I got here."

Parker nodded. "Thank you, Ms. Hayes," his lips barely curled into a grin as he stepped away from her desk.

The door to his office clicked shut behind him, the sound hanging in the still air. On his desk sat the small brown box— unassuming yet perfectly aligned with the edges of his black desk pad. Olivia knew his preferences: everything centered, squared off, no clutter. Parker picked it up, rotating it in his hands. The heavy-stock brown paper was neatly wrapped and anonymous—no postage or return address—just the name 'Parker,' written in precise penmanship. Someone had hand-delivered it.

He placed the box back on his desk, the coarse brown paper scratching against his fingertips. He reached for his leather shoulder bag and removed his appointment book and journal. Parker opened his calendar to today's date and placed it neatly to the left of his desk pad. He thumbed through his journal, stopping at the next blank page before setting it on the right side of the desk. His chrome fountain pen rested in the fold, holding the journal open. The familiar routine grounded Parker, much like the morning light streaming into his condo had earlier, reaffirming his belief everything had returned to normal.

Parker reached for the box again, though his instincts whispered warnings. His hands moved on their own, slicing through the brown kraft paper with the letter opener. Each heartbeat was a countdown to something he couldn't yet see. With steady hands, he lifted the lid and gasped, his fingers freezing around the edges of the box.

Inside, a photograph. A shiver ran up Parker's spine as the significance of the image sank in. Heat flushed his skin, a cold sweat following in its wake. His mind struggled to catch up with the shocking image, the image of him—*Parker*—in an intimate embrace with another man. It slammed into him like someone's fist, pulling him into a dizzying spiral of disbelief.

Parker's pulse thundered in his ears as he pulled a small stack of pictures from the box. He thumbed through them, each more damning than the last, each more explicit, each more compromising. He recognized the setting. Whoever took these had been inside his condo, inside his sanctuary. He wanted to throw the photographs back into the box and slam its lid back on, but doing so would not erase the sense of vulnerability now gripping him.

Beneath the photos, a note—his hands trembled as he reached for it. He unfolded the page and read the neatly penned message, the handwriting matching the name on the box.

"I know what you did."

The words blurred, but the meaning was clear. Parker's weekend—the chaos, what he believed he had concealed or imagined—wasn't gone. It had followed him, creeping back into his life when he thought he was safe. The paranoia he had so confidently buried began to claw its way back to the surface, threatening to overwhelm him.

And then he spotted it—the bloodied watch at the bottom of the box.

Parker stood frozen, the note slipping from his fingers and floating down to join the photographs scattered on his desk. He stared at the vintage timepiece, his breaths coming in short gasps as his mind raced, searching for a way to push the chaos back down where it belonged. *Who could have done this?* His suppressed fear roared to life, louder and more intense than ever.

Using the pressed, neatly folded white handkerchief he kept in his left pocket, Parker tentatively lifted the watch from the box. Familiar and once supple, the leather band was stiff and cold in his grip, marred by a dried but still sticky residue. He examined the blood-spattered face, each crack in the crystal reflecting a crack in his memory and growing anxiety.

His fingers tightened around the band. It wasn't just any watch—it was *his* watch. The shattered crystal and stained band mocked him, a visceral testament to the truth he refused to accept. The hands lay frozen above the Roman numerals on the dial, marking the exact moment his life shattered—the moment he could not outrun.

2

THE NEW CLIENTS

(Eight days earlier, Monday the 2nd)

Parker adjusted the frame of his glasses as he studied the two men seated on the sofa across from him, his demeanor practiced and professional. The gentle rustle of the pages in the journal on his lap made the only sound in the room. He settled into his chair slightly, the familiar creak of the leather grounding him in the space he curated to feel safe for others.

Mark Sutherland's steady gray eyes scanned the space with silent intensity, reflecting seriousness and thoughtfulness. His hair, dark brown with some touches of gray around the temples, suggested experience and maturity. His closely groomed, graying brown beard framed his strong jawline, adding to his masculine but professional appearance. Mark sat upright on one side of the sofa, his hands clasped tightly in his lap, his posture deliberate but tense. Parker sensed an aura of quiet authority about him. Still, his eyes betrayed profound exhaustion as if he carried the weight of years of unresolved conflict. While Mark's presence seemed subdued, Parker sensed it was also a potential storm lingering beneath his surface, subtle but impossible to ignore.

By contrast, Devin Marchand leaned back into the corner of his side of the sofa, his posture loose and relaxed. His boyish good looks, warm brown eyes, and easy smile made him seem approachable and charming. He smiled smugly, as though their first session with Parker was more a victory for him than an attempt to address his relationship issues with Mark. The grin playing on Devin's lips told Parker much of what he needed to know about the couple's dynamic.

"So, gentlemen," Parker began, his tone measured. "Why don't we start by discussing what brought you in today?" It was his job to remain impartial, to guide and not judge. Still, Parker observed Mark's calm waver, like glass under pressure—intact, but only just. He also determined Devin's gaze to be challenging and demanding acknowledgment.

Devin's smirk dissolved as he leaned forward, clasping his hands. "Well, I'll start," he jumped in, glancing briefly at Mark before locking eyes with Parker. "I'm the one who made the appointment. He doesn't see the point." His tone carried an edge of frustration, though he tried to keep it light. "I'm just trying to figure out why it feels like I'm the only one who wants to make this work. You know? If I didn't push for this, we'd just…" Devin paused and glanced at Mark again, "…ignore everything until it falls apart. But maybe I'm just overthinking it, right?"

Mark sighed, his fingers flexing briefly in his lap before tightening again. "I think it's clear we're having some issues with communication. No matter how carefully I phrase things, they always seem wrong. Or worse, it gets twisted into something I didn't mean."

Devin chuckled, his laugh dripping with amusement as he tilted his head toward Mark. "That's because you're always so careful, Mark. So buttoned up. You're so afraid to say something wrong that you don't say anything at all. It's exhausting. You never express what you feel. It's like talking to a robot or a brick wall, sometimes."

Mark's hands clenched tighter, and Parker caught the way his jaw tightened. His voice was low and controlled as he responded. "Let's keep things civil, Devin. We've had enough fights already."

"Civil?" Devin echoed with a playful sneer. "You mean sanitized, right? You keep everything bottled up, always so serious, like you're above dealing with the real stuff. You never let me in. You'd rather drift along and pretend we're this perfect little couple in some perfect world like there's nothing worth talking about." Devin leaned forward, his expression hardening, shaking his head. "But life's not neat, Mark. It's messy. And you—you just don't get that."

"Always and never. Such big words," Mark retorted.

"You know what I'm talking about, Mark. You're not in court right now, Mr. Attorney. Don't be so sarcastic." Devin glanced at Parker, his expression a plea for the arbiter to side with him, filled with hurt and righteousness.

Parker's eyes flickered between the two men, absorbing their words as he shifted slightly in his chair, the dynamic between them becoming more evident with each exchange.

Mark appeared to be in his mid-forties, a strong and stable strength, yet quiet and hesitant. Devin, twenty-four or so, oozed confidence bordering on arrogance. Devin's teasing tone was sharp and laced with challenge. Mark seemed worn down and tired from constantly trying to keep up with Devin, as though he perpetually remained a step behind.

Parker took in the way Mark's shoulders tensed at every

word, the subtle dominance in Devin's voice and posture. *Power dynamics*, he thought, feeling the familiar frustration rise. Mark's weariness was palpable, but the edge in Devin's grin went beyond teasing—it was control masked as charm. Parker understood why they'd come for help. The imbalance was striking.

So you're an attorney, Mark?" Parker asked, trying to bring the couple's focus back with a few simple questions too difficult to debate. He wasn't sure if Devin's previous address of Mark as Mr. Attorney was factual or a snide commentary on Mark's reply regarding the words 'always' and 'never.'

"Yes," Mark answered, "criminal defense attorney."

"Interesting," Parker responded. "Private practice or public defender?"

"I've done both, but currently a court-appointed defender."

"And you, Devin?"

"I'm the Head Maître d' at Mise en Place."

"Very nice restaurant," Parker commented. "I went there once. Great French food. Are you of French descent? Isn't Marchand a French surname?"

Devin's lips curved into a faint simper, his eyes gleaming with a hint of amusement. "It's actually pronounced 'Mar-shon,'" he corrected, his newly found French accent light but detectable. "The 'd' is silent."

"Oh, apologies," responded Parker. He wanted to say 'Excusez-moi, bien sûr," attempting to recall a phrase he learned during two years of foreign language in high school. Still, he passed on the opportunity to demonstrate his rudimentary command of the French language. The diversion of professions and surnames was enough to settle the couple's tension, at least momentarily.

"Gentlemen," Parker continued, "it sounds like you both have professions that depend heavily on communication."

"Agreed," responded Mark.

"Yes, of course," answered Devin. "That's why I wanted to come here. My job is just as important as his. It may not pay as much but deserves as much respect." Devin could have continued had he not been cut off by Parker, preventing the launch into yet another aspect of the couple's challenges.

"And I'm glad you both agreed to come in today," interjected Parker, his voice kind yet firm. He glanced at Devin, who seemed pleased by his agreement. His focus shifted to Mark, who nodded and cast his eyes downward toward his folded hands in his lap. This office was Parker's courtroom, and Mark would have plenty of time to defend himself against accusations.

"It's true," Parker continued, "the number one reason couples attend counseling is communication issues, and you both agreed how important communication is. Most couples— regardless of age, time together, or sexual orientation—struggle with expressing their needs, emotions, and concerns. It's difficult to resolve conflicts and respect boundaries."

Neither couple disputed the statement.

"How long have you two been together?" Parker asked.

"Four years," Devin answered.

Parker set his journal and pen on the table beside his chair, nodding in understanding as he leaned forward. He acknowledged the *four-year mark* to himself—the milestone when the initial 'honeymoon phase' of passion and excitement fades, and couples move into a more settled, long-term relationship. Routines set in and lead to feelings of complacency or boredom if the relationship isn't evolving. Unresolved communication patterns start to create strain. Misunderstandings, unexpressed needs, and poor conflict-resolution skills begin to affect the relationship. Novelty and adventure diminish, leading to routine and predictability. Differences in values and goals overlooked earlier become more apparent. Parker was mentally checking off the long list of possibilities sitting before him.

"Devin, it sounds like you feel Mark is holding back. Something is missing in how he expresses himself. Mark, I hear you're trying to avoid conflict and maintain peace, but your words and actions are sometimes misinterpreted. Is that right?"

As if our issues were that simple, mused Devin, the thought laced with quiet cynicism.

Mark gave a slight nod, his stare steady. "Yes. I've never been one for drama. I want us to be happy, but it feels like I'm failing no matter how hard I try. Devin gets frustrated, so I just back off."

"And when you back off, what happens?" Parker asked.

"He sulks," Devin cut in before Mark could answer. "Or he retreats within himself for days, then expects me to fix everything."

With his fingers intertwined and his palms together, Parker's thumbs tapped lightly against one another. The balance of power was glaringly skewed, and Devin knew how to maintain influence. A flash of annoyance stirred inside Parker, a creeping frustration with how Mark seemed to fold under Devin's words. *Please stand up for yourself*, Parker thought, though he kept his expression neutral.

The session continued, grating on Parker's nerves as it progressed. He maintained his professional façade, but inside, judgments formed. *This relationship isn't going to last.* The words played in his mind, unspoken.

Then, a subtle shift occurred. When Devin's eyes met Parker's, his sharp smile softened into something more cryptic, an almost knowing expression. A flicker of unease came over Parker as if Devin were seeing more than he should. The gaze lingered until Parker shifted his focus, steadying himself before returning attention to the younger client. Devin turned to Mark, his expression faltering for a moment. A glint of vulnerability surfaced in his eyes before he masked it again with a casual shrug.

"Maybe you're trying too hard, Mark. Maybe if you just," he paused, "I don't know, let go a little, you wouldn't feel like you're always failing."

Parker's eyes fixed on Devin, the younger man's disarming charm undeniable. A magnetic quality about him made it hard to resist his draw, and Parker could feel himself pulled into the tension between the two men. Still, Parker did not miss the slight crack in Devin's confident demeanor—his faltering smirk and the trace of vulnerability—an indication that despite his arrogance and outward composure, he was still emotionally invested in the relationship. "Mark, when Devin says these things, what does it bring up for you? What do you feel?"

Mark hesitated. "I feel... dismissed. I feel like my efforts, being here now, for instance, don't matter. I'm trying to make this work, but it feels like Devin waits for me to slip up to prove I can't handle him."

Devin's smile faded, his expression tempering for the first time in the session. "Exactly. You're always trying to *handle* me,

Mark. Like I'm some problem to solve. But I'm not. I just want to be with someone who gets me, not someone who's constantly trying to fix me."

Parker leaned back into his chair, sensing the raw emotion behind their statements. There was more here than what their spoken words revealed. Devin's teasing was a defense, and Mark's silence was a resignation. Where Devin's energy was magnetic and youthful, Mark's aura seemed like the weight of a mountain—immovable but with a potential for sudden force.

"Devin," Parker began, his tone cautious, "it sounds like you're feeling constrained, as if Mark's attempts to maintain stability feel more like neglect than support. Is that accurate?"

Devin shrugged, his gaze flashing briefly to Mark before landing back on Parker. "Maybe. But it's not just that. It's about feeling alive. I want to feel like we're living life, not just going through the motions."

Mark lifted his head, his frustration and gloom unmistakable. "I feel like I'm the only one trying to keep us grounded. Like if I let go, everything will fall apart."

Parker let the silence sit for a moment, the weight of their words lingering. He nodded slowly at the couple. "Maybe we can start by acknowledging you both bring something valuable to this relationship. Mark, your stability and commitment are strengths. Devin, your passion and spontaneity are equally important. The challenge is finding a way to balance those qualities, to create a steady and vibrant relationship."

Devin glanced at Mark, the edge of his usual bravado relaxing. "Maybe. But Mark's got to stop acting like he's my babysitter and start treating me as his partner."

Mark's response was quieter, more resigned. "And Devin's

got to understand I'm not trying to hold him back. I want this to work just as much as he does."

Parker, sensing their words were only scratching the surface of their complex relationship, nodded to signal the end of the session. "I think we've established a good base and made progress today. Remember, this isn't about winning or losing. It's about understanding each other and finding a way to move forward together."

His eyes lingered on Devin as the couple stood to leave. Little doubt, the younger man's attractiveness and charm intrigued him. Devin was charismatic, a sharp contrast to Mark's quiet intensity, and it was hard for Parker not to note the carefree certainty and authority Devin exuded. It was a type of freedom that stirred a deep pull within himself, a feeling he wasn't ready to examine too closely. Not yet, at least.

As the door shut behind them, Parker slumped into his office chair, the cool leather pressing against his back and neck. His gaze lingered on the empty sofa they'd just occupied. The tension from their session hung suspended like a thick fog. He removed his glasses and exhaled slowly, rubbing the bridge of his nose and temples as if trying to nudge the bemusement from the session to the edges of his mind.

A light knock at the door pulled him from his thoughts. It cracked open, and Alyce, her chestnut-brown hair neatly styled in soft waves, poked her head in. "Mind if I come in?" she asked with quiet confidence, stepping inside without waiting for an answer.

"Of course," he motioned her. "Have a seat."

Alyce sat on the end of the sofa where Mark sat earlier, crossing her legs with measured grace. Her simple yet elegant white button-up blouse tucked neatly into tailored slacks reflected her sense of composure and certainty. She leaned in slightly, her expressive brown eyes studying Parker with an attentive, grounded presence.

"Tough session?" she asked with a natural smile, hinting at her empathy and years of experience as a psychotherapist. In her late forties, Alyce Bennett was Parker's peer and mentor at the practice. Her relaxed voice and kind demeanor, balanced with inner strength and assertiveness, came through when needed.

Parker let out a slight chuckle as he put his glasses back on and leaned forward, elbows on his chair arms. "You could maybe say interesting," he replied, running a hand through his dark hair, his mind still tangled in the remnants of the session. "Mark and Devin," he added, "they are going to be a challenge, I think."

Alyce nodded with clarity of thought, understanding instantly. "I caught a glimpse and overheard them on their way out. Like oil and water, aren't they?" Her insight and intuition carried the wisdom Parker had come to rely on since joining the firm.

He leaned back, folding his arms. "Yeah," Parker replied sluggishly, "except neither wants to leave the bottle." His words were uncharacteristically curt, the edges of his frustration peeking through his usual professionalism.

Alyce nodded again and smiled. "Leave the bottle?"

He paused to think about her question, wondering if she was asking for clarification of his metaphor or if this was about to become a mentoring moment. "You said 'like oil and water,' as in incompatible substances that don't mix. The bottle symbolizes the relationship they are both stuck in. Despite the tension, frustration, and incompatibility, they remain together, unwilling to break free or change their circumstances. An unhealthy dynamic of emotional entanglement." Parker assumed she was after a clinical rationalization for his statement. "Of course," he added, "it's a very cursory observation after a single session with them."

"Do they plan to come in regularly?"

"Three times a week," he replied. "Aggressive schedule, I know."

Alyce softened her smile as her strong understanding of human behavior and emotions shone through her narrowing eyes. "And you, Parker? Where do you land in all of that? They aren't just stuck with each other. Your clients will be stuck with you, and you will be with them. What's your strategy?"

Parker exhaled sharply, rubbing the back of his neck. "Honestly? I'm not sure yet. Mark is like this human wall— there's measure in everything he says as if he's scared to let anything slip. He spoke calmly during the session, but I sensed an underlying tension. His calmness seemed hollow. There's no doubt Mark is frustrated, but he also struck me as distant and withdrawn, like he's already emotionally disengaged from Devin and sees the relationship as a burden. Mark said he wanted to work it out, but I don't know. I sense it's out of obligation or guilt, not love."

Alyce sat quietly and leaned in, listening intently to his words and nodding to let Parker know she understood.

"And Devin," he trailed off, drumming his fingers on the arm of his chair. "Devin is all charm and provocation. He seems to enjoy creating chaos just to see what happens next. Trying to find a middle ground between them might be tough."

He paused, leaning forward with a tired sigh. "I know I'm supposed to stay neutral, but I couldn't help wondering how much of this is worth saving. If neither of them wants to change, what's the point?"

"Relationships like theirs are a mirror, Parker. They reflect the parts we try to keep hidden, even from ourselves."

Parker's eyes narrowed, sensing more to her comment. He met her gaze, feeling a tug of curiosity. "How do you mean?"

Alyce shrugged, her smile casual, and Parker knew her well enough to sense the depth behind her insightful words. "I'm saying sometimes we get so caught up in maintaining control, in keeping everything neat and tidy, we forget what's truly driving us. It's not about control itself, but what happens when we lose it."

Parker frowned, the weight of her wisdom settling uncomfortably in his mind. "Fear?"

Alyce nodded, her expression growing more serious. "Exactly. Fear of chaos. Fear of what happens when we lose control, even for a moment." She leaned forward slightly as if sharing a secret. "Here's the thing, Parker. Control is an illusion. We convince ourselves we're in charge—we have everything figured out. But one twist, one unexpected event, and that illusion shatters."

Her words pressed into Parker's thoughts like an uncomfortable truth. He prided himself on maintaining control in his professional and personal life. But here Alyce was, suggesting control was fragile, and chaos was lurking, waiting for the right moment to break through.

He rubbed his temples again, thinking back to Devin's smug

grin, the subtle dominance in his posture, and Mark's quiet weariness. The session was like a power struggle—chaos versus control—but a more profound tension unsettled him.

"So, what are we supposed to do? Just let it all go. Embrace the chaos?"

Alyce's eyes lightened with awareness. "No. It's not about giving up control completely. It's about balance. Too much control, and you become rigid and brittle. Too little, and you're swept away by the whims of the world. Chaos will always exist, but the trick is not letting your fear of it control you."

Her words struck a chord with Parker. Alyce had a way of distilling emotions into clear, actionable advice. He glanced at her, feeling the familiar comfort of her grounded presence and the subtle challenge she always presented him with—an unspoken dare to confront the more profound, messier parts of the human psyche.

"And what if you don't like what you find?" he asked, his voice barely above a whisper. "What if you let go and discover something," he paused, "darker?"

Her expression relaxed as she stood, moving confidently toward his chair. At 5'6", she wasn't physically imposing. Yet, she had an inner strength in how she carried herself, a quiet resilience he admired. She gently placed her palm on his shoulder, her touch firm and professional yet comforting.

"That's the risk we take, Parker. But it's also an opportunity. We need to grow, change, and confront those parts of ourselves we'd rather ignore. We all have a breaking point where the cracks start to show. The question is: what do you do when you see them? Do you crumble, or do you rebuild?"

"True," he murmured, though his thoughts still tangled in the web of words she'd spun. "Thanks, Alyce."

"Anytime," she added, patting him on the shoulder. "I hope it helps you with your couple."

As Alyce left, she paused at the door and glanced over her shoulder. "One last thing, Parker," she said with a knowing smile. "Control and chaos aren't opposites—they're just two sides of the same coin. And the ones holding on the tightest are often the closest to losing it."

Parker nodded slowly, her words settling into place like an archway's keystone: *Control and chaos—two sides of the same coin.* It was an idea echoing through everything he'd witnessed between Mark and Devin.

After Alyce left, Parker remained in his chair, fingers drumming idly on the armrest. The session replayed in his mind. Mark was deliberate and guarded, trying to avoid conflict by clinging to control. Devin was unpredictable and relentless, stirring friction at every turn to feel alive.

Alyce's comment repeated in his ears: *The ones holding on the tightest are often the closest to losing it.*

Parker straightened, thinking of Mark's cautious phrasing and how his shoulders tensed with every word Devin hurled at him. Mark wasn't just keeping the peace; he feared what would happen if he let go. One wrong step, and he feared the relationship would collapse.

And Devin? Parker leaned back again, tapping his pen against his palm. Devin thrived on the disorder. It gave him power, keeping Mark off-balance. But what if chaos wasn't just recklessness? What if it was a way of masking his fear—clinging to what he feared losing? Fear of abandonment and becoming irrelevant the moment the fight was over? Chaos isn't always destruction. Sometimes, it's a desperate attempt to grasp what's slipping away.

Alyce's words clicked into place, bringing Parker an unexpected sense of clarity. Mark's control and Devin's chaos weren't obstacles but defenses. Both men tried to protect themselves, but their methods drove them apart.

Parker reached for his journal and scribbled a note for their next session. His counseling wasn't just about getting them to communicate. It was about helping them realize what lurked beneath their actions—the fears they hid from each other and themselves.

He set the journal aside and exhaled slowly, the tension easing for the first time since the session began. A small smile curled at the edges of his lips. He had a strategy now. Mark and Devin were stuck, but Parker was confident he could show them the way out of the bottle.

3

FRIENDLY ADVICE

The gym buzzed with machines clanging and sneakers squeaking over the rhythmic hum of treadmills. Parker exited the locker room, adjusting the wrist strap of his lifting gloves as he stepped inside the expanse of the fitness center. He scanned the floor for Tim, who was easy to spot. Parker's best friend and workout partner was already in the free weights section, tossing a dumbbell between his hands with the casual ease of someone who had done this for a long time and could do it blindfolded.

"Look at you, running late again," Tim called out with a grin, his voice carrying across the gym. His reddish-brown hair, cropped short and tousled, glinted under the overhead lights. Even after a long workday, his energy was infectious—a combination of enthusiasm and relentless optimism, making him the center of attention without trying.

Parker leered as he laid his towel across the nearest bench. "I'm right on time, actually."

"Barely," Tim chuckled, rolling his shoulders with a dumbbell in each hand, focusing intently on the 5'10" reflection in the floor-to-ceiling mirror. Tim's tone was playful, but he carried warmth in how he said it. He never took anything too seriously. Wearing a black tank top, gray athletic shorts, and well-worn running shoes, Tim radiated ease, every movement deliberate yet unforced. His body was that of a muscular yet agile former rugby player who'd stayed in shape without obsessing over it.

Parker stretched, focusing on his breathing. Tim was in motion around him, grabbing Parker's bench and lying on his towel, preparing to begin his dumbbell bench presses.

"So what's new at the nuthouse, Park?" Tim asked, genuinely interested and always supportive. His carefree approach to life carried a knack for humor and was naturally confident and relaxed. While fun-loving and playful, Tim was also insightful and could typically recognize underlying stresses with Parker.

Parker exhaled, feeling the tension creep back into his shoulders from the previous day's session with Mark and Devin. As the two maneuvered around the gym doing their routine, he filled Tim in on his new clients. Parker withheld names and specifics, of course, and was always careful to honor client confidentiality. The best friends informed each other about their professions, talking shop each time they worked out. They were each other's sounding board on life, offering one another opinions, encouragement, and advice.

Tim released an exaggerated groan as he lifted the dumbbells and racked them. "I don't know how you do it, man. Listening to people complain about their problems or couples fighting all day? I'd lose my mind. You ever want to say, 'Break up already and do us all a favor?'"

Parker shook his head, though a smile tugged at the corner of his mouth. "Not exactly professional, Tim. Do you ever want to tell buyers to 'Do us all a favor and make a decision and buy the house already?'"

Tim grinned, mischief lighting his eyes. "Professionalism is overrated. Real estate is way less emotional drama—unless you count people arguing over closet space or color schemes."

"Tempting," Parker deadpanned, rolling his neck. "But I think I'll stick to counseling."

"Suit yourself," Tim replied, folding his hands behind his head to flex his back and biceps in the mirror. "Speaking of sticking—are you sticking to that story about you and Stephanie 'taking a break?' When will you tell people the real deal, or do you plan to live like a monk? When are you going to start dating again?"

Parker grabbed a heavier weight for his last set. "You always circle back to that."

"That's because it's tragic," Tim said with a laugh, the humor tempered with genuine concern. "Come on, Parker. You're thirty-one now. You can't just work and go to the gym forever."

"Seems to be working out so far," Parker muttered, curling the dumbbell with slow deliberateness.

Tim let the comment hang in the air before responding. "You're impossible, man." His tone was light with an underlying seriousness—a reminder that Tim wasn't just here to crack jokes. "Look, we're leaving for Italy tomorrow—three weeks of pasta, wine, and fun. When we return, I want to hear you've done something fun. Hell, just something outside your routine."

Parker rolled his eyes but couldn't help smiling. "Ah yes, life advice from the man running off to Europe with his wife for three weeks."

Tim grinned, not the least bit offended. "Emma's idea, not mine. She says it's our 'last adventure' before we start trying for kids."

Parker arched an eyebrow. "Kids, huh? You really going through with that?"

"Yup," Tim said, popping the "p" with exaggerated confidence. "Family, dog, house with a fenced-in yard. Going to do it all. We're thirty now, so gotta get started sometime, right?"

"That's," Parker paused, searching for the right word, "ambitious," he finished, grabbing his towel.

"Hey, better ambitious than boring," Tim quipped. Then, glancing at Parker, he added, "You know, it wouldn't kill you to take a risk occasionally. Do something out of your comfort zone."

Parker flung the jump rope over his head, letting it snap against the floor behind him. "Not everyone needs constant excitement to feel alive, Tim." As soon as he said the words, Parker was reminded of what Devin said yesterday about wanting to feel alive and not just move through the motions.

"No, but some excitement wouldn't hurt either," Tim replied. "Come on, Parker. You've got to let yourself want something more than just stability."

Parker paused mid-jump, the rope slack in his hands. "And what exactly is that supposed to mean?"

Tim sat forward on the bench, resting his elbows on his knees as he waited for Parker to finish jumping rope. "It means you can't keep hiding behind your routines, hoping things magically fall into place. Life doesn't work like that. You need to decide what you want—and go after it."

The words landed harder than Parker cared to admit, their weight pressing against the walls he'd purposely built around himself. Tim wasn't wrong.

"And what if I don't know what I want?"

Tim shrugged, his tone light but his gaze unwavering. "Then figure it out. Start small. Do one thing that scares you."

Parker glanced down, tapping the rope against the floor. "Like what?"

"I don't know. Ask someone out. Take a weekend trip. Hell, join a cooking class. Just something. Anything." Tim's eyes sparkled with humor, but he genuinely hoped Parker would take the hint. "When's the last time you did something just because you wanted to, not because you had to?"

Parker exhaled through his nose, trying to brush off the uncomfortable truth in Tim's words. "Easy for you to say, Mr. Adventure."

Tim stood and reached up to squeeze Parker's bicep, his grip warm and solid as he lightly shook his friend's arm. "It's not about ease or adventure, Parker. It's about living."

Parker shook his head, though he couldn't help the small smile that crept onto his face. "I'll think about it."

Tim grinned. "Good man!"

Entering the locker room, Tim grabbed his gym bag from his locker and slung it over his shoulder. Parker, already stripped with a towel around his waist, walked up to him.

"What, no steam or shower tonight?" Parker asked when he realized Tim was ready to leave.

"Can't tonight, Park. I'm off to start laying clothes out to pack. Emma's waiting. Try not to get too lonely without me."

"Not a chance," Parker shot back. "A welcomed break and quality time alone."

Tim gave a mock salute as he headed out of the locker room. "Remember what I said. I want to hear about some adventure in three weeks."

Parker watched him leave, the words lingering long after Tim disappeared. Tim's relentless optimism was annoying and reassuring, like a gentle nudge from the universe, reminding Parker change was inevitable, regardless of whether he was ready for it.

Sweat rolled down Parker's broad shoulders and defined chest in the sauna. He could taste the saltiness streaming down his forehead and face. Parker's toned physique resembled John F. Kennedy, Jr.—athletic and well-proportioned—fit and muscular but not overly thick and bulky like Tim. He grabbed the edge of the wooden bench and leaned back, his pectoral and abdominal muscles tightening as he did. Tim's words echoed Parker's thoughts like seeds of change planted in his mind. *'Decide what you want—and go after it.'*

4

THE BARTENDER

(Tuesday the 3rd)

The restaurant was quiet, with the low murmur of conversations blending with muted silverware clinks. Parker sat in a corner booth by the window, pushing aside his unfinished plate of stir-fried vegetables. His open journal lay beside him, pages filled with notes and half-formed thoughts from the previous two days' sessions. He tapped his pen on the paper absentmindedly, scrolling over session observations as he recalled his gym conversation with Tim two hours earlier.

He glanced at his watch. It was getting late, a familiar scene after his weekday workouts with Tim. He often ate alone at his favorite Thai restaurant before heading home to set up the coffee for the next day's cycle: wake, dress, work, gym, dinner. Closing the journal, Parker slipped it into his satchel, left a tip under his glass, and walked outside into the crisp autumn breeze.

He paused in the small parking lot, thumbing his car keys, while a low bass pulse throbbed through the walls of the building next door. Parker glanced toward the source of the sound: Cityside, neon-red letters lit faintly against the building's brick exterior above the entrance. Men drifted in and out of the bar's entrance, some laughing, others leaning close, their voices drowned beneath the steady beat of the music coming from inside.

Parker stood between the familiar pull toward safety and an unfamiliar urge to understand—something about what Mark and Devin hinted at and why it unsettled him. His fingers tightened around the car keys, temptation festering within him. *Bad idea*, he muttered to himself. *Just get in the car and go home.*

But he didn't move. Instead, he stood there, watching the door swing open and close as if it offered an opportunity to slip into a world not his own. Just one drink, he told himself. Research. Nothing more. Before he could second-guess himself or allow fear to reel him back, Parker crossed the lot and stepped through the entrance.

Inside, the bar was a rush of sound and color. Blue and red lights swept the space, casting a hazy glow over chrome railings and faux leather. Men lounged in booths, others chatted animatedly at the bar, while a few swayed lazily to the beat on the small dance floor. Laughter, music, and chatter filled the space, a cacophony of senses Parker wasn't familiar with but couldn't entirely dismiss.

He slipped onto a barstool, adjusting his glasses while scanning the room. He tried not to feel conspicuous as he shifted uncomfortably on the seat.

"First time?" a smooth voice asked from across the counter, the tone edged with amusement.

Parker's head snapped up, startled, as a young man leaned against the bar on the opposite side, elbows propped on the polished wood. His blond hair was short on the sides, with volume on top, disheveled just enough to seem effortless. His eyes sparkled with mischievous warmth, and his easy smile carried a dangerous charm, hovering just shy of innocent.

Parker blinked. "Is it that obvious?"

The bartender's grin widened. "A little," he responded. "Let me guess. Vodka tonic?" His voice was light and teasing, with an edge of playful flirtation just beneath the surface.

"Perfect," Parker replied. "Again, obvious?"

"Good choice. You didn't look like the beer or whiskey type." As he poured the drink, the bartender's lean frame moved with fluid grace, suggesting he was no stranger to being watched. His T-shirt hugged his toned body, hinting at the wiry strength beneath his casual demeanor. "Name's Nick."

"Parker," he acknowledged back.

Placing a napkin on the counter, Nick set the cocktail in front of Parker, his fingers lingering on the glass for a second longer than needed. "So, what brings you in tonight? I don't think I've seen you in before."

"Long day," Parker muttered, adjusting his glasses.

Nick nodded approvingly, and his smile deepened as if Parker's answer amused him. "Long day, huh? What type of work wears someone out enough to end up here on a Tuesday night?" Nick leaned on the bar, his bright eyes flicking briefly to Parker's satchel before settling back on his face.

Parker exhaled. "Therapist," he admitted, shifting in his seat and wondering why he felt so compelled to be honest.

The twenty-three-year-old bartender let out a pleasing chuckle, resting his chin on one hand. "Ah. So, you spend your days untangling other people's messes." He leaned closer, his brilliant blue eyes hinting at a mix of amusement and curiosity.

29

"Tell me, are you one of those therapists who has it all figured out, or are you just as screwed up as the rest of us?"

Parker couldn't help but smile. "A bit of both, perhaps."

Nick tilted his head, a playful grin dancing across his lips as his gaze lingered on Parker. He leaned back, absently wiping the counter. "And now you're here. So, what's the diagnosis tonight? Care to analyze me?"

Parker shook his head, feeling awkward and strangely at ease at the same time. "No, I think I'm off the clock."

"Okay, fair enough," Nick replied, though his gaze didn't waver, holding Parker's with a steady, playful intensity. Nick arched an eyebrow. "Curiosity is dangerous, anyway. Right? But it can also be fun."

Parker lifted the glass to his lips, hoping the burn of alcohol might settle the unease sweeping over him.

The music shifted, a heavier beat pulsed through the bar, and Nick went to serve another patron. Parker watched him move, admiring the ease with which Nick navigated space—entirely at home here, exuding an effortless confidence Parker envied.

When Nick returned, he leaned on the bar again, close enough for Parker to catch a faint scent of cedarwood and a crisp note reminiscent of fresh mint. Nick's voice dropped just enough to cut through the interference of nearby patrons. "You should come back Friday night," he said, his voice smooth and inviting.

"Friday?"

Nick's grin widened. "I dance then."

Parker raised an eyebrow. "You're a dancer too?"

"Yup." Nick's grin was electric, the kind that could make promises without saying a word. "Nothing too wild, but enough to keep things interesting."

Parker understood the offer for what it was—both an invitation and a test. He shook his head, amused. "I don't think this is my scene," though the conviction in his voice faltered.

Nick shrugged, unbothered. "You never know. You could surprise yourself."

Parker glanced at the door, his pulse quickening. Part of him wanted to leave to escape the unsettling sense of possibility Nick represented. But another part—leading him there initially—wanted to stay.

"Maybe," Parker said, though the word sounded foreign on his tongue.

Nick's smile was slow and knowing as if he'd already won. "I'll hold you to it." He gave Parker a playful wink before disappearing to attend to other customers.

Parker watched him walk away as a strange mix of curiosity and unease settled within him. Nick had a positive energy—a pull hard to ignore, though Parker knew he should. Nick reminded him of Devin—how the two seemed so alike. Both were confident and charming, yet one seemed manipulative while the other was disarming.

When Parker finished his drink and stood to leave, Nick caught his eye from across the bar. "See you Friday."

Parker hesitated, fingers tightening around his satchel strap. Then, against his better judgment, he gave a slight nod. "We'll see."

Outside, the night was colder, the world heavier—less precise and more fluid. Parker leaned against his car for a moment, staring back at the neon sign above the entrance of Cityside. Nick left an impression, and Parker wasn't sure if that was a good thing—or the start of a far more complicated entanglement.

5

The Art of Provocation

(Wednesday the 4th)

The scent of sandalwood and leather burned from the Old Hemingway soy candle, filling Parker's office as he sat back in his chair. Mark and Devin took their places on the sofa, the gulf between them as palpable as the scented silence in the office. The cushion springs groaned faintly under Mark's weight, a subtle reminder of the tension still present from their first appointment two days earlier.

Mark sat upright, arms crossed tightly, his posture rigid. His steely-gray eyes locked onto Parker, unblinking, as if studying his every move. His gaze was unsettling—cold, heavy, patient, like a winter sky. It didn't feel like he was hunting for answers but waiting for them to reveal themselves. Mark wasn't the kind to chase prey; he let it exhaust itself.

At the other end of the couch, Devin sprawled against the armrest, his jeans brushing the sofa's fabric as he shifted to settle in. The scent of something minty clung to him—gum or cologne, Parker couldn't tell which—but it was sharp, a contrast to the earthy tones of Mark. His body language was loose, his slouched sureness radiating physical certainty, and his legs casually spread as if claiming territory. Devin's sneakers thudded rhythmically against the area rug covering the hardwood floors, a deliberate, restless beat. Those sharp, brown eyes glanced toward Parker with amusement—almost a challenge. Devin's lips curved with a hint of private amusement as if he and Parker shared a secret Mark could never understand.

Parker's pen tapped once against his notebook as he cleared his throat and broke the silence. "How have things been since our last session?"

Mark leaned forward, wearing his dusk-blue herringbone tweed jacket like a suit of armor. His elbows rested on his knees as his leather loafers gave a quiet creak to his shifting body. "We're back for another session. That's something, I suppose."

Devin scoffed, his lips curling into a sneer. The sound was pointed, like the snap of a twig. "Barely. He wanted to call it off this morning." His voice was light but laced with mockery, the kind slipping under someone's skin without effort. Devin slouched deeper into the couch, glaring at Mark, daring him to deny it.

Mark's jaw clenched—the muscles shifting beneath his stubble—but his voice remained level. "We're here, aren't we?"

"Under duress," Devin said, a dimple surfacing with his lingering smirk. His glance at Parker teetered on the edge of flirtation. "He's not exactly a team player."

Mark exhaled a slow, deliberate breath through his nose like a boxer sizing up his opponent before the next round. He controlled his expression, though Parker could see the tension coiled beneath the surface. "I'm not interested in playing games."

Devin adjusted his position, casually extending his leg until his shoe brushed Parker's. The touch was casual and fleeting—light, like a breeze—but enough to make Parker's skin prickle, sending an involuntary flicker of heat through him. Parker leaned back, ignoring the sensation and forcing himself not to react, though he noted his pulse quickening. It was an annoying reminder of how easy it was to lose focus around Devin. Still, he reminded himself that Devin's charm was nothing more than a carefully constructed weapon.

"I think you like games more than you admit," Devin murmured amusingly, his eyes gleaming with mischief as they lingered on Parker. The glint in his gaze hinted at both invitation and danger, as if testing Parker's boundaries. Parker found it unsettling, meant to be playful but threatening, like a cat toying with a mouse.

Mark caught the exchange but held his presence as steady and unyielding as a stone wall. He turned to Parker, speaking with the cold precision of someone who measured every word before speaking. "I imagine this isn't how you thought things would go."

Parker shifted in his chair, Mark's words settling in his gut as his fingers tensed against the notepad in his lap. "I'm not here to—"

"You assumed you could fix us, didn't you?" Mark cut him off smoothly, his voice diplomatic but with an edge sharp enough to slice through steel.

The heat on the back of Parker's neck rose, a mix of embarrassment and irritation. The faint hum of the air rushing from the floor registers droned in the background, a reminder of how still the room became. A sliver of doubt crept in—had he said the right thing earlier? Was he guiding them correctly?

His self-doubt nagged him, triggering an old memory of the

day he froze in front of his seventh-grade class while giving a speech. He could still feel the polished edge of the note cards in his sweaty hands, slick with nerves. Parker practiced the presentation countless times, reciting every fact perfectly at home in front of his mirror. But when he stood alone before his classmates, the cards slipped from his grasp, fluttering to the floor in a scattered heap. He stared down at them, helpless, the laughter starting in waves—forgiving at first before building as his teacher urged him to continue. Parker stayed rooted in place; his voice stuck deep in his throat as the classroom swelled with giggles and whispers.

From that day onward, Parker knew control was the only way to ensure he would never feel the sting of humiliation again. If everything stayed orderly—if he stayed ahead of every mistake—he would avoid the spiral of chaos. But now, Parker felt off-balance, questioning whether he was losing control of the session.

"It's not like that," Parker said, maintaining measure in his tone.

Mark's expression didn't shift; it remained tight and pitiful, carrying the weight of an unspoken coldness. "It's not your fault. Devin always has a way of pulling people into his anarchy."

Devin rolled his eyes and scoffed, his sneaker again tapping against the floor like the impatient ticking of a clock. "Right. I'm the problem. As always."

Mark didn't respond at first. His demeanor remained intact, his expression unflinching. It was like the silence before a storm—charged, waiting to break. Finally, he reacted. "You'll learn, Parker, eventually. You can't help someone who doesn't want to be helped."

Mark's comment pierced Parker, brushing too close to truths he'd sooner ignore about himself. He shifted in his chair, pushing the discomfort aside. "Let's try to stay focused," he said, regaining his professional tone. "We're not here to point fingers. We're here to find ways to move forward."

Mark leaned back, his gaze steady and unreadable, as if he already decided moving forward was impossible.

Devin, however, leaned in, narrowing the space between himself and Parker. "So, what's your advice, Doc? What's your plan to fix us?"

The way he said 'Doc' was too relaxed, like a private joke no one let Parker in on. His pulse kicked again, a slow tap against his ribcage. Parker adjusted his glasses, focusing on the words rather than the young man saying them. "The plan," he said evenly, "isn't about fixing anyone. It's about figuring out what's keeping you both stuck in this cycle."

Devin smiled slowly, and Parker hated how it made his heart quicken. Devin possessed a magnetic presence. Every glance and grin were a carefully crafted tool, designed to intrigue and unsettle—to pull people in while keeping them off-balance.

Mark exhaled, rubbing his temples with his thumb and forefinger. The scent of cedar and cologne drifted faintly from him, grounding but heavy. "We've been stuck for years," he muttered.

Devin tilted his head and shifted closer to Mark, his expression revealing a glint of vulnerability for the briefest moment. "We could be unstuck, Mark. If you'd stop holding on so damn tight, clinging to this version of us that doesn't exist."

"And if you'd stop trying to blow everything up just to feel alive," Mark answered.

The room went quiet, the weight of unspoken truths settling between them. Parker watched, forcing himself to stay neutral, absorbing the way Mark's steady control clashed with Devin's restless energy. It was like watching two opposing forces—stability versus disorder—equally destructive in their own way. He glanced at Devin, noticing how his lips quirked upward as if enjoying every second of the tension. Perhaps he did. It reinforced what Parker suspected before: Devin thrived on friction, conflict, and watching people unravel. Parker wasn't immune to it.

"Here's what I suggest," Parker finally said, forcing his focus back to the session. "For the next week, Mark, when you feel the urge to pull away, try leaning in instead. And Devin, when you want to provoke, pause. Ask yourself what it is you sincerely want." Parker paused, waiting for some sign of acknowledgment.

Mark gave a slow nod, though his expression remained guarded. Devin offered a noncommittal shrug, but the gleam in his eye made Parker feel he had already dismissed the suggestion.

As the session ended, Parker stood and shook their hands. Mark's grip was firm, his palm cool and dry—calculated, like everything about him. Devin, however, let his hand linger just a beat too long, just as he did with his gaze toward Parker. The warmth of Devin's palm seeped into Parker's, leaving behind an intimate sensation.

"See you next time," Devin said with a sly, knowing curve of his lips. His voice was low enough to feel like a whisper meant just for Parker.

"Next time," Parker nodded.

Parker fell back into his chair as the door clicked shut behind them. The office was quiet yet still charged, as if the energy Devin left behind still hummed in the air, his presence lingering like a ghost that remained. Parker exhaled slowly, running a hand through his hair. *Control. Chaos.*

It wasn't just Mark and Devin trapped in the cycle. Parker could feel the pull of a dangerous and thrilling force stirring just beneath the surface of his orderly façade. For the first time, he wondered how long he could keep pretending it didn't exist.

6

Big Boys Don't Cry

(Thursday the 5th)

Parker tapped the edge of the fountain pen his father gave him against the open journal, the rhythmic ticks filling the quiet office and marking time in slow, deliberate beats. The fixations over the past few days—his new clients, venturing into Cityside, meeting Nick—all swirled in his mind, each probing deeper into his thoughts. The collar of his button-down pinched at the back of his neck, and he rubbed the tender skin beneath it—a knot of tension refusing to unwind.

His gaze drifted over the orderly lines of his desk, the journals stacked with care, the books arranged by subject, each object exactly where it should be. But today, the familiar order felt suffocating. The door stood slightly ajar, allowing the low hum of voices and the shuffle of footsteps from the hallway to leak in, turning the office's silence strangely oppressive. *Focus,* Parker told himself. *You're a professional.*

He dragged his attention back to the notes in front of him. Mark's name stood out in crisp, neat print—controlled and measured, like the man himself. Beside it, Devin's name scribed in hurried cursive, the way his energy arched unpredictably between charm and commotion. Parker could hear Devin's chuckle behind that playful, knowing smile. It stuck in his mind like the lyrics to a song he didn't want to hum.

"Morning, Parker." Olivia's warm voice drifted in with a light tap on the door. "Got a minute?"

Parker exhaled, flipping the journal closed and pressing the cover shut as if the thoughts inside might spill out if he wasn't careful. "Morning," he replied, glancing at his watch—ten minutes until his next appointment. She was already inside before he could protest, balancing a small stack of files in one hand.

"You look like something's off," Olivia said, setting the files on his desk. "Everything alright?"

Parker leaned back in his chair. "Just busy." He adjusted his glasses, but the frame slipped down the bridge of his nose again, forcing him to push it up with an irritated tap.

Olivia's bracelets jingled as she folded her arms, her expression easy but far from oblivious. "I don't know. You seem…" she paused, her eyes narrowing slightly, "not yourself." Her voice was light, but the concern underneath was unmistakable.

'Not yourself.' The phrase swirled in his head longer than it should have. It brought Parker back—eleven years old, sitting at the dining room table beneath the weight of his mother's disappointment. The homework assignment in front of him sat littered with red marks, corrections slashing through his carefully written essay. He worked on it all weekend, but it wasn't good enough. Nothing ever was.

'This is a B-plus effort, Parker. Is that the best you can do?' His mother's voice was sharp, every word a small, deliberate cut.

If it wasn't perfect, it wasn't good enough. His parents expected high achievement and success. Love and approval were conditional on performance. He learned that mistakes were dangerous, a sign he wasn't paying attention—wasn't good enough. So he made it a habit: bed corners tucked at a perfect angle, the bedroom kept clean and organized, assignments handed in early, and every task completed without flaw. Perfection wasn't just a habit; it was survival.

Parker glanced at Olivia and forced a smile, though the effort was like wearing shoes half a size too small.

Her eyes held his, steady but kind. "A client asked me if you were okay yesterday," she said gently. "People notice, Parker. Whether you think they do or not."

Parker's jaw tightened like his grip tightened around his journal. He didn't need his clients—or Olivia—questioning his emotional state. "I'm fine, Olivia," he replied, sharper than intended. The words escaped before he could reel them in, like a reflex, leaving a bitter bite in his mouth. Regret followed a second too late, but he leaned into the curt statement instead of backpedaling. "I've got it under control."

Still standing at his desk, Olivia gave Parker a small, patient smile, the kind people reserved for children who insist they aren't tired. She wasn't sure what 'it' was. "I'm sorry, I didn't mean—"

"I just have a lot on my plate right now," Parker interjected, tempering his tone.

"You know you're not as invisible as you think, right?" Olivia said gently. "We all see when something's weighing on you."

He released a short, humorless sound, like a chuckle without wit. The warmth of her concern pressed in on him, but instead of comfort, he was annoyed. "I appreciate the concern," he replied, his voice clipped, "but I'm the professional here, Olivia, remember?"

She raised an eyebrow, yet her smile didn't waver. "That you are," she said lightly, though her brow furrowed just enough to signal her disapproval. "Just remember, Parker," she paused before exiting, glancing back over her shoulder with a knowing smile. "Even those who help others find their way can sometimes get lost."

Parker's fingers drummed on his journal as her words sat between them like a challenge. "I appreciate the insight, Olivia." He tried to make it sound like polite dismissal, but it came out flat. A flicker of guilt began to rise, but he shoved it down before it could surface.

Parker was no stranger to suppressing his feelings. He was bullied at school once, but when he told his parents, they dismissed it. They told him to 'toughen up—boys don't cry.' It wasn't a hard lesson to learn, and that's when he began masking his emotions, vowing off vulnerability again. Emotional distance kept things orderly and helped avoid unpredictability.

Olivia gave him a small, understanding smile—a quiet concession. She let the silence settle as if giving him space to fill it. When he didn't, she nodded, adding, "Alright. Just know I'm here for you if you want to talk."

"I'll keep it in mind," Parker replied, opening his journal and returning his attention to the pages. The words tasted hollow in his mouth. He tapped his pen on the page—another nervous habit that didn't escape Olivia's notice.

As she reached the door, Olivia paused, glancing over her shoulder. Her eyes held the same easy warmth though an undercurrent of concern or quiet disappointment lingered. The door shut, and her footsteps receded down the hallway.

Parker exhaled slowly, the dull ache in his temples pulsing under his fingers as he pinched the bridge of his nose. The faint, stale aroma of cold coffee lingered in the air, clinging to his thoughts like a fog refusing to lift.

Instead of relief, however, Devin's image flickered back into his mind—those alluring brown eyes and cocky smile. The inked lines beneath whispered at him—Mark's weary stillness and Devin's grin curled at the edges of his lips like smoke. He pondered how easily Devin shifted between charm and provocation as if he enjoyed keeping people off-balance to watch them stumble. It reminded Parker of how he'd felt sitting across from them—always on guard, never quite knowing when Devin would push too far.

Parker shook his head, reaching for his coffee cup and finding it empty. "Damn it." He stood, the chair scraping against the area rug as he pushed it back. What was it about Devin that kept creeping in—like an itch just under his skin he couldn't scratch? The feeling was ridiculous, even dangerous, but it lingered within him just the same. And Nick—how had Nick's grin already lodged itself in his thoughts, alongside Devin's?

Parker set the notebook aside with more force than necessary before heading for the breakroom. He needed coffee, space, anything to clear the unsettling fog creeping into his thoughts. But as he walked, Olivia's parting words chased him down the hallway: 'Even those who help others find their way can sometimes get lost..'

When Parker returned, he sipped his coffee and told himself it was just another case—another troubled couple tangled in a mess of their own making. Just stay professional, he muttered, readying himself for the next appointment while rubbing the back of his neck. But the feeling of being off-balance clung to him, no matter how hard he tried to shake it. His skin still felt warm, as if the memory of Devin's gaze lingered upon him.

7

BABY STEPS

(Friday the 6ᵗʰ)

The afternoon light filtered through the blinds, casting faint stripes across the office's minimalist furniture and muted walls. Although the air felt lighter than in previous sessions, Parker's guard remained up. He settled into his chair, opening his notebook on his lap, careful not to show how this particular couple lingered on his mind. The faint scent of Devin's cologne still clung in the air from the last session—like bergamot and something sharper—making it hard for Parker to center himself.

Across from him, Mark and Devin sat closer together on the couch than before, and Parker noted an improvement. Devin's arm slung lazily over the backrest behind Mark, his fingers brushing Mark's shoulder. Though still upright and cautious, Mark no longer sat at the couch's edge as if ready to bolt. Parker also noted that his posture was more relaxed—subtle yet present.

"Well," Parker said, keeping his tone neutral. "How have things been since our last session?"

Devin flashed a grin, the corners of his mouth lifting just

enough to show the faintest dimple. "Surprisingly, not terrible." He glanced at Mark, nudging him lightly with his knee. "Right, babe?"

A single chuckle escaped Mark—a sound Parker hadn't heard from him before. "Yeah. Better," he said with a slight shrug. "We tried what you suggested, and it seemed to help."

Parker leaned forward. "That's good to hear. What was different this time?"

Mark exchanged a glance with Devin, something unspoken passing between them. It wasn't exactly warmth, but it wasn't cold indifference, either. "We talked about things instead of arguing," Mark said after a moment. His voice carried a note of disbelief as if communicating without a fight was unfamiliar. "I don't know if it fixed anything, but it was something."

Devin gave a small, self-deprecating laugh. "Baby steps, right?"

"Baby steps are still progress," Parker replied, offering a professional smile. He jotted a few quick notes in his journal, and for a brief moment, optimism crept in. The heaviness that choked their earlier conversations lingered, but it had thinned—enough for both men to breathe.

"And how did it feel?" Parker asked, directing the question to them both. "To make those changes and see some progress?"

Mark hesitated. "We're trying," he admitted. "It's not perfect, but it's better."

Devin tilted his head toward Mark, his smile hinting at sincerity. "We didn't kill each other, which is a win."

Parker noted the shift in their dynamic—how they leaned toward each other rather than away, how the sharp edges in their words softened. It was enough to suggest they were on the right path, though uneven and just beginning. But just as the conversation seemed to settle into a more productive tone, Devin sharpened his expression.

"And what about you, Parker?" Devin asked, his voice carrying a playful lilt. "How have *you* been since our last visit?"

Parker kept his expression carefully neutral, though the question surprised him. "This isn't about me, Devin," he replied smoothly. "We're here to focus on your progress."

Devin's grin didn't falter. If anything, it grew bolder. "Just making conversation." His brown eyes hinted at mischief, gleaming with an inner light attempting to draw Parker closer. "You do look like you could use some fun, though."

Parker ignored the comment, keeping his focus on the couple. His fingers traced the textured leather cover of his journal, the familiar grooves grounding him as Devin's gaze lingered. "Let's talk about what worked for you both this week. What did you do differently?"

Sensing Parker's discomfort, Mark straightened and returned to the conversation. "Well, for one, we made a rule. No bringing up past arguments."

"And that helped?" Parker asked, relieved by the pivot.

Mark nodded. "A little. It kept things from spiraling."

"It was my idea," Devin added, leaning closer to Parker with a conspiratorial grin. "Mark thinks I never listen, but sometimes I surprise him."

Shifting back in his chair to put more space between Devin and himself and redirecting, Parker said, "Progress doesn't have to be perfect. The important thing is you're both making the effort."

Devin let the silence hang before breaking it with a sly smile. "You ever wonder why people stay in relationships even when they know they're doomed?"

Mark shot him a warning glance, but Devin ignored it, his attention still on Parker. "Devin." Mark's tone held a low warning, but Devin only grinned wider.

Parker met Devin's stare, keeping his expression steady. "Relationships are complicated," he said carefully. "And it's not uncommon for people to stay because they believe things can improve."

"Is that what you think?" Devin asked, his tone more relaxed now. "That there's always a chance things will improve?"

"It depends on the situation," Parker answered after clearing his throat.

Devin leaned back, satisfied, as if the conversation went exactly how he wanted. "You're good at this," he said, a hint of admiration slipping into his voice. "I can see why people like talking to you."

Mark exhaled through his nose, clearly annoyed. "Can we just stick to the point, Devin?"

Devin gave Mark a lazy smile, unbothered. "Relax, babe. I'm just saying—it's nice to talk to someone who listens."

Parker checked the time. "We're about done for today. But it sounds like you've made some real progress this week."

Mark stood first, clearly eager to leave. "Yeah. We'll see how long it lasts."

Devin stayed seated and watched Parker with that same

playful glint in his eye. When he stood, he ran his hand downward across his chest and abdomen to smooth the wrinkles out of his shirt. He then tugged at his jeans, smoothing them out, too. His gaze lingered on Parker, a playful dare in his smile.

"You know," Devin casually whispered as he passed close enough to brush his bare forearm against Parker's, "if therapy doesn't work out, maybe you and I could grab a drink sometime. Just to talk."

Parker's heart thudded once, hard, against his ribcage. He kept his expression neutral, though the thin hairs on his skin felt warm where Devin brushed against them. And just like that, Parker was fifteen again, standing at the edge of the school gym locker room.

~

The air smelled like sweat and cheap body spray. Boys were laughing—some towel-snapping each other, others showing off to friends—but Parker hovered near the exit, willing himself to blend into the background.

A voice cut through the noise—casual but sharp as a razor. 'Why are you staring, Grant? You gay or something?'

The words struck like a hard slap. Parker remembered the sting in his throat, the desperate need to deny it, to hide whatever instinct had betrayed him. His face burned as the other boys laughed, more amused by his fumbling denial than the accusation itself.

Parker vowed never to let his guard down again—never to give anyone the chance to suspect. Control. Order. Distance. Those would become his armor.

~

"That wouldn't be appropriate, Devin," Parker said firmly, though his voice lacked the conviction he wanted.

"Relax. I was just kidding." Devin winked, the gesture light but unmistakable. "See you soon, Doc."

Already in the hall, Mark glanced back toward the doorway. "Are you coming, Devin?"

He followed, but not before casting one last glance over his shoulder—another grin, another flicker of intrigue Parker knew he should ignore.

Parker exhaled when the door clicked shut, dragging a hand through his hair. He sat at his desk and reached for his journal, but the words from the session written on the page jumbled together, refusing to make sense. It wasn't just Devin's flirtation unsettling him—it was how easily it frightened him.

With a sigh, Parker closed the journal and leaned back, rubbing the back of his neck. His mind drifted to Devin's playfulness, the lingering sensation of his forearm brushing against his own. He told himself it was just another session—another complicated couple navigating their mess. But the way Devin looked at him and the brush of their skin—those were harder to explain away.

Later, Parker moved through his evening routine at home with mechanical precision, but the rhythm did nothing to settle him. Dinner was a protein shake he barely tasted, followed by a hot shower, leaving his skin warm but his thoughts racing. He slipped into his worn sweatpants from college and the black tee shirt saved for autumn evenings when the air cooled inside the condo. The neatly folded towels, the spotless countertops—everything in its place, but the order felt hollow. None of it was enough to quiet the noise vibrating inside his head.

He sat on the edge of his bed, journal in hand, flipping aimlessly through the week's notes. Mark's skepticism, Devin's charm and inappropriateness, and the subtle push and pull between them looped in his mind, tangled and messy.

Parker finally closed the journal and set it aside on his nightstand. He stared at it, the answers locked within its pages. But the unease clung to him, sticky and persistent. Sleep didn't come easy when he switched the light off and lay back. Devin's grin lingered, a whisper curling at the edges of Parker's mind, infectious and insistent, impossible to ignore.

8

THE DANCE

The clock read 11:17 p.m., and sleep refused to come. Parker sat at the edge of his bed, rubbing his neck and shoulders where the week's tension knotted tight, his muscles aching with a dull persistence. The journal lay closed on the nightstand, the words inside offering no comfort—just the echo of unresolved thoughts. Devin's grin flickered in his mind, sharp and playful. At the same time, Nick's disarming charm lingered behind it, tugging at a notion Parker wasn't ready to consider.

He knew better than to dwell on clients, especially this late in the evening. It was Friday night, the time of the week most thirty-year-olds still consider an early start to their weekend. But Parker wasn't like most thirty-year-olds. He lived his life in clean lines and routines, keeping his world sealed off from anything messy or unpredictable. Yet here he was, restless and awake.

Parker rose, his bare feet cool against the hardwood as he wandered to the living room's glassed wall of windows. The condo remained cloaked in darkness, the only light coming from the Midtown skyline beyond the glass. High-rise buildings such as his gleamed like pillars of ambition, and traffic twenty-six floors below streamed in threads of red and white—headlights chasing taillights on the bustling streets below. People came from somewhere and headed to something. The commotion had a rhythm, an odd comfort in the city's pulse that made sense from a distance, even when Parker's thoughts refused to settle. But tonight was different. Life was moving on without him.

Parker wondered what Tim and Emma were doing in Italy— probably still asleep, about to wake up to another sun-soaked day of adventure. And what about Mark and Devin? Were they fighting over another petty issue, or was tonight one of those rare nights when they weren't at odds, curled up on their sofa, clinging to the image of the couple they claimed they wanted to be?

What about Nick? He was undoubtedly well into his shift at Cityside, weaving through the crowd with effortless charm, moving under the colored strobe lights as if he owned the space—relaxed, confident. Nick's words from Tuesday lingered: "I'll be dancing Friday. You should come by." Parker's noncommittal response hadn't fazed him. Nick had only grinned. "I'll hold you to it."

Parker stared at the glowing streets below, his breath fogging the glass. The curiosity of Cityside troubled him—a place so far outside his world it might as well exist on another planet. He didn't belong in clubs with dancers hustling patrons for lap dances or private moments in back rooms. But again, how would he know? Parker had no idea what happened inside Cityside on Friday nights. He'd never been.

He leaned his forehead against the glass. *People coming from somewhere and headed to something. People went somewhere because they needed something.* Parker mulled over the thought, and the restlessness spread throughout his mind. What did *he* need?

Before logic could anchor him back into the safety of routine, Parker grabbed a pair of jeans and a black polo shirt. His keys jingled in his hand while his heart thumped in quiet defiance. The cool, damp air greeted him in the building's garage, carrying the scent of rain-slick pavement and the faint hum of the city. The drizzle reflected the streetlights in soft halos, painting the night in muted silver. It wasn't enough rain to send anyone home early—just enough to keep the streets shimmering.

Sliding into the driver's seat, Parker gripped the wheel tighter than necessary. He wasn't entirely sure where he was going— just his restlessness needed to go somewhere. It demanded an outlet, pressing against the seams of his caution. He let out a slow breath, turned the key, and drove—headed somewhere because he needed something.

The neon-red letters of Cityside glowed faintly against the brick exterior, a light mist barely falling between Parker and the entrance. Music pulsed from within—low, heavy beats vibrating through his body. The door swung open, releasing a burst of warm air scented with cologne, alcohol, and the faint musk of bodies pressed too close together. Without giving himself time to reconsider, Parker stepped inside.

The nightclub was a world apart from anything Parker knew. Strobe lights cast jagged shadows across the walls, and the bass thrummed beneath his skin—not just a sound, but pressure, vibrating through the soles of his shoes and snaking up his spine. People moved freely, uninhibited, their laughter folding into the music. It was chaotic, a mess of sound and color. And yet, somehow, it was liberating.

Parker made his way to the bar, where Nick stood behind the counter, effortlessly charming patrons with his easy smile.

Nick's eyes lit up when he spotted Parker, and a grin spread across his face. "Look who decided to show up."

Parker adjusted his glasses. "Couldn't sleep," he said, settling atop a stool.

Nick leaned in, his gaze playful. "I told you this place has that effect."

Parker allowed himself a small smile. Nick's voice, trusting and safe, settled some of the restless energy buzzing in him. He handed Parker a vodka tonic without needing to ask. "On the house," Nick said with a wink.

Parker lifted the glass to his lips, letting the burn of alcohol cut through the fog in his thoughts. Before he could finish, Nick had another sitting on the bar top in front of him.

"I thought you were dancing tonight," Parker commented.

I did a set earlier, and you missed it," Nick replied. "I'll be up again later. Get your small bills ready," he jokingly added, busy multitasking behind the bar while focused on Parker.

While Nick worked, Parker's stool slowly swiveled around like a radar collecting signals from all directions, absorbing and analyzing the information collected. The place buzzed with energy that pulsed in rhythm with the bass vibrating through the floorboards. Groups of men—some huddled in tight circles, others lounging casually at high-top tables—filled the bar, their chatter blending into a symphony of low laughter and flirtation. Colored lights flickered intermittently, painting the bar in streaks of blue, green, red, and pink, their glow reflecting off chrome fixtures and glass bottles stacked neatly behind the bar. A thin haze of fog from a nearby machine swirled around the ceiling, catching beams of light and adding an ethereal shimmer to the space.

On the far bar top across the room, shirtless go-go dancers moved with easy confidence, their bodies fluid and unapologetic under the flicker of strobe lights. They were young and wore tight briefs, their skin glistening under a sheen of sweat as they teased the crowd—every sway of their hips or playful dip toward the audience rewarded with applause, hoots, or the flash of a five- or ten-dollar bill waved in anticipation. Parker's gaze darted toward them briefly, feeling both drawn and out of place—like an observer too hesitant to engage in a world operating without apology.

Cityside was a welcoming space known as a friendly twink bar where young men drew the attention of more mature patrons. It catered to various ages and preferences, offering something for everyone. The preppy crowd gravitated toward Blake's; the bears claimed Woofs and The Heretic, while the trance-dance devotees flocked to the Jungle for after-hours revelry. Cityside, by contrast, was far less intimidating. It was the spot people visited after dinner but before the late-night and all-night parties. Groups gathered to celebrate birthdays with cocktails and strippers, treating friends to lap dances as they marked another year. For those newly out of the closet, unsure of what they wanted or needed, Cityside provided a safe space to observe and learn the rhythm of it all.

The air was thick with the scent of men and desire. The sharp tang of citrus and gin cut through the sweetness of spiced rum lingering in the air. Music thumped persistently; a house beat wormed into Parker's chest, syncing with his heartbeat. It was overwhelming but not altogether unpleasant—a strange allure urging him to surrender, to let go.

His hands tightened briefly around the empty plastic cup as he scanned the space. Men of all ages—some his own, some older—mingled freely. A pair of twentysomethings in cropped tanks laughed near the DJ booth while a middle-aged man leaned over the bar, smiling at a dancer with practiced charm. The air buzzed with freedom—an unrestrained energy Parker hadn't experienced in years, if ever. Here, disorder and desire intertwined, untouched by the expectations that weighed so heavily on his carefully ordered life.

As the stool completed its rotation, Parker set his empty cup on the bar and reached for the third drink Nick conveniently prepared, waiting for him to claim it. Nick winked, and this time, Parker smiled and returned the gesture. He let himself sink into the rhythm of the bar. The alcohol dulled his edges, the music loosened the tension coiled in his muscles, and the cold bite of vodka against his tongue calmed a restlessness within him—an unease lurking beneath the surface. The ice clinked softly against the sides of the cup, a quiet, grounding sound amidst the chaos, allowing Parker to drift just enough to stay afloat. As he did, a familiar accent cut through the ambient noise like a wire pulled tight.

"Well, what do we have here," the voice said, his grin spreading across his face with a predatory ease.

Parker's pulse quickened. Devin stood with his usual cocky nonchalance, hands stuffed in his pockets. Just behind him, Mark hovered—a step back but impossible to ignore. His expression was unreadable, his steady presence both gentle and disconcerting. The contrast between them was sharper than ever. Devin radiated energy and recklessness; Mark exuded composure and precision—two forces orbiting a single, inevitable pull.

Devin's leg brushed against Parker's with intentional slowness as he squeezed between occupied barstools. The brief contact sent a jolt up Parker's spine. It was casual enough to ignore yet deliberate and lingered. Parker tensed but said nothing, the heat from Devin's contact radiating through the denim of his jeans. Devin grabbed Parker's exposed biceps below the cuff of his polo shirt, exclaiming, "Wow! Look at those arms. I had no idea, wearing those long-sleeved button-downs at work." The comment embarrassed Parker, pulling his arm out of Devin's grasp.

Mark gave Parker an approving nod as if old friends were meeting by chance. "Out enjoying the night?" Mark asked, sounding genuinely surprised to find Parker outside the office walls.

Parker shifted on his stool. "Couldn't sleep," he answered, lifting his cup to his lips again, finishing the last of his third vodka tonic.

Behind Parker, Nick wiped down the bar top while carefully watching their interaction. His easy smile faltered as he leaned in toward Parker, lowering his voice so only Parker could hear. "Be careful with these two," Nick muttered, a note of caution in his voice. It wasn't just a suggestion—it was a warning.

Despite Nick's discretion, Devin caught his comment. His grin widened, mischief flickering in his eyes like embers ready to ignite. "Aw, Nick," Devin teased, shooting him a playful and pointed glance. "You say that like you're an angel."

Nick returned the comment with an expression of blended frustration and pity before turning to serve another customer down the bar.

Devin shifted his attention back to Parker, his gaze unwavering. "Come dance with us," he said, tilting his head toward the dance floor. Devin's tone carried no hesitation, just the quiet confidence of expected compliance.

"I don't actually—" Parker began, but Devin was already

tugging on Parker's arm, trying to coax him toward the dance floor. He didn't have time to look back at Nick. If he did, he would have seen Nick shaking his head from side to side, signaling him not to let Devin manipulate him. Parker would have seen Nick put both hands on the bar top as if the lean bartender would leap over it to intervene and save him.

"C'mon, Doc. It'll be fun," Devin insisted, the invitation floating between them, a subtle challenge wrapped in enticement. His hand kept trying to grab Parker's while Parker resisted. "C'mon, Mark's okay with it," he added. "Aren't you, Baby?"

He had no intention of dancing with Devin. Still, when Parker glanced at Mark and the two locked eyes, he noted Mark's expression was as steady as during each session. It was absent of jealousy—only an acceptance making the moment feel more surreal—as if Mark knew how this would likely play out and was content to let it happen.

The shout behind his shoulder broke Parker's focus on Mark's puzzling response to Devin's tenacity. "Here ya go, buddy," Nick called out, setting a fresh vodka tonic behind Parker. He hoped it would keep Parker where he was, and it did for a few moments. The vodka's sharpness cut through the restraint lingering in the back of his throat, leaving a clean burn mirroring his fraying composure.

"C'mon, Doc," Devin persisted, dancing in place beside him.

Parker knew Devin's tendency to stay in motion mirrored his emotional volatility. His seeming inability to stay still suggested a mind constantly working, searching for ways to control or manipulate a situation. During sessions, Parker observed how, when confronted by Mark, Devin often deflected with physical movements—pacing, leaning against furniture, and playing with his hair or clothing. These restless movements highlighted his unpredictability. Now Devin was doing it to Parker.

"Not now, Devin," Parker replied, taking three large sips of his fresh drink to consume most of it.

In response, Devin pouted with youthful innocence, a victim of harsh rejection when all he was trying to do was bring joy and happiness to all around him. After a few moments, his dimples and boyish grin returned, and he raised his hand toward Parker, politely inviting Parker to the dance floor to keep him company while he alone danced.

Swallowing the rest of his fourth cocktail, Parker slammed the empty cup on the bar, the ice rattling as it hit. The alcohol hummed through his veins, dulling the edges of his usual restraint and leaving his thoughts loose and untethered. The air around him was warm, and his judgment blurred as his defenses slipped beyond reach. He gazed into Devin's eyes and hesitated. He told himself it was just a dance, nothing more. But the hairs on his neck prickled when Parker stood and followed Devin to the dance floor. He knew, deep down, this wasn't just a dance.

The music shifted as they stepped into the mass of bodies, slowing to a sultry, hypnotic beat. Devin was already moving, his body fluid and confident, hips swaying to the rhythm. He spun toward Parker, and a grin tugged at the corner of his mouth as the distance between them closed. Devin's hands ran lightly up Parker's muscular arms, along his broad shoulders, and across his well-defined chest.

Parker's heart raced, and he momentarily lost himself in the movement. The nightclub's flashing lights erased the edges of reality. The heat from the crowd pressed against his skin, damp and heavy, blurring the boundaries between his body and theirs, personal and professional, right and wrong.

Circling them slowly, Mark followed them out to the dancefloor. He stayed close, his movements deliberate and measured. His hand rested on the small of Parker's back—not forceful but present enough to make it clear he was part of this, too. It wasn't possessive; it was more like permission.

When Devin leaned in, he stood on his toes to reach Parker's head. At first, the quick movement stunned Parker, and he jolted back. However, when he realized Devin was trying to speak to him, he leaned forward again and lowered his head. Devin's lips brushed close to his ear as he did, his voice a warm whisper over the music. "See? I told you it'd be fun."

The words were lighthearted on the surface but rooted in deeper significance. Devin's hand on Parker's shoulder was casual and deliberate, as though gauging the boundaries of Parker's self-control.

Across the swirling lights, Mark's gaze met Parker's again, composed and approving—no malice, no anger—only a quiet understanding. Parker found it unsettling how effortlessly it all seemed for the couple.

The heat between them was building—too much, too fast. The pulse of the music, the closeness of their bodies, and the blurring of boundaries Parker spent years reinforcing were dangerous and intoxicating.

And then, like a cord pulled too tight, it snapped.

"I—" Parker stammered, his voice thick with panic as he pulled back abruptly. His heart pounded against his ribs, the air around him too hot, too heavy. "I need to go."

Devin's expression flashed with disappointment—a brief crack in his carefree demeanor. Still, he recovered quickly, flashing a grin hinting at more. "See you around, Doc," he said with a playful salute as if this was only the beginning.

Mark, still steady and composed, gave Parker a slight nod. "Take care, Parker," he said, his voice low and relaxed, as though he understood no line crossed couldn't be uncrossed.

Turning sharply and pulling away from the couple, Parker threaded his way back toward the bar, his pulse drumming in his ears. Nick was waiting for him when he reached the bar, his arms folded, his expression unreadable.

"You okay?" Nick asked, though his tone suggested he already knew the answer.

Nodding, Parker replied, "Yeah. Just need some air."

"You sure you know what you're doing with them?" Nick asked, sliding a bottle of water across the counter.

Parker exhaled and sipped the water, the cold liquid sharp against his throat. "No," he admitted quietly. "But I'll figure it out."

Nick studied him for a moment longer, his gaze cutting through Parker's facade with unsettling precision. "Just be careful," he said, his voice carrying the weight of experience. "They're not as simple as they seem."

"Nothing ever is," Parker murmured, setting the bottle down.

He cast one last glance at the dance floor. Mark and Devin had already melted back into the crowd, their figures distorted by the flashing lights. The world tilted slightly beneath his feet, the edges of his vision blending like the smudged lines of a watercolor painting. His pulse drummed louder than the music, an uneven rhythm making Parker believe he drank more than he should have. Everything blurred: the lights, the crowd, his judgment. A strange heaviness settled in his limbs like he was floating outside himself, detached and unsteady. The cool air outside called to him, but trying to reach the door was like walking through water, and that was the moment Parker went under.

9

THE SURPRISE

(Saturday the 7ᵗʰ)

The sound of running water roused Parker from sleep. He stirred slowly, the back of his skull throbbing with a dull ache. His tongue felt thick in his dry mouth, and the stale taste of vodka lingered like regret. As he lay atop sweat-soaked sheets, he rolled on his side and reached for his watch—10:34 a.m.. Parker never slept this late, even on the weekends.

He sat up slowly, disoriented, rubbing at his temples. His brain swam with fragments of last night: lights, music, Nick's smile, Mark's knowing glances, Devin's touch. The lingering remnants of the alcohol clouded his thoughts as if the drinks wove threads of fog, dulling his senses. The hiss of the shower mingled with the splashing of water against the tile, resounding in the otherwise silent condo.

Confusion first anchored Parker to the mattress, but as he listened intently, the nature and source of the sound became apparent. Could he have been *that* drunk as to have left the shower running after getting home and washing the stench of the bar's smoke and anxiety from his body? It could explain awakening to the feeling he laid upon damp sheets all night.

Parker swung his legs over the side of the bed, feeling the ache in his muscles as he moved—a dull stiffness from too much alcohol and too little sense. The events from the night filtered through his mind in uneven flashes: Nick's generosity, the bass thumping beneath his skin, Devin's hand brushing against his body. *Think, Parker*, he willed himself. Did Nick drive him home? No, he would have remembered that. Did he remember locking his front door after coming home? An uncomfortable chill coiled through him, unease flowing through the gaps in his memory.

He forced himself to stand. Moving slowly, as if any sudden motion might shatter his little clarity, Parker crept toward the bathroom door. Steam rolled out from beneath it, the scent of lavender soap in the steam like a ghostly presence, its sweetness foreign and unsettling in the sterile familiarity of Parker's home.

His fingers hesitated on the doorframe, uncertainty knotting in his chest as the flowing water amplified the strangeness of the moment. The thoughts running through his mind were irrational and strangely compelling.

Haze spilled out as Parker eased the door open, warm and dense, like the breath of a new presence stirring to life. Through the misted glass of the shower, he saw him standing under the cascade—his head tipped back as water traced the contours of his body, illuminated by the shimmer of the polished white tiles.

The figure in the shower stood with casual ease, the water tracing over his shoulders and running down his torso. He wasn't as lean or defined as a dancer, yet his build had a natural strength—a body shaped more by movement than weights. His upper body was smooth, not broad, but proportionate. The faint outline of his ribs shifted with each breath, giving way to the subtle contours of his abdomen—not chiseled muscle but taut as if sculpted by constant motion. His real strength was in his legs: powerful thighs and firm glutes carved like those of a speed skater or someone used to gliding through space. They gave him a grounded presence, a contrast to his playful demeanor.

Devin?

The wet cascade traced over his back, gliding down the curve of his hips and the length of his legs, emphasizing the quiet confidence in how he held himself—a man who didn't need exaggerated muscle to command attention. He seemed at ease, fully inhabiting his skin, as if entirely aware of the effect his presence, clothed or not, had on anyone watching.

Parker watched him clearly and wholly—the moment was intimate. His mind reached for logic, desperate for a tether to reality, a way to explain this impossible scene, but reasoning slipped through his fingers like sand. All Parker could do was stare, caught between the urge to leave and the compulsion to stay.

He watched Devin's graceful movements. The water's warmth belonged to him—soap trailing lazily down the lines of his torso, gathering briefly at the curve of his hip before slipping away to his powerful lower extremities. His body was a study in contrast: limber but strong, every movement deliberate yet relaxed. Parker's throat tightened. He should've said something, but words refused to come.

Parker blinked, convinced for a moment his mind was playing a trick on him, that the alcohol was still affecting his perception. *What the hell is Devin doing in my shower?*

Devin caught Parker's reflection in the mirror above the sink and unabashedly grinned as if his presence was the most natural thing in the world. "Morning, sleepyhead."

Parker's response was slow and hesitant. "What are you doing here?"

Devin chuckled, the sound relaxed, like a shared joke. "Where else would I be, silly?" He pushed the shower door open, water dripping from his hair in lazy rivulets as he reached for his towel. His skin glistened under the bathroom light, each movement deliberate and unhurried. His eyes sparkled with the same playful energy Parker saw before—mischief wrapped in charm. "You're funny when you're hungover, you know that?"

"Seriously, Devin, what the hell are you doing here?"

Devin tilted his head, a playful grin curling at the edges of his lips. "Seriously, Babe. What do you *think* I'm doing here? I live here. Are you *that* hungover, or did you hit your head last night?"

"What?" Parker shook his head as if the simple gesture could dispel the absurdity of the moment. "We—" He stumbled over the words. "We aren't together."

Devin dried his body and wrapped the towel loosely around his hips, humoring Parker's little morning charade. "Um, we sure are."

The words landed like a slap. Parker's stomach clenched. "This can't be real," he whispered, the words barely audible.

"Babe," Devin uttered as if humoring a child. "You always get like this when you're stressed. It's okay."

"I'm not stressed," Parker insisted.

Devin's grin didn't falter. If anything, it deepened with an indulgent and endearing affection. "Sure, babe. Keep telling yourself that."

He moved through the space with the ease of someone who perfected this moment, each step a quiet declaration of belonging. The floral sweetness lingered in the steam, faintly clinging to his skin. Devin was much too close again, and Parker's instincts urged him to step back. But his bare feet remained rooted to the marble floor, trapped between confusion and a sensation teetering on the edge of desire.

"You've been acting weird lately," Devin said, his statement sincere as he studied Parker. "Is it work again? You always get a little weird when work stresses you out. But we've talked about that, haven't we?"

Parker's jaw clenched. "Devin, you don't live here," his voice cracking under disbelief, the words stumbling out, brittle and uncertain. "You never have."

Devin gave him a patient smile, suggesting he'd heard this argument a dozen times before. "Then whose clothes are those?" He gestured toward the closet, where several unfamiliar shirts hung neatly beside Parker's. "And the pictures in the living room?"

The adjoining closet doorway stood open, revealing neatly hung clothes—and interspersed between them, clothing that didn't belong to him—clothing he'd never seen yet hung as if they belonged. Parker's heart pounded as if he stood precariously on the edge of a cliff, the ground beneath him shifting dangerously. He forced himself to step away from Devin, moving toward the bedroom like a man drowning in the unknown. He pulled open a drawer. T-shirts—Parker's folded with precision, yet interspersed between them, others he didn't recognize. His mind scrambled for explanations.

"This isn't possible," Parker whispered. "I'd remember."

"I know it's a lot," Devin said sympathetically. "You get caught up in your own head sometimes. But I'm here." His voice dipped lower, tender and reassuring like someone coaxing a frightened animal or reassuring someone awakened by a bad dream. "I've always been here for you."

The words unraveled Parker further, tugging at the frayed edges of his sense of reality. His hands trembled as he reached into the drawer again, pulling out one of the unfamiliar shirts. He stared at it, searching for meaning in the fabric as everything he believed he knew was slipping away.

Devin closed the distance between them again, his hand brushing Parker's shoulder in an unsettlingly natural touch. Parker's mind teetered between panic and a warmer emotion he couldn't quite name. He pulled away, but Devin followed, deliberately maintaining the closeness. It was like a dance—one step forward, one step back—with Devin confidently leading.

"I don't remember—" Parker trailed off, his pulse pounding in his ears as the room tilted under the weight of his confusion and the surreal conversation. He wanted to pull away, to escape, but Devin's presence rooted him in place. It was the way Devin's nearness crept into Parker's senses, like a warm, enveloping fog, disarming him with ease. His scent—clean, inviting, and familiar—wrapped around Parker. At the same time, the faint pressure of his touch ignited sparks dancing along Parker's skin.

"You don't have to fight this," Devin whispered, his gaze unwavering. "You know you don't."

Parker's heart hammered painfully. *This isn't real.* But the warmth in Devin's embrace said otherwise.

And then, for a moment—a dangerous, fleeting moment— Parker let himself believe it. He allowed himself to think maybe this *was* real.

10

The New Past

Parker wandered through the condo in a strange and slow trance, his fingers grazing surfaces as though to ground himself. With each step, his senses grew sharper, like he was walking through someone else's life, someone wearing his face and answering his name. The small details tugged at his attention— a key ring with a charm he didn't recognize, a coffee mug with his initials etched alongside Devin's. He let his fingertips brush over them as if their mere touch might provide clarity. They were strangely familiar, yet out of place, as though someone subtly rearranged the pieces of his life without asking.

Devin watched him from across the kitchen, his mug cradled in his hand and his eyes following Parker's every move. "You're quieter than usual," he remarked with a gentle smile, his gaze remaining uncomfortably steady, a flicker of concern shadowing it. "I know we have our routines," Devin hesitated, "but if you need a little time to yourself, I get it."

Nodding, Parker watched the heat swirl from the fresh cup of coffee Devin poured into the mug with their initials. His fingers curled tight around the handle, needing the steady heat to keep him anchored. "It's just... you ever feel like you're dreaming while you're awake?" His voice sounded brittle, even to his ears.

"Only when I'm lucky enough to wake up next to you." Devin's response sounded genuine and unguarded, and it might have reassured Parker if it hadn't also sounded so perfectly timed, as if Devin knew what Parker needed to hear.

Parker was unsure how to respond. His mind circled back to the only way he knew to resolve uncertainty—uncover facts and gather evidence that would stand up to scrutiny in the courtroom of his mind. "I think I just need a minute," he said, attempting a faint smile as he gestured hesitantly toward the rest of the condo. He hoped moving through the space would help him find clarity—anything to ground his scattered thoughts.

Devin nodded in quiet understanding. "Of course. I get it," he said with empathy, standing back to give Parker space. He sipped his coffee, a quiet presence, supportive but unobtrusive. "Take all the time you need, babe. I'll be right here."

As Parker moved through the condo, items seemed placed just so—a framed photo of them at a beach with Devin's hand on his shoulder, Parker laughing casually and unguarded. Another picture of him at some family event, his arm around Devin's shoulders while a group of people stood behind them, smiling at the camera. The images looked real, but how could they be? He didn't remember any of it. And yet, they existed behind the picture frame's glass, preserved as memories. He could almost hear laughter—his own, mingled with Devin's— but the memory was too dim, like an old photograph faded by time.

Still dressed in only his black boxer briefs from the night before, Parker reached for his phone and walked outside onto the balcony. It was a chilly Saturday morning, an overcast remnant from the night before. Still, Parker was unaffected, his thumb hovering over Tim's contact. Each unanswered ring tightened the knot in the back of his neck. The ringing echoed in the stillness until Tim's cheerful voicemail greeting replaced it. He was still in Italy with Emma, of course. Parker knew that, yet the absence of his friend's answering made the stillness of the open-air balcony more isolating.

"Babe, don't you want to put some clothes on?" the voice from inside shouted through the glass doors. Parker heard him but already pressed the call button again, deciding whether to leave a message this time. What could he say that would sound halfway sensible during a thirty-second voicemail?

"You're calling Tim?" Devin asked as he leaned casually against the open doorframe behind Parker, watching him as though he was reading his mind. "There's a time difference, you know." Devin's tone was breezy, yet his gaze was unwavering and too knowing.

Turning around, Parker was caught off-guard by Devin's familiarity with Tim. "Yeah," he said slowly, trying to keep his voice steady. "Just thought I'd check in."

Devin nodded thoughtfully, but a crease formed between his brows, a hint of concern threading through his otherwise relaxed expression. "Well, you don't usually worry about him like this. It's sweet, though." The statement carried an undertone that Parker couldn't quite place. It was supportive but expectant, as though Devin was waiting for him to come to some silent understanding. "But I get it," Devin continued, "It's been a strange morning." Devin reached out, his fingers lightly rubbing Parker's forearm and bicep, a touch meant to soothe.

"Guess I'm just… I don't know, out of sorts." Parker's voice faltered slightly, betraying the uncertainty he fought to suppress.

Every rational part of him screamed this wasn't real and he should question everything. But the way Devin looked at him, the warmth in his touch, all felt disturbingly genuine and desired.

They walked together toward the living room, and Devin gestured to the bookshelf lining the wall. "Look," he said, running his finger along the spines—books arranged alphabetically, precisely as Parker preferred. "You always liked keeping things just so," he remarked. "It's one of the things I love most about you, even if I'm not as meticulous as you are." His brown eyes carried a quiet kindness, offering unspoken comfort and understanding. Yet, beneath the warmth ran a faint gleam of satisfaction.

Parker stared at the shelves, feeling a tug of recognition both comforting and unsettling. The books were, in fact, perfectly ordered, the titles blending in the familiar arrangement he favored. "I didn't realize you noticed things like that," he said as if the words were present, but his mind was elsewhere.

"You know me. I see everything. I'm just subtle about it," Devin replied playfully.

As Parker moved to the desk, his eyes landed on a neat stack of paperwork and files—his handwriting scrawled across the top page, his signature at the bottom of a document, unmistakably in his style. He lifted a few sheets, eyes scanning the ink, his name printed alongside Devin's in a way that implied permanence and commitment. Each detail fell into place too perfectly, like a script tailored to soothe his mind rather than challenge it.

"How long," he began, his voice catching. "How long have we—?"

Devin stepped closer, his voice low and warm. "We've been through a lot, haven't we babe?" His hand reached up, rubbing

Parker's broad shoulders and bare back with a comforting gentleness.

Parker swallowed, grappling with the familiarity Devin claimed and the blank space in his memory. "I should remember all of this. These aren't the kinds of things anyone forgets."

Devin's expression bent into concern. "Maybe we should go to the ER. You're acting strangely, and it's starting to scare me."

"No," Parker shot back. "It's nothing. It's just a hangover, I guess. You know I don't drink." For the moment, Parker didn't focus on the snippets of memory from last night. His mind was too consumed with the events of the past thirty minutes to piece together the flashes of Devin, Mark, Nick, Cityside, and the dance.

"Memory is strange, babe, especially when you work as hard as you have lately. You know you hate stress. Don't push yourself. Just let it come back naturally," Devin murmured. His demeanor was too understanding, as though he already considered every possibility, every reaction.

Parker's gaze dropped to the floor, the weight of Devin's words settling over him. Every instinct told him to resist, question, and find a logical answer. And yet, the tenderness in Devin's eyes and touch spoke to a truth he couldn't easily dismiss. His concerns were slowly fading as if Devin's gentle assurances were nudging him into a reality he hadn't consented to but couldn't entirely deny.

Walking into the kitchen, Parker leaned against the center island, rubbing the bridge of his nose as he took a slow, grounding breath, willing the remnants of his hangover to fade. The morning's surreal events clung to him like a dream he couldn't shake, the hazy unease lingering long after waking.

Glancing toward Devin, who now sat comfortably on the sofa with a coffee mug in hand, Parker chose his words carefully.

"I need to head into the office for a bit," he finally said, trying to keep his voice steady. "There's a lot I need to sort through."

"On a Saturday? I thought we had plans to relax today," he said, his tone layered with surprise and concern. "Especially after last night."

Parker hesitated, trying to shake the nagging confusion, his mind scrambling for an answer to explain this new reality. "It's something I didn't get to this week," he replied, careful to avoid specifics. "Shouldn't be too long."

Devin's brows knitted as he took a slow sip of his coffee, studying Parker with quiet scrutiny. "Are you sure you're in condition to go anywhere, let alone work?" His tone carried a gentle rebuke as though Parker's well-being was his familiar responsibility.

"I'll feel better once I get cleaned up," Parker answered, shrugging off Devin's concern. "Don't worry."

Devin nodded with a practiced acceptance. "Of course. I know how dedicated you are," he said, his gaze warm and oddly knowing as though this Saturday trip to the office was his well-known habit. "Just promise me you'll take it easy. You don't need to always bury yourself in other people's problems."

Something about Devin's words, a mix of endearment and routine like a friendly reminder, twisted uneasily in Parker's stomach. He forced a nod, keeping his tone casual. "Right, thanks. I won't be too long."

Devin stood, crossing the room to rest a reassuring hand on Parker's arm. "Good," he said with gentle insistence. "I'll be here when you get back, and then we can relax."

Parker mustered a tight-lipped smile, but his unease only deepened. The tenderness in Devin's voice and the familiar way his hand lingered on his arm was warm and disorientating, like a ritual they'd shared countless times. Parker nodded while his mind raced, walking to the bedroom to clean up and dress. A thousand questions rattled in his mind. He needed to go to the office, find evidence to ground him and confirm that his mind and life weren't unraveling.

The office was closed on the weekends, and as Parker entered, his steps echoed against the polished hardwood of the renovated house. He walked down the hall, the framed art and décor in its rightful place—the normalcy starkly contrasting what was happening at home.

Entering his office, he found it undisturbed, the early afternoon light casting a warm glow over his desk and the meticulously arranged items on its surface. He set his satchel down carefully, scanning the room as if searching for disruption. He exhaled slowly, savoring the stillness as it calmed the turmoil in his mind. As he sank into his chair, the need for evidence—a confirmation his remembrances held firm—became paramount.

With a sense of purpose, Parker opened his laptop and scrolled through emails, glancing at each subject line and sender with a tense eagerness. He was searching for some evidence of this 'relationship' with Devin. Old appointments, billing reminders, and a message from Olivia about a scheduling conflict. Nothing unusual. He moved to his calendar, scanning for any mention of Devin or any sign of this relationship he was supposedly a part of. As his fingers scrolled through entries on the monitor, he noted his familiar schedule—sessions with clients, updates from administrative staff, reminders from Dr. Warren—but nothing suggested Devin was anything more than a client. There were no mysterious gaps in his calendar and no appointments with Devin beyond the standard appointment confirmations. Every entry was clinical; every session notated with practiced efficiency. He saw only his meticulously organized routine, just as he remembered it.

Parker drummed his fingers restlessly on his desk. It made no sense. The physical evidence—clothes in his condo and shared photographs—suggested one reality. His office, with its neatly organized emails, calendar, and furnishings, untouched by any hint of a relationship with Devin, offered another. Devin's story of their relationship remained unsubstantiated. Every document and entry confirmed the truth he remembered. Devin was merely a client, nothing more. But the lack of evidence was as unsettling as the alternative.

Pulling his phone from his pocket, Parker scrolled through his photograph gallery, searching for any trace of Devin. It contained only familiar photos he remembered. Parker wanted to check his journal next but feared he had left it on his nightstand where he last reviewed it. Relief quickly swept him as he recalled slipping it into his bag after dressing to come in.

Reaching down, Parker retrieved the notebook from his satchel and flipped it open on his desk. He skimmed through his notes on Devin and Mark's sessions, rereading his observations. They were sharp, professional, and untouched by anything remotely personal. Nothing here suggested he'd blurred the line between therapist and lover. Only one session entry caught his eye: '*Client exhibits an uncanny understanding of personal routines—possible manipulation?*' It was an observation he'd dismissed as another of Devin's manipulative traits. Now, however, the words took on a different tone. It read less like professional insight and more like intimate intuition.

That's when the idea hit him: *call Mark Sutherland*. That would answer all of his questions. It was so simple he wondered why it hadn't occurred to him sooner. Parker considered what he might say—why he would call a client on a Saturday afternoon. It was highly unusual, something he had never done before. Perhaps he could frame it as a professional check-in after an unusual three-session week. But how would he broach—or maneuver around—the topic of Devin's whereabouts?

"Parker?"

The voice startled him, and his head jerked up. Dr. Warren stood in the doorway, his gaze sweeping over Parker's tense posture. A man whose presence commanded quiet respect, Dr. Warren carried a gentle authority at sixty-eight. His neatly trimmed, thinning gray hair framed a thoughtful expression, and behind wire-rimmed glasses not unlike Parker's, his round features held a balance of kindness and wisdom, tempering his sometimes-rigid expectations.

"Dr. Warren," Parker replied, his voice still shaken as he quickly closed his journal and cleared his throat.

Parker's boss stepped inside, his posture as poised as ever. He was alone in the office on the weekend, yet dressed in his usual attire: a plaid tweed jacket, vest, tie, and aged but polished shoes that barely made a sound when he walked on the old hardwoods. "I wasn't expecting to see you here on a Saturday." His voice was gentle, but his eyes—keen and watchful—missed nothing. "I assume you came in to catch up on some work?"

Parker's fingers tapped the edge of his journal before he folded his hands in his lap, forcing a casual tone. "Yes, just reviewing some client notes and emails."

Dr. Warren's gaze remained steady, the corners of his mouth dipping slightly. "Given your recent workload, I'd expect you to be taking some rest." His eyes studied Parker's face, noting the signs of fatigue and the unshaven stubble. Dr. Warren's expression contained an additional layer, subtle but unvoiced.

"I thought it'd be best to stay on top of things," Parker replied, his voice sounding distant to himself. He felt exposed under Dr. Warren's steady scrutiny, as if the owner could sense the turmoil beneath his composed exterior.

Dr. Warren nodded, though his expression betrayed a hint of doubt. "Work is important, but so is balance." He took a step closer, his voice dropping slightly. "Is everything alright, Parker?"

Parker shifted uncomfortably and glanced down. "Yes, of course," he said, attempting to inject confidence into his tone. "Everything's fine."

Dr. Warren's question lingered in the room, the silence probing. "Good, then," he finally replied, though unconvincing. "Remember, even therapists are entitled to feel unsteady. Part of being in this profession means recognizing your limits."

Parker met his gaze and understood the underlying message—a gentle nudge to confide, to let his mentor in. But he couldn't voice the questions disturbing him, the unraveling sense of self taking hold. The seasoned therapist patiently waited until Parker replied, "I'm sorry, sir. I've just been dealing with some unexpected changes and needed a few quiet hours in the office to sort things out. I didn't realize you were in today." His voice sounded thin and unsteady, clenching his jaw as he spoke and hating the sound of vulnerability seeping through.

Dr. Warren's brow furrowed, a slight but unmistakable sign of concern. "Well, you know that my door is always open. If there's anything on your mind—anything troubling you."

Parker's pulse quickened. He nodded though his throat constricted. "Thank you, Dr. Warren. I appreciate it."

Dr. Warren's gaze lingered on him a moment longer before he straightened, offering Parker a reassuring nod. "Very well. Remember to take care of yourself. The practice relies on each of us being at our best." He gave Parker a final glance, contemplating whether to say more, but only added, "Have a good weekend, Parker," before closing the door behind him.

Parker's hands relaxed. He'd weathered the conversation, though he sensed Dr. Warren remained unconvinced. He had already steadily climbed a never-ending slope of questions and self-doubt today.

Taking a steadying breath, Parker forced his focus back to his journal, opening it to his last session with Mark and Devin. Perhaps some overlooked detail or passing comment would align with Devin's claims from the morning.

A sliver of paper protruded from the fore-edge of the journal, barely visible between the pages. Parker flipped the pages to find a yellow Post-it note stuck to a blank page—one he would eventually turn to and write on. His curiosity became shock as he read the note.

"Miss you. Love you. Dev-"

Parker's hand reached for his phone. With a pang of apprehension, he pressed the call button and waited, each ring heightening his anxiety. But it went to voicemail—Tim's cheerful invitation to leave a message recorded in Italian. Parker hung up without leaving one, frustrated that his closest friend—

the one person he could rely on to anchor and reassure him—
wasn't available to confirm the memories slipping through his
fingers.

Slowly, he leaned back in his chair, staring at the ceiling as his
mind churned. He searched every document and verified every
entry. Still, Devin's presence in his life remained as enigmatic as
ever, undeniable and impossible. And now, the note.

When the phone buzzed, it jolted him. He expected Tim's
name to be displayed when he glanced down. It was just a
notification, however—another reminder that his wanted
answers would not come easily. And for the first time, his
office—a place he'd cultivated to be a place of order, control,
and grounding—felt like it held secrets he couldn't untangle.

11

A Toast to Us

The doors slid open, and Parker stepped into his quiet, dimly lit hallway, the steady hum of the elevator fading behind him. Each step toward his condo was a small surrender to an increasingly tempting reality; the scent of garlic and rosemary drifted from the kitchen to meet him at the door as he entered. Devin was cooking dinner as if it were the most natural thing in the world.

Parker's body still carried the ache from last night and this morning. But now, it settled differently—a slow resignation sinking into his muscles, a quiet surrender. He set his satchel down and watched Devin at the stove, absorbed in his work. He wore an apron over the fitted polo shirt that hugged his frame. The kitchen lighting cast a warm glow over the young figure. Devin moved with practiced ease—how he maneuvered around the counter, familiar with the location of each utensil and ingredient, as if he'd done this a thousand times before.

"Hey," Parker managed, unsure what else to say.

Devin's smile was warm and inviting. "Hey, you're back," he said, wiping his hands on a kitchen towel before giving Parker a light peck on the cheek. It was both strange and incredibly normal simultaneously, making Parker's stomach tighten with conflicting emotions.

"You, uh, made dinner?' Parker asked, keeping his tone casual despite his surprise at the unexpected gesture. He hadn't considered what to expect when he arrived home after his encounter with Dr. Warren and the contradictions lurking in the evidence at the office. Emails and calendars offered no insight into Devin's claims, yet the note in his journal was clear and direct. Parker considered showing it to Devin but hesitated. Not yet.

Devin nodded, motioning toward the kitchen counter where two glasses of red wine awaited them, along with two plates of chicken marsala nestled beside creamy garlic mashed potatoes and a garnish of fresh rosemary. Each element of the meal was perfectly crafted and thoughtfully plated, the savory scents blending to make Parker's stomach rumble despite his anxiety.

"Thought we could have a quiet dinner outside," Devin said. "It's chilly but nice out. Grab a plate, babe."

Parker nodded, feeling a mixture of gratitude and wariness. He hadn't entirely accepted this reality, but Devin's serene presence made resisting difficult. Reaching for the bottle of wine, Parker walked outside. Devin was already setting the dishes on the balcony's small bistro table.

The city lights shimmered against the evening sky, casting a relaxed glow over the balcony. Parker joined Devin, each taking a seat. As Devin handed him his glass, Parker hesitated. *Hadn't Devin always preferred Merlot?* he wondered, watching the deep purple hue of the Malbec swirl in the glass. Devin poured it without hesitation, raising his glass with a smile as if it were his favorite. The thought snagged in Parker's mind, but he let it go, chalking it up to the disjointed haze clouding his thoughts.

The first sip washed over Parker, dulling the remnants of his hangover and the uncertainty still fogging his mind.

Devin raised his glass again, offering a toast. "To us," he said, his gaze steady, the warmth in his eyes igniting an unfamiliar but profound sensation within Parker.

As Parker raised his glass, his gaze lingered on Devin's easy smile. It should have felt wrong, but instead, it was like slipping into a dream that had been waiting for him all along. The warmth of the wine spread through him, loosening the tension in his shoulders. He exhaled, only now realizing he'd been holding his breath, the strangeness of the moment settling like a shadow just out of reach.

As Devin set his glass back on the table, his hand brushed Parker's. It was a fleeting touch, but the warmth lingered on Parker, an unexpected gentleness. Devin caught Parker's gaze across the table and paused briefly. An unspoken emotion briefly flickered in Devin's eyes before glancing away.

For Devin, it was like opening a door to the past he'd tried to keep locked for years—the image from a night years ago before Mark, the last night he'd seen Leo, ingrained in his memory. They'd sat across from each other in the flickering candlelight of Leo's tiny kitchen, their laughter and easy affection filling the room. But there was tension beneath it all— a tension Devin refused to acknowledge.

~

"So, what happens now?" Leo said, his voice vulnerable as he set his fork down and stared at Devin with an intensity that demanded an answer. Leo wanted more—something real and permanent—but Devin hadn't known how to give it to him. He'd always kept things light, kept his distance, and never let anyone in too far.

"I thought we were just having fun, Leo. Why does everything need a label?" Devin tried to make it sound like a joke, but his words fell flat. He could still see the hurt in Leo's eyes, the silent understanding that whatever he meant to him wasn't enough.

The candlelight cast shadows across Leo's face as he nodded, quietly accepting the limits of Devin's affection. "Guess I just believed we were more," Leo had said, his voice barely above a whisper. Devin left before dawn the following day, slipping away without a word. They never spoke again.

~

The memory of Leo forced Devin to confront a vulnerability he long avoided. Beneath his carefree exterior lived the weight of having dismissed genuine affection, haunted by his decision to downplay his connection with Leo as mere fun. But with Parker, there was an undeniable intensity—a solace requiring no armor or distance. Devin felt a profound connection in this quiet moment: a sense of comfort rooted in authenticity and permanence. This time, he wasn't willing to let it slip away.

Devin blinked, the memory of Leo fading like smoke in the candlelight of that distant kitchen. He shifted back to Parker, meeting his gaze with a feeling of openness as unfamiliar as it was welcome. But this time, Devin wouldn't retreat into the safety of lightheartedness. Instead, he held Parker's gaze, feeling the magic of this moment—a quiet invitation to rewrite his story, to lean in rather than let love slip away.

Devin and Parker ate the rest of their meal in relative quiet; the only sound was the occasional clink of silverware and the distant hum of city life below. Parker stole glances at Devin, who seemed entirely at ease, savoring each bite with quiet pleasure, which only added to Parker's confusion. He wanted to ask questions, to probe, but every time he opened his mouth, the words of inquiry died, leaving him with a strange sense of contentment he didn't expect.

"Doesn't it feel good just to relax?" Devin asked as they finished their meal. "Sometimes words aren't necessary. It's the comfort of just being together."

Parker hesitated, his fingers tracing the rim of his glass. "I suppose, yes. It's just—." He paused to restrain the unease within. "I can't shake the feeling I'm living someone else's life."

Devin's gaze softened. "Babe, you're overthinking it, as usual." He leaned forward, placing a hand over Parker's, the touch warm and grounding. "Just let yourself be with me. You don't have to understand everything to enjoy it."

Parker let out a long exhale, nodding as he laced his fingers with Devin's. "I don't know why it feels so foreign, though."

Devin's thumb traced circles on the back of Parker's hand, his expression gentle but intense. "Maybe because you don't let yourself feel things often enough. You're too focused on ensuring every detail is right or helping people fix their problems." He gave Parker's hand a reassuring squeeze. "That's so admirable and great, but it's also exhausting. You are allowed to relax, too, babe."

Parker managed a small smile, feeling his defenses slip further. This was what he always wanted, what he was experiencing right now—a genuine connection, someone who seemed to understand him without words. It was what he dreamed of in his loneliest moments.

The silence between the two stretched, and Devin took a sip of his wine as he gazed out upon the lit cityscape. He could feel

Parker watching him, curious and confused. He took a deep breath and glanced back across the table.

"You know," Devin said, his voice quieter than usual, "I've never really been one to play by the rules." His mouth curved into a smile, yet there was a sadness behind it. "Sometimes, I guess I just wanted things to stay simple. But simple doesn't always mean easy."

Parker held his gaze, a quiet understanding passing between them. As Devin's mask began to slip, the practiced charm yielded a vulnerability he usually kept hidden.

Parker's voice was quiet, his tone a mix of understanding and curiosity. "So, what is it you're expecting, Devin?"

The question hung in the air, and for a moment, Devin wasn't sure how to respond. He glanced down at his plate, feeling the weight of Parker's attention on him. "Maybe...someone who doesn't turn away." He spoke tenderly, shaking his head, the words sounding foreign. "Someone who sees more than what's on the surface."

The honesty of the statement surprised him. Devin looked back up, meeting Parker's eyes, feeling the closeness forming between them. For the first time in years, he hoped this time could be different.

After dinner, they cleared the table together, moving through the kitchen in an easy rhythm that looked choreographed. Devin washed while Parker dried, their movements synchronized, their silences comfortable. After putting everything in the kitchen away, they settled on the couch, a movie flickering on the TV screen as they sipped the last of their wine.

Parker's mind was hazy with a mixture of fatigue and curiosity. He followed Devin to the bedroom, his heart pounding with each step. He'd always feared and desired this in equal measure—an intimacy he only allowed himself to imagine.

Their hands explored, each touch uncovering a hidden depth, a piece of desire Parker hadn't dared to acknowledge. Devin was tender and hungry, guiding Parker with a confidence that left him breathless. Parker yielded, surrendering himself to the moment, his thoughts dissolving in the warmth of Devin's embrace.

As they settled, Parker lay behind Devin and spooned him. Unexpected warmth spread through every point of contact. The steady rise and fall of Devin's breathing was smooth and grounding. But as Parker's eyes drifted shut, a sharp memory surfaced with an abruptness and cruelty he didn't expect.

~

He was sixteen, lying curled in a tent on a winter camping trip with his friend Brandon. The wind picked up that night, whipping against the tent's thin walls. The cold crept in so slowly that he hadn't realized he was shivering. He drowsily shifted closer to Brandon during the night, instinctively seeking warmth. Parker's arm settled over his friend at some point, their bodies drawn together in the narrow space, the closeness comforting against the harsh chill outside and the unspoken forces of curiosity and desire of adolescence within.

The nylon tent walls flapped under the wind's bite, and the air inside carried the damp, earthy scent of snow-soaked ground. Parker remembered how the cold seeped into his bones despite his layers. Brandon's warmth had been the only shield against it—a closeness that felt natural in the dark but grew jagged and sharp in the morning light.

When daylight came, Parker was violently awoken by an elbow into his chest, followed by a shove. His thin sleeping bag slipped from his shoulders as Brandon pushed him away, his face twisted in disgust and anger. "What the hell, Parker? Are you gay or something? Get the fuck away!"

The words stung and lodged somewhere deep within. Parker mumbled an apology, trying to shrug off the morning arousal that afflicted all teenage boys. He scrambled out of the tent, stumbling in the snow outside, trying to escape the hurt in Brandon's voice. The memory stayed, lodged like a splinter he could never entirely remove, one reminding him to keep his distance and guard his actions.

~

Now, with his arm around Devin, that old ache lingered, but this was different—without rejection or disgust—just warmth and acceptance. Parker thought he could finally rest here, free from the echoes of shame; the last traces of that old memory dissolved as he sank deeper into the comfort of the present. This moment with Devin was what Parker unknowingly longed for. He shifted, letting his head relax against the pillow as Devin pulled him closer, feeling, for the first time, that he could let go without the exhausting need to maintain his walls and barriers.

Much of the night was a blur of sensations, reality and dream bleeding into each other until Parker could no longer tell where one ended and the other began. And when they finished, tangled together in bed, Parker closed his eyes with a contented sigh. Whatever questions lingered at the edges of his mind could wait until tomorrow. For now, he was where and who he wanted to be.

As Parker's breathing slowed, his gaze drifted to the bedroom mirror, where faint moonlight glimmered off its surface. For an instant, he sensed a flicker of movement—a sharp and fleeting glint like light off the edge of a blade. He blinked, his body spent with satisfaction, unable to respond. When his eyes opened again, the mirror was still, its surface blank and undisturbed. The fleeting impression faded like reality curling into the dark as sleep overcame him.

12

THE KISS OF DEATH

(Sunday the 8th)

Morning arrived with the sun's glow slipping through the windows, filling the bedroom with light and the promise of a new day's transparency. Parker blinked, his eyes heavy from a deep sleep engulfing him after the night's intimacy. The warmth of Devin's body was still beside him, sleeping peacefully, an anchor to this new reality Parker was slowly settling into. It was a feeling of belonging and warmth he hadn't experienced before. For a moment, everything was peaceful and normal. For a moment, everything was perfect.

Parker studied Devin's features as he slept. He saw contentment and genuine happiness, along with vulnerability. They were things Parker hadn't seen in him before. When Devin finally stirred and opened his eyes, he gazed at Parker with warmth, as if waking up like this was the most natural thing in the world.

"Morning, gorgeous," Devin murmured, his voice still rough with sleep. He leaned in to press a kiss to Parker's forehead. "Hope you're not thinking of running off to the office again today."

Parker rested his head back upon the pillow. "No. No work today." He could feel Devin's smile against his skin, the weight of the last few days seeming to dissolve as he allowed himself to relax, enjoying the feeling of having someone there—someone who genuinely cared.

Devin slipped out of bed and offered to make breakfast—his comfort in Parker's home still disorienting in the bright light of morning. He stretched as he moved toward the kitchen, entirely at home and wearing only a pair of Parker's pajamas, his muscles flexing as he reached into the cupboard for coffee.

Devin's cheerful humming echoed from the kitchen as Parker sat on the sofa and nursed a cup of coffee. He watched Devin move around the kitchen with ease, frying eggs and slicing bread to toast. Devin knew where everything was— where Parker kept the olive oil, salt, and cloth napkins. The familiarity was still both comforting and unsettling to Parker.

Devin noticed Parker watching him and returned an affectionate smile. "You look lost in thought, babe."

There was an undercurrent Prker couldn't quite identify, a subtle tension beneath the surface leaving him uneasy. Though he couldn't put his finger on it, the sensation gnawed at him and made him restless. He wanted to embrace this new reality, to let go and enjoy what was in front of him. Forcing a nod and a smile, Parker said, "Just getting used to... all of this," gesturing vaguely around the kitchen.

"You better," Devin replied.

Reaching for his laptop, Parker opened it on his knees. He told himself it was just to check emails and get a jump on the upcoming workweek. Instead, Parker clicked on his banking app after a small curiosity emerged.

He typed in his password, waiting for the screen to load. Devin's muted voice in the background, calling him to breakfast, filled the space between them. The numbers appeared, and Parker's eyes narrowed. The balance was much lower than he expected—than he knew it should be. As he scrolled through the transaction history, he made mental notes of charges he didn't recognize. Transfers and ATM withdrawals, large and frequent, made over the last two days, nearly emptied his checking account.

"Parker?" Devin's voice snapped him back to the present, and he quickly closed the laptop. Devin stood in the doorway, holding a plate of eggs and toast, his face bright and open.

"Breakfast is ready," Devin said, walking over and setting the plate in front of Parker on the coffee table. He leaned over and planted a gentle kiss on Parker's cheek. "You look a little pale."

Parker hesitated, his heart pounding in his chest. He nodded slowly, trying to keep his expression neutral. "Yeah, I'm fine. Just checking some work stuff."

Devin brushed a hand through Parker's hair, reminding him he worked too hard. "Today is supposed to be about us, remember?"

Parker nodded, his eyes trailing Devin as he moved back toward the kitchen. He could still feel the warmth of Devin's lips on his forehead, but now it was different. Parker needed more information. He needed to understand what was happening.

After breakfast, he retreated to the second bedroom, a guest room he often used as a study, under the guise of needing to finish some paperwork. Devin didn't question it. Instead, he planted another kiss on Parker's cheek and told him he'd be in the living room if he needed anything. The ease of Devin's demeanor and the casual way he moved through his space began to bother him, a sense of wrongness deep in his gut.

Parker closed the door and opened his laptop again. His eyes scanned the inbox of senders and subject lines, searching for something—anything. He wasn't sure what. He opened an email from his bank, his eyes widening at the words on the screen— warnings indicating his account balance was dangerously low.

Parker's mind raced. He sat still, listening for any evidence of movement from the living room over the beating of his heart. He logged into his American Express account next, quickly scanning the recent charges from online retailers, luxury stores, and airlines—all things he hadn't bought. The knot in his stomach twisted tighter, rising in his throat as a realization set in. *It isn't possible*, Parker thought. His bank account and credit cards were all protected by text notifications when charges posted above certain limits or balances fell below specific minimums. He had received none of those.

Parker remembered Mark's words from their counseling sessions—his frustration and exhaustion when he spoke about Devin. At the time, Parker thought Mark was struggling to communicate or maybe even exaggerating. Now, staring at the evidence before him, Parker understood Mark's previous comments.

A soft knock on the bedroom door made Parker jump. He quickly closed the laptop as Devin peeked his head in.

"Hey, everything okay?" Devin asked, his eyes filled with concern. "Why's the door closed?"

Parker forced a smile, "Yeah, just finishing up. I'll be out in a minute."

Devin nodded. "Take your time. I'll wait." He pulled the door handle gently behind him, failing to close it entirely, leaving a slit of exposure between the two rooms. Parker watched him walk back into the living room and sit, shooting an inquisitive glance in Parker's direction as he did.

Parker released a shaky sigh and ran his hands through his tousled hair. He needed to talk to someone and make sense of what was happening. Reaching for his phone, Parker scrolled through recent calls to Tim's name. He hesitated momentarily without pressing the call button, staring at the door cracked open and Devin beyond it. Without sufficient privacy, he didn't, switching the phone off and tossing it onto the bed.

Parker stood, his mind still racing. He needed to confront Devin to understand what was happening. But as Parker considered the way Devin looked at him with such love and warmth, his resolve wavered. He wanted to believe this was all some misunderstanding—that some explanation existed. Deep down, however, he knew there was none.

Rubbing the back of his neck, Parker recalled dinner the night before, how Devin smiled and had eyes filled with affection. He remembered how tender their touch was, how gentle their kisses, how warm their embraces. It was so real. It was so right. But now Parker didn't know what to believe with this newfound evidence.

Parker took a couple of deep breaths, grounding himself in the present moment—precisely what he would advise his clients to do. He sensed a wrongness lingering beneath the surface but needed clarity. He needed the truth.

Reaching for his laptop, he opened it again and continued going through his emails. He scrolled further to several unread messages from his mother and Tim—messages he'd somehow missed. He opened one from Tim, his eyes widening as he read the words.

"Why haven't you returned my calls? What's going on?"

Parker grimaced, scrolling to the following email from his mother.

"Are you really not coming for the holidays? I don't understand why you've been so distant. Please call me."

A cold sense of dread settled over Parker. He hadn't sent any messages to cancel holiday plans. He hadn't ignored Tim. Everything he uncovered pointed to a disturbing reality: his life was being distorted, piece by piece.

Parker scrolled through his social media, noticing changes there, too. Posts he didn't remember writing, pictures with Devin he had no memory of taking. It was as if someone else was curating his online presence to fit a narrative he didn't recognize. The unease tormented him, leaving him unmoored.

Parker also considered another possibility. Could he have experienced an injury or illness that affected his memory? Olivia, Dr. Warren, and Devin all mentioned him seeming 'off' lately. They each expressed concern. He knew it himself. Was this what the beginning of a mental impairment was like?

Parker set his laptop aside and took another deep breath, standing up and heading for the door. He needed answers and wouldn't find them sitting here, second-guessing himself. Parker needed to confront Devin and get answers. He couldn't keep pretending everything was fine, couldn't keep ignoring the truth. Steeling himself, he opened the door and stepped into the living room.

Devin lounged on the couch, scrolling through his phone, feet propped on the coffee table. He glanced up at the sound of the door, his face brightening when he saw Parker. "Hey, there you are," Devin said, smiling. "Everything okay?"

Parker swallowed hard, his heart pounding faster than usual. We need to talk," he said.

Devin's smile faltered, his eyes narrowing slightly. "What's wrong, babe?" He sat up and placed his phone, screen down, on the coffee table. "Come sit," he said, patting the space beside him.

Parker remained standing and steadied himself, leaning against the back of the sofa. "I just need to understand what's going on. With us. With everything." He peered into Devin's eyes, the warmth there enough to make him forget everything he saw. Almost.

"Of course. Are you still feeling out of sorts? Whatever it is, we can figure it out together."

"I hope so," Parker said, his voice apprehensive. "I truly do."

Parker hesitated before sitting down, and Devin immediately wrapped an arm around him when he did. "You're always worrying," Devin murmured, his hand brushing against Parker's temple and through his hair before resting on the back of his neck to gently rub it. "Just relax, okay? I'm here. Everything's good."

Parker wanted to believe him—to let go of his doubts. But he couldn't and pulled away from Devin's affection.

"Hey, don't pull away," Devin said gently, his hand resting on Parker's knee instead. "I know you're confused, but I'm here. Whatever it is, we can deal with it."

Parker glanced at Devin's phone lying on the coffee table. He hesitated before reaching for it, swiping the screen impulsively—a desperate act entirely out of character. It was locked, and although Parker felt a sharp pang of defeat, he wasn't ready to give up. He had to know.

"Parker!" Devin's voice cut through the quiet, making Parker jump. "What the hell is going on?" he cried out, grabbing his phone out of Parker's hand.

"That's what I want to know. What the hell is going on here, Devin," he shouted back. Parker stood, towering over the boy on the sofa, cowering into a protective ball and holding his phone close to his chest.

Devin's affectionate demeanor and adoration for Parker immediately went to shock and confusion. Devin scurried to get his feet under himself to retreat, putting the back of the sofa between himself and Parker.

Parker's body trembled with anger and confusion, his breath ragged gasps as he watched Devin scurry back. His mind was in turmoil, torn between wanting answers and trying to understand his life's surreal turn.

Devin's eyes were wide, a mix of fear and disbelief flickering behind them, his confidence replaced with fragility. "What is going on with you?" Devin stammered, keeping the sofa between them. His voice dripped with feigned concern. "Why are you acting like this? You're scaring me."

Parker's entire body shook as he tried to keep himself composed. "Don't try to turn this around on me. Don't you dare!" He stepped forward, his voice rising. "You've been lying to me, draining my accounts, blocking my phone contacts—no wonder I hadn't heard back from Tim. And you emailed my mother! You're messing with my life. Why?

Devin's lips trembled briefly before a strange calmness settled over him like someone at gunpoint negotiating for his freedom. He held his hands up, palms facing Parker. "Listen to yourself, babe. You sound paranoid. You've been off for weeks now. Everyone's noticed it. Maybe—maybe something's wrong. Maybe you need help," he suggested, his voice tempered but patronizing, as if trying to talk down someone on the edge.

Parker's vision blurred with rage. He could feel the ground beneath him slipping away. Devin's words splashed him like cold water on a grease fire, only intensifying the flames of his frustration. "Stop it," he shouted, his voice breaking. "Stop trying to manipulate me. I know what I saw."

"Parker, please," Devin pleaded, slowly moving from behind the sofa and backing toward the kitchen. "I love you, okay? We can figure this out. Just—" he asserted, his palms still raised to guard against Parker's advance, "just let's take a breath."

Devin's eyes widened as Parker confronted him, his previously magnetic presence now flickering with desperation. Devin's youthful appearance—his expressive eyes, once full of mischief, now filled with fear. He fought to maintain composure, but his physicality could no longer manipulate or control the situation. Devin's most powerful attributes, charm and confidence, were failing him.

Parker shook his head, moving toward Devin, chasing him as he retreated into the kitchen. He could feel his pulse in his temples, his vision narrowing, his thoughts nothing more than a chaotic jumble. Devin's presence in his home and constant insistence that everything was normal were too much.

Devin stopped and changed his tact. "Babe, please, let's just calm down," he begged. "I love you." He stepped closer now, his arm reaching out as if to embrace Parker, to pull him into the peace he so desperately sought to regain. Devin stepped too close. That's when Parker caught a glimpse of the object's shiny edge concealed in Devin's other hand, drawn low and behind his right leg, ready to whip around and drive deep into his heart as he drew Parker into one last lie of an embrace.

Parker's control snapped. He lunged to the side, instinct taking over as he grabbed the small but heavy crystal bowl on the kitchen's center island. The bowl was cold and solid in his hands, and he swung it with all his might without hesitation.

The bowl came down before he could stop himself, connecting with the side of Devin's head in a sickening thud. The force of the blow sent the boy reeling backward. Time slowed as Parker watched Devin's eyes widen in shock, his body crumpling to the floor in an awkward heap. The thick crystal bowl bounced off the hardwood. It echoed through the otherwise silent condo, mixing with the dull, final thud of Devin's body hitting the floor.

The blade flashed in the light again as the knife bounced around the hard kitchen floor. Or did it?

Parker stood frozen, the adrenaline in his veins giving way to a cold, sinking dread. Devin lay motionless, his body splayed awkwardly, blood pooling beneath his head—dark and viscous against the polished floor. Parker's gaze landed on the cell phone—shiny, silent, harmless.

"No!" Parker cried out, stumbling backward, his legs unexpectedly weak, his breath caught in his throat. "No. No. No."

Parker fell to his knees, his eyes fixed on Devin's lifeless form. Realizing what he did hit him like a wave, crashing over him, drowning him in disbelief. His hands trembled, his heart pounding painfully in his chest. He didn't mean to—this wasn't supposed to happen—this couldn't be real.

He crawled toward Devin's motionless body, his vision blurring with tears. His trembling hand brushed against Devin's arm—finding only cold, unresponsive skin. The irreversible truth of what he did settled in as shock and denial gave way to deep, aching guilt.

"What have I done?" he whispered, his voice barely rising above his broken sobs. His carefully constructed world surrounded him, offering no comfort for the turmoil and blood he now sat beside. His panting filled the absence of sound from the boy now lying next to him.

Just moments before, Devin pleaded with him, telling him he loved him and everything would be alright, and they would work it out together. Now Parker's breathing was ragged and uneven, each breath a struggle. He crossed a line, one he could never come back from. Everything he worked for—his career, reputation, sanity—was gone, shattered in a moment of rage.

Or was it?

13

The Body

(Nineteen years earlier)

The playground was bustling during recess, filled with childhood laughter and the steady scuffle of sneakers on the hardened earth. Twelve-year-old Parker Grant stood apart, leaning against the chain-link fence, observing the commotion of boys playing tag and girls screeching and laughing as they took turns at jump rope. His glasses slid down his nose, and each time they did, he pushed them back with the tip of his finger.

Parker's eyes focused on a small group gathering near the jungle gym, the scene tugging at his nerves. At the center of the ring of boys stood Scott, a quiet classmate, his backpack discarded and its contents scattered across the dirt. Andrew, a larger boy known for targeting the vulnerable, stood over him with a sneer. The expression on Scott's face—a blend of fear and quiet resignation—struck Parker with an unsettling intensity, like a sharp gust of wind.

"Hey! Give it back!" Scott's voice trembled as he reached for his textbook, but Andrew stepped on it, pinning it to the ground. The boys' laughter around them rang out, harsh and reverberating in Parker's ears.

Even at twelve, Parker sensed indignation rising within—he was already judging people, dissecting their behaviors, and analyzing situations through a scrutinizing lens. In his young mind, there was a right way and a wrong way for everything, and this—what he was witnessing—was undeniably wrong.

His eyes scanned the playground, expecting a teacher to step in. Undoubtedly, one of them would intervene with their whistles and strict rules. But they remained engrossed in their conversations at the far end of the yard, oblivious to the commotion. Their negligence grated on Parker just as much as the injustice of the mob surrounding Scott did.

The laughter grew louder as he watched the group, their faces twisted in amusement at someone else's expense. Parker's stomach knotted. He despised the disorder of it all, how things could spiral out of control when no one adhered to a basic code of decency. It wasn't just the bullying that annoyed him; it was the lack of structure and the failure of the school's adults to uphold the rules he obeyed. He couldn't comprehend how people could be so indifferent, so blind to what was unfolding right in front of them. There were rules for this, and someone should enforce them. The teachers weren't watching, but the rules still mattered. It felt wrong, like a stain on the playground no one cared about.

Parker was not a brave boy, and a voice inside him whispered this wasn't his fight—he should stay out of it—but he couldn't ignore it. To him, passivity was as good as participation. Every instinct told him someone needed to restore order. He wasn't just upset but determined; he had an innate responsibility for setting things right when the world became disorderly. Right now, there was disorder.

Parker's gaze hardened as he decided he couldn't just stand there and watch. It wasn't perfect or safe, but it was the right thing to do. If the adults weren't going to fix it, he would.

Taking a deep breath, Parker pushed away from the fence and approached the group. His tall but slim frame seemed comically mismatched against Andrew's bulk, but he didn't let it stop him. Parker stepped in front of Scott, his green eyes locking onto the assailant.

"Leave him alone," Parker demanded. His voice was firm despite the unease twisting inside him. The air around them shifted as the other boys fell silent, their eyes snapping to him.

Andrew's taunting became scorn as he faced Parker. "Or what? You gonna stop me?" He lifted his foot from Scott's workbook, only to nudge it further away with the tip of his sneaker.

Parker held his ground. "Just stop." He glanced down at Scott, his eyes wide and shaken. "You're just being mean," he shouted at Andrew.

Their world stood still for a moment, and there was silence. Andrew sneered as he leaned closer to Parker, testing his resolve, then rolled his eyes and stepped back with an exaggerated sigh. "Whatever, Parker. You're no fun," he said, raising his hands in a mockingly dismissive gesture. "Not worth it."

Andrew backed up and motioned for the others to follow. The group slowly dispersed, muttering as they left. Parker waited until he was sure they were gone before he knelt to help Scott gather his scattered books, their edges coated with a thin layer of playground dirt. He handed them back to the boy, who took them with shaky hands.

"Thanks," Scott mumbled, his voice barely audible.

"No problem. Just don't let those assholes get to you, okay?"

Scott nodded, his eyes still downcast, and Parker patted him on the shoulder as he helped the boy stand. Scott met Parker's eyes with a faint but growing smile of relief, the first spark of confidence creeping into his expression.

As Parker walked away, a swirl of emotions filled him—anger, relief, and a flicker of pride in taking action, no matter how small. He couldn't bear to witness others in pain, couldn't stand by and do nothing while someone suffered. Not if there was a way he could intervene.

Parker returned to his spot by the fence. The children's laughter returned, carried on the wind, and blended with the bright afternoon sunshine. Everything seemed normal again, but the image of Scott's frightened expression lingered. Parker's heart raced as he recalled the scene. He stood up to the bully and made things right—but why did it feel so heavy, like the weight of responsibility would hang over him forever?

(Sunday evening the 8th)

Parker remained motionless on the floor, his back pressed against the center island. He stared blankly at the lifeless form sprawled before him. Seconds became minutes, and an hour passed, though time now seemed meaningless. The sun, slowly descending, painted the living room in long, creeping shades of darkness, encroaching like a physical presence.

The contrast was morbid. That morning, Parker had wrapped his arms around Devin's warmth, comforted by his presence beside him. Now, there was only cold stillness. Sunlight had flooded Parker's bedroom while hope filled his soul. But now, despair crept into every corner, unraveling the fragile order he clung to.

Shock coursed through Parker's veins, freezing him in place. His thoughts whirled like shattered fragments, refusing to piece together, and his senses dulled. His mind refused to accept the reality before him, scrambling for any explanation to prove this wasn't real—that he wasn't responsible. He blinked, desperate to wake from this nightmare, but he couldn't escape the sight of Devin's motionless body. His pretty young face became pale while bruises bloomed like stains against his skin. The silence in the apartment was suffocating, broken only by Parker's ragged, uneven breaths and the occasional whimper escaping his throat. He wanted to scream, wanted to cry out, but his voice caught in his throat, choked off by fear.

The sharp metallic tang of blood hung heavily in the air. Each inhale made Parker's stomach churn. His fingers still trembled, smeared with the crimson mark of Devin's blood—a visceral reminder of the irreversible act he'd committed. He clenched his hands, wringing them together, staring at his palms as if the red stain might fade if he willed it hard enough. He wiped his hands on his shirt, the crimson stain smearing across the fabric, but nothing changed. The stain was there, permanent. And so was the truth. Nothing would ever change that.

Parker closed his eyes and leaned his head back against the sides of the island cabinets. He tried to imagine a world where this never happened. In his mind, Parker rewound the day and remembered Devin's smile that morning, the two of them waking up together in the bedroom. He wished he could step back, undo it all, and make a different choice. But no matter how much he wished, reality remained beside him.

Parker drew a deep breath, holding it momentarily before exhaling slowly. He coached clients through this process countless times—wives reeling from betrayal, husbands grappling with loss, and teenagers fighting the grip of addiction. He'd been their anchor, guiding them back from the brink. Now, Parker needed to be his own anchor. He needed to soothe the storm raging inside him, to focus. Parker needed to think logically and weigh his options, just as he had often helped others do in therapy. He had seen enough crime shows to know he could piece together something, anything, to help him now.

There was one option—it floated in the back of Parker's mind like a whisper. Call the police to report what happened. It was an accident. He could tell them it was self-defense. He wasn't a killer, after all. The police would understand he wasn't a threat, just a man who lost control for a split second while defending himself. But as Parker considered it, he only saw his future disintegrating. His career. His reputation. His freedom. Everything he worked for—everything he spent his life building; shattered in an instant. No one would understand.

The weight of those consequences pressed against him, squeezing his lungs and leaving him gasping for air. Parker opened his eyes, the room around him swimming in and out of focus. He needed to think. He needed to make a plan. Parker couldn't afford to lose himself in this spiral. His gaze drifted to Devin's body again, forcing himself to take in the reality of it— to see Devin as he was now, a lifeless form that didn't belong there in the first place and needed to disappear.

Parker's body shifted to autopilot, his mind detaching from his actions as if he were watching someone else—someone far removed from who he used to be. He pushed himself off the floor, his legs shaky beneath him. He took one step forward, followed by another, until he stood above Devin. Parker had no time to clean up, no time to dwell. He had to act now while still capable of acting—before his courage slipped away.

He stared down at Devin, his gaze unsteady, his thoughts jumbled. Parker's mind continued to fight against the truth, but the cold reality was inescapable. He needed to get the body out of his condo; only then would the order be restored.

His fingers were numb as he knelt beside Devin, his eyes wandering over the bruises now darkening across the skin of his face and neck. Parker swallowed, bile threatening to rise, but he forced it down. There was no room for hesitation now—no room for weakness.

Parker's hands trembled as he reached for Devin, feeling the dead weight of his body as he tried to shift him. The head lolled to the side, his features slack and empty. Parker clenched his jaw, refusing to let his emotions rise again. He couldn't think of Devin as a person—as someone he shared his bed with little more than twelve hours ago. Devin was now just a task, a problem Parker needed to solve. He was good at solving problems, he reminded himself.

The tang of coagulating blood lingered, clinging to Parker's nostrils with every breath. He grunted, his muscles straining as he lifted Devin's limp body. As he did, he stepped into the puddle of blood, feeling that it had thickened into a jelly-like consistency as it transitioned from liquid to semi-solid. Devin was heavier than anticipated, the dead weight resisting Parker. He struggled to secure a good grip, his hands slipping as he dragged Devin across the floor. Devin's bare heels squeaking against the hardwood sent a shiver up Parker's spine—they sounded like a high-pitched cry—too real in the suffocating silence of his home.

Parker paused momentarily, breathing heavily, sweat beading on his forehead. His heart pounded; each beat reminded him of what he had just done. He closed his eyes and forced himself to focus. He couldn't fall apart now. Parker needed to get Devin out of his home and his life. He took another deep breath and resumed the task of dragging Devin inch by inch toward the hallway, painting two thin, sporadic blood trails behind him.

Pausing at the door, Parker carefully leaned Devin's body against the wall in the hallway. He knew there was no turning back once he opened the door—he would be carrying Devin out into the world, risking everything. It was apparent he couldn't use the elevator into the lobby—too many cameras and the risk of running into someone along the way. He considered the service elevator going straight down to the garage, used primarily for owners and tenants to move in and out of their units. No, that wouldn't work either, he concluded. Use of the service elevator required time reservations with the management company and a key for operation.

There was only one other way out. They would need to use the stairwell down twenty-six floors—twenty-eight, to be exact, counting the two extra floors to the garage. He knew there was little risk of being seen, and there were no cameras, at least not until entering the parking garage. Parker used the stairwell regularly, once or twice a week as part of his fitness routine, running down the twenty-six floors from his condo to the lobby and back up again. Depending on the weather, he mixed stair climbing with jogging in Piedmont Park across the street or using the treadmill at the gym. It would not be easy with a hundred and sixty pounds of dead weight, but at least descending, he knew he was fit enough to do it. Parker had no other choice.

He glanced at his watch but wasn't wearing it. He turned to the digital numerals on the microwave instead—9:40 p.m.. Hours had passed since hitting the floor in the kitchen, and the time-lapse puzzled him. Devin's wounds had stopped bleeding some time ago, but the muscles in his jaw and fingers were stiffening. Parker needed to pick up the pace.

As he scanned the body, his mind worked to solve issues and consider options. The young man was no longer a client, an object of attraction, or even a person. The slumped figure leaning against the hallway wall was a messy intruder in Parker's space—little more than trash that needed dumping.

Parker considered a large trash bag, but it wouldn't have worked. He only had tall white kitchen bags in the house, the ones residents used to throw their garbage down the trash shoot, listening to it fall twenty-eight floors to the compactor in the garage.

The compactor? *That could work*, Parker thought. Flesh, muscle, and bones compressed and packed between layers of resident trash and garbage, hidden from view. Since it was Sunday night, the trash company would pick up and exchange the dumpster soon after the weekend when most people were home. The body would be gone, in all likelihood, before it decomposed and drew attention.

The idea was a strong option, but it had issues. Parker couldn't risk standing in the hallway trying to slide a body into the trash shoot. The opening wasn't large enough anyway, especially with rigor mortice setting in. Even if he could stuff it in, the falling corpse would likely become caught or hung up, blocking the shoot and drawing immediate attention to the problem. With trash bags piling up above the blockage, someone would discover the problem too quickly. The floors above the blockage would receive immediate suspicion, and the victim too traceable to Parker.

What about a large suitcase? Parker owned several older bags he used for long trips when he checked bags with the airline. One was a longer, red duffle-style with wheels on the bottom and a sturdy telescoping handle at the top. Still, he knew it was too small to stuff a frame this size into without breaking joints or cutting the body into pieces. Although an excellent packer, he knew the boy's frame was too large to arrange the parts, however neat and organized, into the travel duffle.

Parker considered an alternative to bypass the trash shoot entirely—carry the body down the stairwell to the compacter itself—but he knew the doors to the compacter and dumpster would be sealed. The dumpster was also behind a locked, chain link fence to prevent residents and outsiders from throwing large pieces of trash into the dumpster directly, which is what Parker wanted to do. No, as he considered it, Parker concluded he needed to move the body as far away from his home and himself as possible, and he needed to do it soon.

After a moment of hesitation, Parker sprang into action. He went to the kitchen drawer and grabbed a small dispenser of two-inch clear packing tape, which he used to seal boxes before shipping. Parker ran to his bedroom closet next and pulled out one of his old ball caps, its bill folded and worn from years of use. As he turned to leave, his eyes landed on Devin's blue hooded sweatshirt draped over the chair in the corner—the one Devin called his 'hoodie jumper,' a souvenir from his one trip overseas to London. Parker grabbed it, too.

Getting the jumper around Devin and his arms and hands through the sleeves wasn't as tricky as Parker expected it might be, though he noted the continued stiffening of the intruder's joints and muscles. It was the taping of his head that proved more difficult, but only in terms of trying not to focus on the wound itself. Parker wound the clear tape around Devin's head to keep the gash closed and pieces of flesh intact. The screech of the tape unwinding from the spool sounded unnerving—just like the sound of Devin's bare heels dragging across the polished floors or the shriek of fear he let out just before having his head bashed in with a single, wide-arching blow. The garage was a long descent down a winding staircase, leaving no room for hesitation or error if the head struck or caught on an obstacle while descending.

Parker placed his ballcap on the head and pulled the jumper's hood over it, concealing any concern someone might have should they be seen. The stranger in his apartment was ready to go—until Parker moved behind him to lift and saw the body's bare feet and red, blood-stained heels. They had been in the condo all day, and Devin hadn't put any shoes on, instead lounging around barefoot since getting out of bed. Setting him back down, Parker retrieved Devin's white sneakers from under the bedroom chair where his hoodie rested. He forced Devin's feet into them, proving more difficult than putting the jumper on, considering the ever-stiffening state of the ankles and toes.

Standing once more to lift the body, Parker caught another detail. Devin's phone—the object that had sparked the scuffle—still lay on the kitchen floor, untouched by the crimson pool. It remained where it had landed when Devin's body collapsed. Parker stared at it. That was what he had lunged for, what he had been so sure Devin was about to plunge into his heart. The knife behind Devin's right leg had never existed.

Oh shit, Parker muttered. Devin used it when Parker confronted him in the living room—time-stamped evidence of Devin's location. Parker ran to pick it up, quickly mashing the side button to power it down and switch it off. The phone's screen transitioned to black, like Devin's eyes when struck on the side of the head with the heavy crystal bowl. Parker studied it, wondering if he should use a thumbprint to unlock the phone and scan its contents for later use as evidence. It could prove his suspicions about the deceit were correct. He would decide later, shoving the phone into his jacket pocket. Right now, time was of the essence.

Parker picked the lifeless body up and held it with one arm around Devin's torso under his arms while fumbling with the deadbolt behind himself with the other. His fingers were clumsy, the latch slipping in his grip before he finally managed to turn it. The deadbolt clicked, and Parker hesitated, his hand resting on the doorknob. This was it. He twisted the knob, and the door creaked open.

The carpeted hallway outside the apartment was empty. Parker glanced both ways, his heart pounding in his ears. He could hear the distant hum of the elevator and the muffled sounds of life from other units, but no one was in sight. Parker shifted Devin in his grip, still propping him up with one arm around his torso. He threw one of Devin's arms around his neck, supported by his broad shoulders. He was about to help his drunk friend down to his car to drive him home.

It was a struggle to move Devin through the doorway, but with some maneuvering soon got the knack of assisting someone who had overindulged to the point of unconsciousness. The air in the hallway was cooler and fresher—a stark contrast to the oppressive heat inside the apartment. The scent of antiseptic from the freshly cleaned carpet mingled with sweat and caution radiating off Parker's skin. He moved as quickly as he could, his eyes darting nervously down the hallway. Each step was labored, the distance to the stairwell farther than he anticipated, his arms aching as he dragged the unnatural weight along the narrow corridor. He could feel his resolve beginning to crack, the weight of his exposure and what he was doing pressing down upon him with every step.

The stairwell was at the end of the hallway, a heavy, industrial door taunting him as he approached it. Despite the chill of the hallway, Parker could feel the sweat dripping down his back and his shirt clinging to his skin. His fingers and hands numbed, gripping and holding Devin's cold body upright so the feet did not float in the air nor drag on the ground. It was like trying to lift and pull a stone statue. Devin's weight was solid and uncooperative.

Finally, Parker reached the stairwell and its door's push handle. He glanced down the hallway one last time to ensure he was alone before he pushed his way through the door. The sound of the metal door unlatching made Parker jump, his heart leaping into his throat. When it slammed shut, the sound echoed throughout the concrete silo, and a wave of relief swept over him. Parker just liberated his sanctuary and was halfway to regaining control over his sanity.

Parker moved as though his body were no longer his own, each action mechanical, driven by instinct rather than thought. It was the only way to keep from collapsing under the weight of it all. He bent over and slung Devin's body over his shoulders, weaving one hand and arm through Devin's legs; the other gripped Devin's arm for stability. It was called a fireman's carry, a maneuver Parker learned in Boy Scouts—a sound way to carry a victim long distances with minimum effort.

Parker swallowed hard and began his descent, the body slung over his shoulders, allowing him to see each step before him. He took it slowly, step by step, floor by floor. He stopped and leaned against the wall every five floors or so, resting briefly to catch his breath and rest his legs before proceeding. Each step bore the weight of his actions. Still, Parker shut it all out, focusing only on the next stair step.

When they finally reached the parking level, Parker lowered Devin and propped him against the wall long enough to slide his arm back around Devin's body to walk him into the garage upright. He pushed the doors open as the dimly lit space stretched before them, its emptiness parallelling his isolation. A rush of cool autumn air and the scent of gasoline and oil hit them as he glanced toward his Bronco parked in the corner, its familiar shape and proximity comforting.

Parker's legs ached, his body shaking with exhaustion as he assisted his drunk-like friend hanging from his arms across the concrete cavern. The sound of their movement echoed through the garage. The occasional scrape of Devin's shoes against the concrete when Parker allowed his body to hang too low was a subtle reminder of the reality of what he was doing. Parker could feel his resolve wavering, the weight of Devin's body too much to bear. The garage lights above flickered, casting distorted flashes of light and dark, mocking his struggle and symbolizing his flickering hope of escaping the horror of what he did.

Finally, they reached the truck, and Parker leaned Devin's body against the side as he fumbled through his pockets for the keys. He thought he had left them upstairs for a moment but found them as he patted his pockets with his shaking hands. His breath coming in ragged gasps and his heart pounding, Parker bent down to lift him one last time. With a grunt of effort, Parker heaved Devin into the back of the sport-utility vehicle's cargo area, his body collapsing into a fetal position.

Parker stood there, his breath shaky and uneven. He stared down at Devin and couldn't help but remember how those same arms wrapped around him, pulling him close in the early morning light. Now they hung limp, lifeless, betraying him in their stillness.

He did it. He successfully moved Devin and got him out of the apartment. But now what?

Parker scanned his surroundings before slamming the tailgate, the sound echoing through the garage. He stood there, his body quivering while his mind refused to process what came next. Parker felt Devin's phone in his jacket pocket; its screen was dark, but its secrets were there to be revealed.

There was no plan, no clear path forward—only the Bronco, the body, and the uncertainty of the night ahead.

14

The Forest

The 1971 Signature Series Ford Bronco was beautiful with its anvil gray-blue exterior and hickory-colored low-back seats. Impeccably maintained, Parker had washed and waxed it routinely since he was a young teen. His parents bought the Bronco new, and it was the rugged ride Parker loved to take with his father to the hardware store or on family camping trips. Parker purchased it for $300 from them at sixteen, using his earnings from his first part-time job stocking shelves and bagging groceries. He cherished the classic lines of the Bronco. It was like his appreciation for his vintage round-face watch with its slender lizard-skin band, his wire-rimmed eyeglasses, and the chrome fountain pen his father gifted him for college graduation. These objects had a sense of timelessness, a reassuring permanence speaking to Parker's need for stability in an unpredictable world.

Parker drove north into the darkness, his knuckles white as he gripped the steering wheel. The rhythmic vibration of the road beneath the tire's hum offered a strange, hypnotic solace, lulling him into a state that allowed him to keep moving forward despite the fear gnawing at his insides. Parker switched the radio off; he wanted no distractions and no attention drawn to him while focusing on driving. Each mile took him farther away from Atlanta, the city lights disappearing in his rearview mirror, replaced by the dim glow of the dashboard and the endless stretch of asphalt before him.

For a brief moment, Parker wondered if he was still in bed, tangled in his sheets, the world beyond his windshield nothing more than the remnants of a vivid nightmare.

There was a place about an hour north of the city where Parker camped and hiked on the north side of Lake Lanier, off an isolated road near River Forks Park and a boat ramp. He wasn't sure why he drove north when he exited the parking garage. There were plenty of options for dumping a body inside the city limits: run down and vacant houses, dark alleyways, under bridges spanning creeks and waterways. But for some reason, Parker instinctively headed north, away from the urban disorder and toward a place of quiet beauty and solitude— where the silence might swallow the terrible truth of his actions. Maybe the familiarity of the site was of comfort, a lifeline to a time when his life was simpler and untouched by this nightmare. He remembered the trailhead, where the air was crisp, and the scent of pine needles coated his senses.

The winding roads leading to that section of the lake were deserted, the thick canopy of trees making the darkness more impenetrable. Parker's heart pounded as he turned off the main road. The Bronco's headlights cut narrow paths through the forest, the beams bouncing with each bump in the dirt road, briefly illuminating the skeletal trees that loomed overhead. He sensed the forest's judgment—every shadow and every rustle in the trees was a whispered condemnation. The sensation distressed him, irrational but undeniable, as if the darkness peered into his soul and knew what he did. He knew what to do, but every fiber of morality screamed against it.

Parker pulled off onto a narrow dirt path, the wheels of the Bronco slowly crunching over gravel and leaves. He killed the engine, and silence took over, pressing against his eardrums as if deep underwater. Parker closed his eyes, trying to steady his breathing, his fingers nervously tapping against the steering wheel. He could feel the forest leaning closer, waiting for him to carry out the monstrous act.

Parker sat and waited. He rolled the windows down and took in the cool night air, the sounds of the forest flooding in. The constant chorus of crickets weaved through the trees, their rhythm loud and unapologetic. Somewhere nearby, the haunting hoot of an owl cut through the night, an alarming reminder of unseen predators lurking around him. The rustling of leaves came in unpredictable swells as a light breeze wound through the underbrush. Occasionally, the snap of a twig broke the monotony—a reminder that the forest was alive with movement, hidden creatures scurrying about. The distant splash of water against the lake's edge added a rhythmic pulse. The forest was anything but silent—its symphony of sounds was a primal reminder he was not alone, and the world continued its relentless march, indifferent to the darkness of his actions.

Grabbing the flashlight from the glovebox, Parker stepped into the cool night, the crisp air biting at his skin. He moved to the back of the Bronco and hesitated for a heartbeat before lowering the tailgate.

Devin's body lay there, a motionless lump beneath the dark plaid blanket Parker had thrown over him for concealment. The sight of that still form—hidden yet unmistakably human—sent a shudder through him, his instincts recoiling against what he had set out to do. The metallic tang of blood still clung to the air, mingling with the damp earthiness of the woods.

Bile burned at the back of his throat. He fought the urge to retch as his gaze locked on the consequence of his anger and misjudgment.

Parker swallowed hard, his gaze shifting to the trees. He needed to move quickly; he couldn't stay longer than necessary. The cold steel of the tailgate bit into his thighs as Parker leaned in to grab the blanket, straining to free the stiffened body. The odor of sweat, blood, and pine needles filled his nose, a cocktail of life and death. He tried to slide it toward him, struggling to pull the dead weight from the front of the cargo area. His muscles strained as he did, and every inch of progress was a monumental task, the lifeless mass resisting him and refusing to cooperate.

As Parker pulled and heaved, the blanket slipped slightly, revealing Devin's face—pale, eyes closed, a haunting stillness etched into his features. The sight practically broke Parker, a flash of memory playing in his mind of Devin's laughter, his smile—moments now lost forever. He jerked his head to the side, fighting to keep his composure.

Manhandling the stiffening carcass into the woods, Parker needed to only go far enough from the gravel and dirt path to remain undiscovered. He sometimes lifted and carried it like a lifeguard carrying a child out of the ocean toward the beach. When it became too laborious, he dragged it along the ground like a heavy garbage bag of yard clippings to the curb for pickup. The rustling leaves and snapping branches beneath him echoed in the night, joining the sound of swaying trees and distant animal calls—each one a reminder of his exposure. Parker stopped to listen; his eyes darted around, his ears straining for any sign of another person. When he heard none, he moved deeper into the trees, his feet slipping on the uneven ground as his heart pounded louder with every step. Gloominess stretched unnaturally between the trees, the separation of light and dark curling like accusing fingers.

When he finally reached a small clearing, Parker paused, his lungs heaving from the effort. He didn't have a shovel. Panic began mounting, but he forced it down, scanning the ground for anything he could use. He considered leaving his blanket and its contents on the ground where he stood. Animals would undoubtedly find it, dismantling and partially eating it, making identification more difficult.

Identification, Parker thought. He made a mental note to remove anything that might aid quick identification.

He contemplated dumping the body into the lake but quickly dismissed the idea. He had no way of getting out to the lake's center and nothing to weigh down the body to sink it. Could it be made to appear as an accidental drowning? Unlikely, he concluded, considering the clear packing tape wrapped around the victim's head to conceal a deep head wound. Besides, forensics would quickly show the victim did not die of water aspiration but blunt force trauma to the head. No, it needed to go into the ground, concealed to decompose and disappear forever.

Parker scanned the area again, his eyes locking onto the outline of his dark Bronco in the distance. His vision had sharpened, adjusting to the deep darkness of the forest since his arrival. His pupils, now fully dilated, drank in every trace of light, activating the rod cells in his retina to detect even the faintest shadows. It was called dark adaptation, and Parker chuckled at the irony. *Dark Adaptation*. He couldn't remember where he learned that fact or why it surfaced now—useless trivia—his mind's way of distracting him from the grim reality. He focused on the Bronco. It held something he could use.

Reaching into the back of the truck, Parker retrieved the tire iron and jack stowed in the truck's hidden compartment. Their weight was grim reassurance in his hands, heavy and solid—perfect for digging through the stubborn, red clay earth. His gaze caught the tire impressions left in the gravel and dirt path, and he made a mental note to brush clean those tracks before leaving this place.

Returning to the spot, he dropped to his knees and scraped at the earth. He plunged the tire iron into the ground to loosen it, scraping and pushing away the dirt with the flat plate of the jack. The soil was cold and damp, moistened by the drizzling rains of the weekend, making the task easier. The clay resisted him, clinging to his hands as if the earth fought against the burial, a silent protest of the secret he was asking it to keep.

Each drag of the jack against the earth echoed in the darkness, the grating sound amplifying the moment's weight. Each plunge of the tire iron and each scrape of the jack against the ground was a brutal reminder of what he did and was about to do. The sharp edges of the tire iron dug into his palms and left angry red indentations. The dampness of the earth seeped through his jeans, chilling his knees and solidifying his connection to the grave he was digging.

Parker knew the hole was shallow—too shallow—but his arms ached, and his fingers numbed from the effort. He glanced at the body wrapped in the dark blanket lying a few feet away. Parker had to finish this. He couldn't stop now. His breath fogged in the cold night air; each exhale was a testament to his exhaustion, the weight of his actions pulling him deeper into the hole he dug.

Parker pushed himself to his feet, losing his balance slightly as he stumbled toward the covered corpse. Reaching to brace himself, his hands landed on the lump and quickly recoiled. He gazed at it for a moment, nausea churning within his stomach. When he finally grabbed the edge of the blanket, he dragged it toward the newly dug hole. The rustle of the fabric against the forest floor resonated through the trees, a ghostly reminder of what he was about to do. He stopped at the edge of the hole, his heart hammering in his chest.

Remove any identification, Parker reminded himself.

Parker pulled the blanket back slowly and looked down at Devin. His vision blurred with tears as soon as he did. Parker didn't want to do this—he didn't want any of it, but now there was no other option. He sat for a minute and wept, allowing the moment's emotion to sweep over him, if only briefly. The sobs sounded raw and jagged, each one scraping his throat like a tire jack grinding through dirt, a harsh release for the agony threatening to consume him whole.

When he composed himself, he searched Devin's clothing, gently patting him down over his jeans and jumper. He found Devin's wallet in the pocket of his jumper, still in it from when Devin slung it over the bedroom chair the night before. *Good*, Parker thought, relieved it was not still in his condo.

Parker thought about Devin's cell phone. Was it still back at the condo? No. He remembered picking it up from the kitchen floor, switching it off, and slipping it into his jacket pocket—now lying on the forest floor beside him.

He retrieved it and swung the tire iron down with all his strength. Glass shattered beneath the force of the blow, tiny shards scattering into the dirt. He struck it repeatedly, each impact releasing the fear and anger coiled inside him. Whatever evidence the phone held—whatever answers it might contain about the past two days—wasn't worth the risk of being caught with it.

The sound of metal meeting plastic dulled against the pine needles as he kept swinging until the device broke apart. Breathing hard, he scooped up the pieces and walked to the water's edge, hurling them as far as he could. They hit with hollow plunks, sending ripples across the surface before sinking—swallowed by the depths, lost in the tangle of weeds and gritty silt below.

He returned and mechanically removed his ball cap from Devin's head. He couldn't leave evidence in the hole. Clenching his jaw, Parker grabbed the blanket's corners and pulled Devin into the hole. The body landed with a dull thud, the sound reverberating through Parker's bones, a finality making his stomach twist. He paused to stare down at the lifeless form, his mind turning blank and his heart aching with a feeling of sorrow.

A cold breeze swept through the clearing, rustling the leaves, and Parker shivered despite the energy he was expending. The air was thicker now, charged with energy, making the hairs on his arms stand up. It was as if the earth was rejecting what he was about to do.

Parker stared at the blanket. Should he take it with him or leave it to keep Devin warm and comfortable? It was sure to contain Devin's DNA, dirty and torn from being drug over the dirt and twigs. The blanket now had a connection to the body and this place; he would not bring it back home. He had no intention of keeping it in the truck to use again. And what if he left it? It was an old blanket, stained with oil and worn from use as a cargo mat. The blanket had no identifying marks to tie it back to Parker. Still, it was better to leave it. The fabric might serve as a shroud to shield Devin from the earth's cold, an absurd notion but one that Parker found comfort in.

His actions grew heavier with each slow, deliberate movement as if Parker were trying to stave off the inevitable. He folded the limbs tightly, compressing them into a compact shape. As he worked, he felt Devin's watch on his wrist beneath his sleeve, a small relief knowing it was one less piece of evidence left in his apartment. Parker tucked the blanket neatly around the edges of the body, pulling it tight with the precision of making a bed—corners fitted and tucked. The orderliness brought him a sliver of reassurance. The blanket enveloped Devin in a final shroud, concealing the bruises and lifeless form, reducing him to an unrecognizable shape—a neutral object, no longer the person Parker briefly held.

Slowly, Parker covered the body with the loose dirt scraped away. Each handful landed like a final betrayal on Devin's still form. The soil was cold and damp, clumping as it fell, muffling the impact sound. Parker's hands shook as he scooped, each movement deliberate, the weight of the earth a physical manifestation of the burden now lodged within him. He paused, his resolve wavering as the reality of what he was doing returned to hit him all at once. This body was Devin—someone he imagined he could love one day, someone who had made him feel alive in a way no one else did, no matter how briefly. Now, he was erasing him from existence.

That's when it hit Parker—the memory of Devin from the night before, how their bodies fit together in a moment of intimacy now impossibly distant. He gripped the memory of making love to Devin the night before and held onto it. The evidence was inside the young boy in the shallow hole in the ground in the middle of the forest.

That's when Parker finally did vomit, throwing up the remnants of the last meal Devin made for him that morning, before Parker confronted him, before the argument, and before

126

the accident. The acidic burn scorched his throat, the taste lingering bitterly on his tongue, an acrid reminder of his body's revolt against his mind's resolve. Tears blurred his vision as he vomited, his soul retching to reject the horror of what transpired, trying to expel the memory of the past twenty-four hours.

There was no more time to think about it. Parker knew if he allowed himself to dwell and give into the pain, he'd fall apart entirely. Not here. Not now. Parker's hands shook as he quickly threw handfuls of dirt into the grave, his vision swimming with tears.

He wanted to stop, turn back, and undo everything that happened. But he couldn't. He again sensed the forest close around him, shadows growing darker, the air colder, the world rejecting what he had done. The rustle of the branches above grew louder, and the wind became icy. The earth itself was trying to push him away.

Parker pressed the ground with his hands, each motion sealing a part of himself with Devin beneath the earth. He patted the uneven ground flat and stomped on it repeatedly to pack the mound tight as though he were trying to bury his guilt. Parker dropped a nearby rock on it and redistributed pine needles and twigs over the site, blending the forest floor to conceal the sins beneath him. He stepped back, examining the patch of earth, hoping it blended into the forest's natural floor. When it did, Parker's arms fell limp to his sides. He stared at the grave, his breath coming in short, ragged gasps. It was done. Devin was gone. A hollow emptiness gutted him as the reality of his actions set in.

Parker picked up his jacket, grabbed the tire iron and jack, and stumbled away from the grave. His legs were like jelly, barely holding him upright. Each step was heavier than the last. It was as if the ground resisted his leaving, a tether pulling at his ankles, the memory of what lay beneath clawing to keep him there.

When Parker reached the Bronco, he brushed the dirt and death off himself and leaned against it, his body trembling. The weight of what he had just done settled over him like a suffocating blanket of his own.

The forest grew silent as if holding its breath.

Parker wiped the tools clean and returned them to their storage places in the Bronco. It was finished. He buried Devin. Still, the sense of relief he hoped for did not come. Parker only felt dread, a deep trepidation twisting in his gut.

He brushed away the tire tracks half-heartedly, his mind too frayed to detect the faint impressions remaining, the kind that might catch the attention of someone who examined them too closely.

Climbing into the Bronco and turning the key, the engine roared to life, the sound startling in the stillness of the night. Parker drew in some deep breaths. The air in the Bronco smelled stale, thick with the scent of sweat and dirt, but at least it was safe here—away from the body and evidence of what he'd done. His eyes stung with tears as he pulled away from the clearing, leaving Devin—and a piece of himself—behind.

15

A Safe Shelter

(Monday the 9ᵗʰ)

The early morning darkness stretched out in front of Parker as he drove south towards Atlanta. The empty road extended endlessly before him, the occasional pothole jolting the Bronco's frame and Parker's already frayed nerves. The windshield speckled with condensation, the faint hum of the tires on asphalt filling the silence. Outside, the horizon began to hint at a faint, grayish-blue hue, teasing the arrival of dawn. Its light offered no promise of clarity, however. For a fleeting moment, Parker had the unsettling sensation that the road was looping back on itself, the same mile stretching out repeatedly, as if trapped in a dream he couldn't wake from.

The radio remained off, and the quiet of the pre-dawn hour provided no solace, only a suffocating blanket of isolation. Parker could feel the dirt under his nails, the phantom weight of Devin's lifeless body, and his muscles aching with exhaustion—physical and emotional. His throat was dry, his eyes stinging from a mixture of fatigue and tears he now refused to shed.

Gripping the steering wheel tightly, Parker tried to keep his focus on the road and his thoughts in check. Still, the reality of his actions was relentless, his mind replaying every moment with brutal clarity. He couldn't go back to the condo—not yet. The anxiety over walking through the door and facing the scene he left behind sent a shiver down his spine. He needed distance, clarity, and time to determine his next steps.

Parker considered his options. Tim was still in Italy, likely sipping espresso on some cobblestoned terrace, oblivious to the chaos Parker was drowning in. His mother? Out of the question. She would recognize vulnerability as a failure, another crack in the pristine image she expected him to uphold.

His colleagues at the firm, Dr. Warren, Olivia, and Alyce, were off limits too—Parker couldn't bring this mess into the office and threaten his reputation and career. Besides, who would believe him? He would sound like an unbalanced fool who lost his mind if he told anyone half of what he had just experienced. Wake up to a relationship he had no memory of? Have same-sex relations with a client? Commit murder, even if in self-defense and accidental, and bury the body in the woods in the dead of night? Parker knew it was all true, but repeating it silently in his mind made him feel insane.

Parker drove thirty more miles before picking up his phone, a storm of doubt raging in his mind. Nick wasn't a friend, not really—a bartender and dancer Parker met a handful of times, whose charm seemed effortless but whose life Parker knew little about. And yet, the distance made Nick feel safe—someone who wouldn't pry too deeply or didn't know Parker well enough to judge him for the wreckage he was becoming.

His fingers trembled as he scrolled through his contacts, pausing when he found Nick's name. It was a ridiculous idea. Yet, a quality about Nick made Parker feel he could reach out to him. Maybe it was the way Nick's gaze lingered, calm and steady, or the effortless confidence with which he navigated the lively chaos of the bar. Perhaps it was Nick's care two nights ago when Mark and Devin stumbled into Parker at Cityside.

Parker had no intention of telling Nick what happened. He just needed somewhere to go until he was ready to face what awaited him at home. He couldn't be alone with his own thoughts just yet.

[Still at the bar?] he typed.

The response came quicker than he expected. [Just closing. What's up?]

Parker paused, his fingers hovering over the screen. After a moment's hesitation, he drew in a steadying breath and typed: [Can I stop by?]

There was a long pause before a reply. [Sure. Heading back to my place. Meet there?]

Parker exhaled slowly, forcing the tension to ease. He texted a thumbs-up emoji, followed by [Drop a pin, please.] He didn't know where Nick lived, but he remembered Nick mentioning it was in an apartment on the south side of Midtown, not far from his condo.

When the text notification chimed, he tossed his phone on the passenger seat and focused on the dark road ahead. Parker sensed this was a bad idea. He knew he should go home to fix the mess created earlier in the evening. He couldn't do it, though. Not yet. He needed a moment of reprieve from the person who killed Devin.

The drive to Nick's apartment was a haze, city lights smearing past as the Bronco rolled down empty streets. Parker found a parking spot a block away—a rare stroke of luck, given the old building's lack of a garage.

He killed the engine and sat still, staring ahead. The drive had been simple, but convincing himself this was the right decision was far more challenging. The urban street lay silent at 3:40 a.m., the artificially lit air thick with a bleak emptiness—so different from the restless, nocturnal life of the deep, dark woods.

Parker stepped out, his legs unsteady as he approached the building's entrance.

[Here] he texted Nick.

Nick buzzed him in without hesitation, and Parker made his way up the staircase. The door to 3B was slightly ajar. Parker tapped lightly with his knuckles while gently pushing it open to step inside. The apartment was small but cozy, the scent of incense lingering in the air. Nick stood in the living room, his eyes lighting up with curiosity and concern as Parker entered.

"Hey," Nick said, his voice cautious, scanning Parker from head to toe. Nick's brow furrowed at the sight: Parker's clothes smeared with dirt, his hair disheveled and damp, and a musty, earthy scent clung to him. Nick saw the faint tremor in Parker's hands and noticed the hollowness in his eyes as if he hadn't slept in days. "What the hell happened? You okay?"

Parker swallowed, still standing just inside the open door. His throat was tight. "No," he admitted, his voice barely above a whisper. "Not really."

Nick's expression shifted, concern etching lines across his forehead. He stepped closer and rested his hand on Parker's shoulder, gently pulling him into the apartment. "You look like you've been through hell."

Nick guided Parker in, attempting to steer him toward the sofa to relax, but Parker shook his head, too aware of the filth covering him. Instead, he walked into the kitchen, his body weighed down with exhaustion. He leaned against the counter while Nick filled a glass with water.

When Nick handed Parker the glass, he couldn't help but take in the man before him. Parker appeared utterly broken. It wasn't the first time Nick welcomed someone into his apartment in the middle of the night, but this time was different—it wasn't about fun. Seeing someone who usually seemed so composed and in control now unraveling before him was disorienting. The haunted look in Parker's eyes, the visible fight to maintain even a shred of composure, stirred a deep ache within Nick, one he couldn't ignore.

Realizing he couldn't remember when he'd last drank anything, Parker took a small sip before gulping it down wholly. The cool water soothed his dry throat, though it did nothing to douse the turmoil burning inside him.

Nick stood beside him, his eyes searching Parker's face. "Do you want to talk about it?" he asked, his voice gentle, no pressure, just an open invitation.

Parker hesitated, his gaze dropping to the floor. He wanted to tell Nick and spill everything—the fear, guilt, and horror of what he'd done. But the words caught in his throat, a lump of shame refusing to budge. He couldn't say it. He couldn't admit to the thing now defining him.

"I just," he paused, "I just can't go home," Parker finished, his voice cracking. "Not yet."

Nick nodded, his expression relaxing after the surprise at seeing Parker at his door at this hour. "It's fine, Park," he responded. "Take your time, no questions. Just whatever you need."

Parker gazed into Nick's eyes, and a flicker of emotion passed through him—perhaps gratitude or a fragile thread of hope. In that moment, the quiet sense of refuge kept him from unraveling.

Nick didn't know the full weight of what Parker was carrying, didn't know the darkness shadowing him now, but he was offering a quiet reprieve. Nick's relaxed openness and steady patience, free of judgment or demands, allowed Parker a rare sense of safety.

"Thanks," Parker whispered, his voice thick with emotion.

Nick gave him a small smile and patted Parker's arm briefly with his palm. "You look like you could use a shower," he said, his tone light and teasing. "Go ahead. I'll find you something to wear."

Parker nodded, grateful for the distraction and ability to wash away the dirt, sweat, and blood clinging to him.

His legs wobbled as he passed Nick's open bedroom door, a fleeting idea curling like smoke in the back of his mind—a dark, malicious suggestion sickened him the moment it took shape. What if Nick wasn't just someone to lean on? What if Nick could shoulder more than just Parker's guilt, taking the burden of this whole nightmare off his hands?

Parker floated the idea to himself. He was alone in the back of Nick's apartment, covered in dirt from the scene. There was undoubtedly some of Devin's DNA on his clothing. In that brief moment, Parker wished he hadn't smashed Devin's phone and tossed it into the lake.

The thought clawed at him, insidious and seductive, before Parker crushed it with a surge of revulsion. He swallowed hard as he stepped into the bathroom, ashamed of the devious seed momentarily taking root in his mind. He wondered how much of his morality he buried in those dark woods and how much cowardice he returned to the city with.

The sound of water running filled the apartment as Nick sat on the sofa, his ears tuned to the shower spray. He remembered when he began working at the bar—the night he first danced for tips. The lights, the crowd, and the attention were thrilling at first. The men leaned close, whispering things into his ear, trying to claim a piece of him with their gaze. It eventually became noise to Nick, shallow and easily deflected. He'd gotten good at turning them away with a smile, giving them just enough to satisfy without ever letting them in.

But Parker was different. In Nick's apartment, he hadn't postured, demanded, or sought to impress. He wasn't projecting masculinity or asserting control—he was just there. Unshielded. Present. And that raw openness stirred something in Nick, something unfamiliar yet magnetic, pulling him in before he could name it.

The shower was small, but the water was blessedly hot as it cascaded over his skin. Steam filled the air as Parker closed his eyes, letting the water scald his raw, dirt-etched skin. Each drop felt like a needle against his back, sharp and relentless, a poor attempt to scrub away the guilt embedded in his pores—and his conscience. His hands trembled as they passed over his face, the memory of Devin's lifeless eyes flashing behind his lids. He scrubbed his skin until it was raw, trying to cleanse himself of the guilt, the fear, the reality of what he did. He scrubbed and rinsed until the water ran as cold as a deep, shadowy lake on a chilly autumn night.

When Parker emerged from the shower, virtue rolled out with him. Nick was waiting in the doorway, and his eyes immediately locked on the handsome figure standing naked in his bathroom. Water droplets flew from the ends of Parker's waves as he shook them free, cupping his hands and running them back to squeeze the water from his locks. His skin flushed from the hot water, and he appeared less lost—cleaner, more composed.

Nick couldn't deny how his breath caught in his chest, the slight tightening tugging at his core. He stepped forward to hand Parker a fresh towel and some clothes, which he heated in the dryer for comfort. His fingers brushed against Parker's briefly, warmth spreading up his arm. He could feel the tension in his body, the urge to close the space between them. But he wouldn't do it—not while Parker was weak and vulnerable.

"Here," Nick said softly, his voice measured and calm. "These should fit." He steadied himself, determined not to let his tone falter. Tonight wasn't about him—it was about creating a space where Parker could feel grounded, free from the weight of fear or uncertainty. Nick focused on being what Parker needed: a presence he could trust without expectations or demands.

Parker slipped into the sweatpants, and Nick handed him a tee shirt too large for himself, but one Parker's frame filled out entirely. The clothes were soft, the fabric worn and comforting. They provided a slight sense of relief as he put them on.

A cup of hot tea was sitting on the coffee table when Parker emerged. Nick was sitting on the couch, a cup already in his hands. He flashed Parker a small smile. "Feel better?"

Parker nodded. He did feel better, though his stiffness hadn't wholly eased. He sat beside Nick, his eyes staring at the steam rising from the cup of tea Nick handed him. A heavy silence lingered, loaded with everything Nick wanted to ask and Parker couldn't say.

Nick broke the silence first, his voice understanding. "Whatever it is, you don't have to go into it now if you don't want to. We can just sit." They did sit, each holding a cup of tea, the steam rising in delicate tendrils, the warm liquid providing some comfort against the chill of the early morning. Nick studied Parker intently, taking in the way he was staring at his reflection in the cup.

Nick wanted Parker to lean on him. And now, sitting near him, watching Parker struggle with whatever had happened tonight, Nick had an overwhelming urge to bridge the distance between them. He wanted to reach out to let Parker know he wasn't alone. But Nick could also see Parker was on edge, barely holding himself together. He saw it in the way Parker's hands still quivered and the glazed, haunted void in his eyes.

"You look better," Nick said, his voice offering unforced warmth. "Just take it easy, alright? You're safe here."

Parker's throat tightened, his eyes watering. He blinked, trying to push back the tears threatening to fall. He wasn't used to this—wasn't used to weakness, to letting someone see the cracks in his strong façade. But Parker sensed his defenses were crumbling in the dim light of Nick's apartment, the force of what he had done to Devin squeezing him. His mind raced. Should he say it? Should he let Nick in on the truth weighing on him like a heavy chain?

Parker recalled Olivia's words: 'Even those who help others find their way can sometimes get lost.' One word, one sentence, and everything would change. Nick could walk away, could reject him the moment he knew the reality of Parker's evil actions. And yet, there was no one else. Parker's heart ached with the risk, the fear of losing this new and fragile, uncertain connection.

Parker hesitated, the words sticking to his throat like shards of glass. He gripped the mug tighter, staring into the swirling tea as if it held answers he couldn't find in himself. "I did something," he whispered, the weight of the admission pulling his voice down like an anchor. His fingers trembled, the tea rippling in the cup as he clutched it like a lifeline. "Something terrible. I don't even know how to start explaining it."

At first, Nick was quiet. He reached out, his hand resting gently on Parker's knee. "We all do things we're not proud of," he said, his voice steady. "But whatever it is, it will be alright."

Parker's gaze met Nick's, noticing the redness and weariness etched into Nick's eyes from the long, smoke-filled shift at Cityside. Yet, despite the fatigue, Parker saw no trace of judgment. Instead, Parker found understanding in Nick's expression, along with a glimmer of what seemed to be hope.

"I don't know if I can fix this," Parker whispered, his voice breaking. "I don't know if there's a way out."

Nick wanted to ask Parker a hundred questions to understand what happened to him and why he was at his door at four in the morning. But he didn't. He didn't need to. Not yet.

Nick's grip on Parker's knee tightened, his eyes locked on Parker's. "Then we'll make one," he said, his voice filled with confident determination. "Whatever it takes. We'll make a way out for you."

For a fleeting second, Parker allowed himself to hope. The

dark despair gripping him loosened, and he wanted to trust Nick—not just because he needed help but because he wanted someone who could see through the darkness in him and still be there.

Parker swallowed, the tears finally spilling over as he nodded. He didn't know if Nick was right or if he could return from what he'd done. But with Nick's hand on his leg and the promise of help in his eyes, Parker wanted to believe it was possible—he wanted to believe he wasn't completely lost.

16

NOTHING TO SEE HERE

Before the first light of dawn broke the horizon, Parker checked his phone—6:00 a.m., Monday morning. Although Nick offered and urged him to, Parker knew he couldn't stay. He had been there long enough. It was time to gather his composure and go home. The night seemed like a distant memory, a blur of panic, but Parker hoped the little respite at Nick's apartment would help muster the courage for what he faced next.

A chill crept over Parker despite the hallway's warmth, unease clinging to him like a shadow. Each step toward his door felt labored as if an unseen force were pressing against him, urging him not to enter. It was the same feeling he'd had in the woods—a strong breeze pushing, whispering for him to leave before it was too late.

The key hovered above the lock as Parker stood before his condo's door. The faint scent of Nick's shower soap clung to him as he hesitated, feeling a sense of dread as his fingers trembled around the key. *You can do this*, he reminded himself. *You must do this.* Cleaning the scene was the final step, the only thing between him and getting his old life back. Once the orderliness returned, he could convince himself he was Parker Grant again.

As he opened the door, his heart pounded. He stepped inside, silence cloaking him, shattered only by the softened gray clouds of the morning's light filtering through the glass. He stood frozen in the entryway, his gaze sweeping the kitchen first and the living room beyond. Parker braced himself for the inevitable mess—the intermittent trail marks from Devin's heels leading to the hallway, the heavy crystal bowl still on the kitchen floor, the half-empty coffee mugs on the coffee table, and worst of all, the large, smeared pool of dried blood, defiling the perfect order he cherished. He prepared himself to face it, to clean up the chaos left in the wake of the struggle. Parker visualized every stain, every misplaced item, the guilt seeping through every corner of his mind like the gray clouds hanging outside his windows.

But what greeted him inside made his heart stop cold.

Nothing.

The condo was immaculate.

Parker's eyes widened as he took in the impossible sight before him. The kitchen's floor was clean and polished. There were no pools of blood, no stains or smears. The air carried a faint scent of lemon, sharp and clean-smelling as if mocking his memory of the coppery tang of blood that hung there hours before. The faint hum of the refrigerator was the only sound, its rhythm unnervingly typical in the eerie stillness.

The heavy crystal bowl was intact, set atop the long center island, on the side nearest the living room, where it always set. The table in the living room lacked coffee mugs, and there were no signs of any struggle. Everything was in place as if nothing had happened. Parker's pulse thudded in his ears, a drumbeat of bewilderment in an otherwise silent room. He stepped forward and scanned his surroundings, searching for traces of what happened barely twelve hours before.

There was a jarring sense of dissonance in the room. Parker's ears strained for sounds absent—the crash of the crystal bowl, the muffled thud of Devin's body hitting the floor. But the room's silence mocked him, as if the condo was holding its breath.

Parker cautiously strode through the kitchen, running his fingers along the cool granite top as he passed. It was clean and polished, just like he kept it. His gaze fell on the coffee table, the place where the struggle began. Parker carefully examined the fluffed pillows on the corners of the sofa and the neatly vacuumed lines in the area rug. It was all clean and smooth, with no signs of disturbance or violence. Parker's heart continued pounding while his mind raced, his breath growing shallow as disbelief coursed through his veins. *How was this possible?* He stood while his eyes darted around the room. How could it all have vanished?

He returned to the kitchen, to the spot where his hands had trembled, covered in Devin's blood. He glanced into the sink, expecting the smears of red he left behind, the evidence of what he did. But there was nothing. No blood, no mess. Everything was spotless. Parker's stomach twisted as he gripped the counter's edge to reconcile his swirling memory with the moment's calmness. He clenched his jaw, his teeth grinding together as panic bubbled beneath the surface, a raw ache clawing at his throat.

"No," Parker whispered, his voice cracking. "No, this can't be right." He pushed away from the counter and moved back into the living room. He probed the space again, his mind struggling to understand what was there and what wasn't. His head pounded as confusion overwhelmed him. It had to be here.

There had to be something. Parker moved to the hallway, his gaze falling on the open doorway to the bedroom, hesitating before walking in.

The bedroom was just as he left it each morning, weekdays and weekends—the bed neatly made, the pillows arranged with precision. Parker stared at it, his mind flashing back to Saturday night—the way Devin smiled at him, the warmth of his unclothed body pressed against his own. Devin's presence lingered in the room's quiet, his laughter still humming. Parker closed his eyes. He knew it had to have been real. But standing there now, the memory hovered between a blessing and a nightmare, something that had never truly existed.

Turning toward the closet, Parker reached for the doors. He pulled them open while his eyes scanned inside. There was no sign of Devin's clothes hanging there. Parker moved to the dresser and opened the drawer where he had seen Devin's folded clothes. It contained only his now—no sign Devin's clothes were ever there. *What else?* Where else could he search?

Parker sprinted to the bathroom as if to glimpse an item belonging to Devin before it disappeared. Devin's toothbrush and the bottle of cologne were missing. Parker glanced toward the large marble shower, the spot where he first laid eyes on Devin's wet, glistening body, strands of water flowing down his powerful thighs and calves. It was dry now, clean, and white, sanitized of any memory from two mornings ago. *Had only two mornings passed,* he asked himself.

Parker ran his hands through his hair as his mind spiraled. He squatted, leaning against the bathroom cabinets, and slid slowly to the floor. *How could it be gone? How could everything have vanished?* His hands curled into fists, nails biting into his palms as frustration sharpened into a searing rage—rage at the betrayal of his mind and the cruelty of his memory's failure. A scream threatened to erupt, clawing its way up his throat, but he swallowed it, his teeth clenched as the oppressive silence closed in around him.

His eyes trained on the wall ahead as he sat. He buried Devin—drove out to the woods, and buried him. Parker could still feel the weight of the crowbar and jack in his hands, the dirt clinging to his skin, and the cold air biting at his face. But now, it felt like a lie, a cruel trick his mind was playing on him. He ached under the weight of doubt, an empty void where his certainty once resided.

Parker rose and walked back into the living room. He stood in the center and scanned the space, his mind racing. Parker needed to find some evidence it had happened, proof he wasn't losing his mind. He walked to the bookshelf, his fingertips grazing over the spines of the books, searching for anything out of place. Everything was in order, however, just as it should be. The familiar titles offered no comfort, only a sense of disorientation as if the world around him had been rewritten once again.

The unmistakable coppery scent of blood drifted through the air for an instant. Parker froze when he sensed it, his nostrils flaring as he sniffed, trying to catch it again. It was gone. Only the scent of floor polish and lemon remained.

The walls of his sanctuary pressed in on Parker, the weight of the confusion pushing down on him. He needed out. He needed air. His eyes fell on the balcony door, his hands unsteady as he unlocked it and slid it open. The cool morning air rushed in when he did, filling his lungs as he stepped onto the balcony, his hands gripping the railing while staring at the city below. The sky was a muted shade of gray, the sun creeping over the horizon behind the clouds like a hesitant promise.

Closing his eyes, Parker tried to steady his breathing. It wasn't real. *It couldn't have been real*, the thoughts repeated. But he was sure of what he had felt—every moment, every emotion. His hands tightened around the railing. If it wasn't real, what was happening to him? As dots danced across Parker's vision, lightheadedness threatened to topple him. He blinked rapidly, trying to shake the dizziness, his hands slick with sweat.

The wind bit sharply against his face as Parker gripped the railing for balance, his knuckles pale with tension. He stared out over the city below. For one brief, chilling moment, he imagined letting go—stepping off and surrendering to the uncertainty. Would the confusion finally end? Would the guilt dissolve if he embraced the silence below? But something rooted him in place. Not fear, exactly, but a stubborn flicker of defiance—a fragile yet resolute belief he could wrest control back from whatever force was unraveling his life. He closed his eyes and shook his head, forcing the thought into retreat. Yet, the dizzying sense of vertigo lingered as though the twenty-six concrete floors beneath him might crumble into nothingness.

Parker opened his eyes. *I buried Devin. I drove out to the woods and buried him.* He was sure it had happened, but was it merely a cruel trick his mind had played on him?

He once more imagined the quiet stillness of the world slipping away beneath him. No more confusion. No more guilt. Just peace. But the image was as terrifying as it was tempting. He couldn't—he wouldn't let it end like that.

Parker pushed himself away from the railing and stepped back inside. Everything was as it should be—as if the condo conspired to mock him with its orderliness. But Parker knew better. Things didn't just disappear—memories didn't warp, and blood didn't evaporate. Still, here he was, staring at a space that defied logic and dared him to question the foundations of his reality.

Scanning the condo, Parker needed to find some proof it happened and that he wasn't losing his mind. He moved to his desk and brushed over the surface, searching for anything out of place—still nothing, no sign of the framed picture of the two, together and happy. Everything was as it should be.

Parker drew a deep breath, releasing it slowly as his jaw tightened with determination. He needed to uncover the truth and untangle this twisted nightmare's threads. If the world insisted on toying with him, he resolved to push back with equal force, refusing to let things return to normal without clarity or answers.

17

New Day, Fresh Opportunity

The blaring sound of the alarm cut through the early Monday darkness, bringing Olivia Hayes out of an all-too-brief slumber and into the familiar darkness of 5:30 a.m.. She switched it off before it disturbed her boys in the other room, allowing them another hour or so to sleep.

Lying in bed a few moments longer, she stared at the ceiling and ran down a mental list of today's activities: the kids off to school, her commute to work, a full day at the office followed by her night class, home to make dinner, and finally, everyone sitting at the kitchen table for homework. Olivia took a slow, deep breath, letting the morning air fill her lungs before slowly exhaling. Then, her lips curled into a smile: a new day and a fresh opportunity.

After showering and dressing, Olivia caught the aroma of coffee from the kitchen and sighed with gratitude. Her eldest was already up and had at least managed to start the pot. One less thing for her to do. In the kitchen, she found Marcus, seventeen, lanky, already wearing his earbuds, nodding his head to a song's beat.

"Morning, Mom," he mumbled, barely glancing up as he scrolled on his phone. Olivia smiled and patted his arm as she moved toward the coffee maker.

"Morning, baby," she replied, pouring herself a cup. She took a sip, savoring the warmth spreading through her. "Did you finish your English paper last night?"

Marcus shrugged. "Almost. I'll get it done during study hall."

Olivia closed her eyes for a beat, wanting to hold back the urge to lecture, but didn't. "You're up early," she replied, "how about we finish it now, okay?"

Glancing over to the worn textbook left open last night on the kitchen table, she closed it and set it aside, giving Marcus some space. She only made it halfway through her economics assignment over the weekend but would have time to finish it during her lunch hour today. Balancing school, work, and raising two boys was challenging, but Olivia didn't let herself feel overwhelmed. She reminded herself every day's step forward was still progress, no matter how small.

"Yeah, yeah," Marcus muttered, lost in whatever he was watching on his phone, and took the earbuds out.

"Tyler!" Olivia called out, her voice carrying through the small apartment. "Get up, baby! We can't be late!"

Her thirteen-year-old youngest groaned from his bedroom. Olivia shook her head, taking another sip of coffee before setting the mug down and marching to his door. She pushed it open, revealing the mess of clothes, video game controllers, and schoolbooks scattered across the floor. Tyler was still bundled under his blanket, only a tuft of his hair visible.

"Tyler, come on now," Olivia said, her tone gentle but firm as she yanked the blanket off him. "You got five minutes, or I'm coming back with a bucket of cold water." She chuckled but was half-serious.

With a dramatic groan, Tyler rolled out of bed, his feet hitting the floor as he stumbled toward the bathroom. Olivia watched him for a moment, a pang of sympathy softening her stern expression. She knew what tired was. They were all tired—doing their best to make it through each day—but there was no time for rest when there was so much to do.

Olivia returned to the kitchen, glancing at the clock on the wall—7:10 a.m.. "You want some breakfast?" she asked Marcus, who moved to the kitchen table, his eyes glued to his notebook. He shook his head, still focused on his cell phone lying in the fold between the open pages.

"Nah, I'm good."

"Uh-huh," Olivia muttered, opening the fridge and pulling out a carton of eggs. "You're going to eat something, even if it's just scrambled eggs. You have a long day ahead of you."

She cracked the eggs into a bowl, whisking them with quick efficiency. The sizzle of the skillet filled the kitchen, the sound grounding her as she moved through the motions. She glanced over her shoulder at Marcus, focused intently on his assignment. He gave her a small, appreciative smile without looking up, and Olivia's heart swelled.

"Thanks, Mom," he said, his teenage indifference waning momentarily.

Olivia smiled back, nodding. "You're welcome, baby."

Tyler shuffled into the kitchen, his hair still messy but at least dressed for school. Olivia handed him a plate with eggs and toast, and as he passed, he took it to the table. She moved through the kitchen efficiently, grabbing backpacks, checking lunch bags, and ensuring everything was ready for the day ahead.

"Alright, boys," she said, her voice carrying an edge of urgency. "We've gotta leave in ten if you don't want to miss the bus. Let's go, please."

The boys, oblivious to the weight on their mother's shoulders, continued eating, their attention fixed on whatever was capturing their amusement on Marcus's phone.

Olivia watched them, her heart aching with love and exhaustion. She returned to her coffee, taking another sip as she glanced at the clock again. She plastered on a smile, her voice bright as she clapped her hands.

"Alright, let's move, Hayes boys. We have a world to conquer today."

"Mom, I've got a test today," her youngest grumbled as he stood and took his dishes to the sink.

"And you're going to crush it." She squeezed Tyler's shoulder. "You've been studying hard, and I'm so proud of you already."

Olivia's positivity was her armor, which she wore daily to protect herself and her kids from the force of the world's challenges. She knew how hard it was being a single mother, but she learned to face her obstacles head-on, taking a slow and steady approach. There were no shortcuts; that fact never bothered her. She knew the path was hers to walk, and that was all that mattered.

As they piled out the door, Olivia kissed both her sons on the forehead. "I love you. Be good. Be smart. Make today count." She watched as they walked toward the bus stop, her heart swelling with pride and hope.

Arriving at work, Olivia paused momentarily before heading to her desk. She took a deep, cleansing breath, savoring the early morning quiet, the stillness before the hustle. Today would be another busy day; Mondays typically were. Olivia would do her part to keep the office running smoothly, always supporting Dr. Warren, Alyce, and Parker.

Setting her things down, Olivia moved around the office, tidying up the reception area, turning on the printers and copiers, and making coffee. She neatly arranged today's files with sticky notes assigned to each one. As the sun rose higher and cleared the bushes in the front yard, it filled the office with natural light.

As Olivia settled into the morning rhythm, she smiled to herself. Her responsibilities at the practice gave her a sense of control over her life, one she didn't always feel in the sometimes chaotic home life of single parenthood. Her life wasn't easy, but it was hers, and she was determined to live it fully.

Olivia settled into her chair, ready to transcribe notes and listen to weekend voicemails. When her phone rang, she glanced at the screen and raised an eyebrow. It was Parker's name lit up. He was usually in by this time, always the conscientious associate second to the office in the mornings.

"Good morning, Parker." She glanced toward his closed door as they spoke. Olivia assumed he was already in his office when she arrived, but it was obvious now he wasn't.

"Olivia?"

"Hey, Parker, yeah. What's wrong, Hun?"

"Olivia," he paused. His voice sounded distant, distracted. "Hey, I'm... I'm not feeling well today. I'm...," another uncomfortably long break followed, "I won't be coming in."

"Oh, okay." The pause was Olivia's now. She had never known Parker to call in sick. It wasn't like him waiting until the last minute, either—for anything. "Are you okay? I can bring you some files or reschedule some appointments to be conference calls if you—"

"No," he interrupted her. "I can't."

"Are you sure you're okay, Parker? You don't sound like yourself." Olivia's voice was warm, but her tone gave an edge of worry, lingering like a question left unanswered. "If there's anything you need..." She trailed off, her unease growing as the silence stretched between them.

Parker closed his eyes, forcing himself to keep his voice steady. "I'm fine. I just need a day. It's personal. I'll be in tomorrow."

"Alright, sure," she said, though the hesitation in her voice was unmistakable. "Take care of yourself, okay?"

"Yeah. Thanks," Parker muttered before hanging up. He exhaled a long breath before the phone slipped from his hand and landed with a thud on the area rug in the living room.

Olivia gently placed the handset in the cradle. She glanced toward Parker's closed door again, listening to his words replay in her thoughts. She considered what she could do for him, though he asked her for nothing. Olivia greeted Dr. Warren and Alyce as they walked into the lobby, informing them of Parker's absence and setting out to reschedule his clients.

When Parker woke up, mired in grogginess, it was as dark inside his condo as it was outside, with only the faint glow of the city below casting dim sparks of light across the shadows where he lay. His neck was stiff, his back sore from lying in a twisted position for so long, bent awkwardly against the sofa's armrest. The textured fabric pressed against his cheek. Parker blinked, disoriented, his vision blurry as his thoughts struggled to surface. The distant hum of traffic reached him—a low, constant buzz piercing the room's silent stillness. Slowly, painfully, he sat up, his joints protesting as the room and his awareness gradually came into focus.

He searched for his phone, patting the coffee table first and fumbling around the cushions. Finally, Parker found it on the floor beneath him, right where it slipped from his grasp after he'd hung up with Olivia this morning. Wait—*this morning?*

The memory pierced through any remaining grogginess as he pressed his thumb to the screen, the glow illuminating his face—8:45 p.m.. He stared at the time in disbelief. He'd slept for over twelve hours. The shock of lost time swept through him, though it shouldn't have come as a surprise.

Parker was out late Friday night, drinking until he lost consciousness. He had awoken to Devin in his shower on Saturday, spending most of the night tangled in an unexpected and intriguing encounter. And Sunday? There had been no sleep at all—only chaos, violence, and the desperate hours that followed: killing Devin, burying him in the forest, and spending the early morning hours at Nick's place.

A sleep deprivation crisis, he thought. It was no wonder his body gave out after calling Olivia. It also helped to explain the other symptoms—hallucinations, impaired judgment, and cognitive decline. It all made grim sense. It explained the entire day of deep, reparative sleep. But it did nothing to help Parker understand what he experienced with Devin—if he had, in fact, experienced anything at all. And, if it had, where was the evidence?

Parker rubbed his temples as he stood, his body protesting each slight movement. He was stiff from sleeping so many hours in a near-upright position. He stepped forward, stretching as he moved through the living room, his eyes scanning his surroundings in the near darkness.

Parker wandered into the kitchen, his fingers brushing the smooth granite counter. The cold surface sent a faint chill through his skin. The refrigerator's hum buzzed in his ears, too loud in the oppressive silence, as the lingering scent of floor polish mingled with the ghost of coppery blood in his mind.

The pristine condition of his home mocked him, a sterile reflection of the life he built, hollow and unyielding. It was as if the condo conspired to erase Devin's presence and every shred of evidence Parker's world had fractured. Parker's gaze shifted to the hallway and his bedroom, and he moved toward them.

Pausing in the doorway, Parker looked at the bed, perfectly made, the throw pillows arranged neatly at the headboard. He entered the room, his eyes scanning the space for any sign—a wrinkle in the bedspread, an object out of place, anything suggesting what he believed he experienced happened. But there was nothing. Like the rest of his condo, the room was just as he kept it—no trace of Devin's belongings or anyone else having been there.

He released a shaky breath, a sense of uneasy relief beginning to unfurl within him. None of it ever happened. His time with Devin, the argument, the violence—it was all a hallucination, a twisted, stress-induced illusion brought on by exhaustion and sleep deprivation. He had been overwhelmed, his mind playing cruel tricks on him, creating a reality that never existed. Parker wasn't a monster. He wasn't capable of such a thing. He was a therapist—someone who helped people, not someone who hurt them.

The mind worked in strange ways, even for those trained to understand it. Parker knew that well. He spent years studying the mind's complexities, guiding his clients through their struggles. Now, he fell victim to the same fragility he so often observed in others. His training taught him that stress could manifest in many ways—hallucinations, delusions, and loss of control. It wasn't a sign of weakness. It was just the mind trying to cope.

He wasn't going to entertain the idea he lost control of his mental faculties—the idea he did those things. No, he couldn't allow himself to think it. He was Parker Grant, in control of his thoughts and actions. The condo was as it usually was, neat and clean, untouched by the madness he imagined, and he was grateful for it.

Parker's stomach growled, pulling him from his thoughts. He hadn't eaten anything since—when? Sunday morning? No, that was the breakfast he imagined Devin made for him, and Saturday's dinner on the balcony must not have happened either. The hunger reminded him to care for himself and return to his routine. He moved to the kitchen and made himself a protein shake, shaking it vigorously before pouring it into a glass, the familiar motion grounding him in the present.

Leaning against the counter as he drank, Parker's gaze drifted toward the windows and the city's lights twinkling against the darkness. He was awake now, rested and restless. He wanted to go out and move, to make up for the lost hours and weekend stent disconnected from his routines. Maybe a workout at the gym would help clear his mind and bring him back to complete normalcy. It was late, and Parker needed to go to work in the morning, but after sleeping all day, he was wide awake. He wanted to burn off whatever crazy anxiety remained from the distorted weekend.

Parker finished the shake and grabbed his gym bag. Before heading out, he picked up his phone—several missed calls and text messages awaited. He swiped to his voicemail and held the phone to his ear.

"Hey, Parker, it's Olivia. I just wanted to check on you. I hope you're feeling better. Call me when you can." Olivia's voice was warm, her concern genuine, bringing a small smile to Parker's lips. He appreciated her more than he told her.

The following message was from his mom, her familiar voice filling his ear. *"Hi, sweetheart. It's Mom. Just calling to see how you are. I hope you're doing well. Give me a call when you get a chance. Love you."* It was their Sunday routine to chat and catch up, and a pang of guilt ran through him for missing it.

The final message was a text from Nick. *"Hey, Park. Just wondering how ya feel?"* Parker assumed Nick was referring to Friday night at the club. Nick knew Parker hadn't been in the best shape that night, and it was good of Nick to check in on him.

Parker lowered the phone, a sense of quiet washing over him. Everything was normal. Everything was as it should be. He chuckled, now thinking back to earlier when he awoke. Parker considered, for a moment, driving out to the spot on the north side of Lake Lanier—in the woods near where he camped before—to see, to close the door on the possibility once and for all. He knew now it would have been a waste of time and was glad he dismissed the idea as quickly as it came.

He grabbed his keys from the counter and slipped them into his hoodie as he headed for the door. It was over. Whatever had happened—or hadn't happened—was behind him now. He was moving forward. It was a 'new day and a fresh opportunity,' as Olivia was fond of saying.

18

THE PACKAGE

(Tuesday the 10ᵗʰ)

Olivia wished Parker a good morning as he walked in. There was a happy tone to her greeting. "Feeling better today?"

"One hundred percent, thanks," Parker replied, stopping at her desk long enough to assure her of his recovery.

Her gaze lingered on him, the suggestion of disbelief perceptible in her expression. Olivia could read people better than most and didn't need a therapist license to know when someone was withholding.

Parker's smile wavered. "I'm fine. Really."

"I'm glad to hear it," she replied, though her tone carried doubt. "Did Stephanie take good care of you this weekend?"

"No," he replied. "We're not seeing much of each other these days."

Parker remembered his last conversation with Stephanie all too well—the uncomfortable silence filling the room as she sat across from him, her eyes wide and searching, desperate to understand what had gone wrong. He'd said it wasn't her; it was him. The cliché fell from his lips, stale and hollow. It was easier to lean on that overused excuse than to speak the truth.

~

Stephanie was everything one could ask for: kind, supportive, understanding. She genuinely adored him, and Parker tried to reciprocate. But the longer they dated, the more glaring the divide became. He wasn't interested in her the way she deserved. Not honestly. He didn't feel the passion others spoke of when they found the one. Their weekends spent together, the plans she casually hinted at, the gentleness of her touch—none of it made his heart leap the way it was supposed to.

He'd spent his whole life striving for perfection. His parents' perfectionism, etched into Parker early on, taught him anything less than flawless wasn't acceptable. He'd taken that lesson to heart, holding himself to impossible standards and, by extension, everyone around him. It was why no one ever measured up. Stephanie was no different, though it wasn't her fault. Parker cherished control over his space and emotions more than sharing a less-perfect version with anyone else.

There was another truth he could never admit—not to Stephanie and certainly not to himself if he could avoid it. He recalled his college years, sitting among the guys as they boasted about their conquests and their desires for women. He would smile, nod, and laugh along, but it was all a performance. The experiences they described were foreign to him, like a language he couldn't speak. Parker carried a deep secret inside, a longing he dared not name. He fought to suppress it and convinced himself it was just a phase or a fleeting illusion he could outgrow.

Control over his environment, his meticulously organized home, his career, his independence—these were the things

Parker clung to. Stephanie was, albeit gentle, an intrusion into the life he'd built for himself. It wasn't her fault she couldn't fit into the narrow confines he'd made, nor could she break through the walls he'd built around the truth of his desires.

When Parker ended things, he saw the hurt in her eyes. She'd asked him why—what had gone wrong, what she could have done differently—but he had no honest answer to give her. He only muttered that he needed space and things weren't working out. He knew she deserved better and hoped she would find someone to give her the love she sought. But it would not be from him. It could never be from him.

~

"Hey, before I forget," Olivia added, "there's a package for you on your desk. It was outside the front door this morning when I got here."

Parker nodded. "Thank you, Ms. Hayes," his lips slightly curled into a grin as he stepped away from her desk.

The door to Parker's office clicked shut behind him, the sound hanging in the room's stillness. His gaze swept over the space—his second sanctuary after his condo—where he could manage every detail, a place of order and healing shaped by logic and structure. Parker had ninety minutes before his first appointment. It was a welcomed opportunity to reflect on prior sessions and prepare for this week's upcoming appointments. He was eager to focus on work again, returning to an orderly environment where he could manage every detail of his day.

The small brown box sat unassuming in the center of his desk, perfectly aligned with the edges of his black desk pad. Olivia knew his preferences—everything centered, squared off, no clutter. He picked it up and flipped it around, searching for other markings on the heavy-stock brown paper neatly wrapped around the box. Only the name '*Parker*' was written on it in neat penmanship. It had no postage marks or delivery labels, meaning someone had hand-delivered it.

Parker placed the box back on his desk, the coarse brown paper scratching against his fingertips. He reached for the leather shoulder bag and removed his appointment book and journal. Parker opened his calendar to today's date and placed it neatly to the left of his desk pad—four sixty-minute sessions and no other commitments. Given his absence yesterday and the workload he needed to catch up on, he welcomed the relatively light schedule.

He thumbed through his journal, stopping at the next blank page before setting it on the right side of the desk pad. His chrome fountain pen rested in the fold, holding the journal open, a familiar weight anchoring him to routine.

Parker picked the package up again and used his letter opener to neatly slice the brown kraft paper, revealing the cardboard box. With steady hands, he lifted the lid and gasped, his fingers freezing around the edges of the box. His heart pounded, each beat louder than the last, immediately setting the box back down on his desk.

Inside, a photograph. A shiver ran up Parker's spine as the significance of the image sank in. His chest tightened like a vise as his mind struggled to catch up with the shocking image, the image of him—**Parker**—in an intimate embrace with Devin. The image slammed into him like someone's fist, pulling him into a dizzying spiral of disbelief.

Parker's pulse thundered in his ears as he pulled out the small stack of pictures from the box. He quickly thumbed through them, his grip tightening around the edges of the stack as each was more damning than the last—each more explicit, each more compromising. He studied them carefully and recognized the setting. Whoever took them had been inside his condo, inside his sanctuary. The images seared into his mind, and he wanted to throw the photographs back into the box and slam the lid back on it. Still, doing so would not erase the sense of vulnerability now gripping him.

Glancing around his office, Parker verified the door was still closed. His hands trembled as he reached for the note tucked beneath the photos. He unfolded it and read the neatly penned message.

"I know what you did."

The words blurred, but the meaning was clear. Parker's weekend, the chaos, what he believed he had concealed or imagined—wasn't gone. It followed him, creeping back into his life when he presumed he was safe. The paranoia he so confidently buried began to claw its way back to the surface and threatened to overwhelm him.

And then he spotted it—the bloodied watch at the bottom of the box.

For a moment, Parker stood frozen, the note slipping from his fingers and floating down to join the photographs scattered on his desk. He stared at the vintage timepiece, his breaths coming in short gasps. His mind raced, searching for a way to regain control, to push the chaos back down where it belonged. But the realization his life was unraveling was inescapable. Parker tried to piece together what happened. *Who could have done this?* The fear he suppressed for days roared back to life, louder and more insistent than ever.

Using the pressed, neatly folded white handkerchief he kept in his left pocket, Parker tentatively lifted the watch from the box. Once supple and familiar, the leather band was now stiff and cold in his grip, marred by a dried but still sticky residue. He examined the blood-spattered face, each crack in the crystal reflecting a crack in his memory and growing anxiety. The hands lay frozen above the Roman numerals on the dial.

The watch's familiar design yanked at his memory, but it wasn't until he checked his bare wrist that the truth slammed into him. The bloodied, fractured timepiece wasn't just any watch. It was *his* watch. Its shattered face and marred leather band mocked him, a visceral testament to the truth he refused to accept. No amount of control could undo what he had done at 10:09 a.m., the moment he could never outrun.

"Parker?" A sharp two-knuckled tap on the door snapped him back into the present. "Your appointment is here," Olivia called from the hallway.

He jolted, dropping the watch into its box and covering it with his monogrammed handkerchief. He scrambled to collect the note and photographs, returning them to the box. Parker slammed the lid back on, forcing himself to breathe, pushing the panic back down where it belonged. But the realization that his control was not as absolute as he believed gnawed at him— a dark truth he could no longer ignore. It was a disturbing fear refusing to be silenced.

The young therapist swallowed hard, willing his voice to steady. "Thank you," he managed, hastily shoving the small box into his desk drawer. As he did, Parker's eyes caught on the pale strip of skin circling his left wrist, exposed beneath the cuff of his Oxford shirt, while reaching down to hide the box and its kraft paper wrapping in the bottom drawer.

The office door creaked, and his first client of the day stepped into the room.

Parker stepped from his desk and extended a hand to greet John. His palms were clammy, and he hoped John didn't notice it. Every part of him wanted to retreat behind his locked office door to sift through the disturbing contents of the box in solitude. But he had a role to play—an image to uphold. Normalcy was a performance, and he couldn't afford to break character.

John's voice ebbed and flowed, a dissonant backdrop to Parker's spiraling thoughts. His client spoke of strained relationships and mounting pressure at work—words that should have sparked Parker's professional interest. Instead, Parker's mind fixated on the box in his desk drawer, pressing against his focus like a constant, unwelcome reminder. He forced himself to nod, to respond, though each word felt hollow, a script delivered by someone else entirely.

"Parker?" John's voice broke through, his brows knitting together as he peered at Parker with a hint of concern. "Did you get that?"

Parker blinked, snapping his attention back. "Yes, sorry, John. I was thinking about what you said." He forced an acknowledging smile, hoping it looked genuine.

John offered a patient nod as he continued.

The rest of the session dragged on, Parker's forced engagement and attempts at reassurance only serving to heighten his anxiety. When the hour finally ended, he saw John out. Parker immediately returned to his office and shut the door, leaning heavily against it, the lingering sound of John's monotone soliloquy echoing in his head.

He moved toward his desk, his fingers pausing above the handle, the chill of dread spreading across his skin. He needed to deal with the package. The photographs and his watch couldn't remain there, festering like a looming threat waiting to explode.

Parker paced the length of his office, his dress shoes tapping against the polished wood floors. He could take the box with him at the end of the day and dispose of it somehow, but what about the reality of its contents? What about the sender?

A knock on the door startled him, his heart jumping into his throat. He quickly stepped away from the drawer, shoving his hands into his pockets as Olivia opened it slightly.

"Hey, Parker," she said, her eyes scanning his face. "I made a fresh pot. Do you want a refill?" She stepped into the room and noticed the cup of cold coffee still sitting on his desk from when he first arrived. She paused and made a gesture, offering to pick it up to refill it. "Are you sure you're feeling better today?" Olivia asked, her gaze lingering, flickering with concern Parker couldn't entirely dismiss. It was as if she could see the cracks forming beneath his polished exterior. Her presence, though kind, felt like a spotlight on his fraying composure.

Parker swallowed, nodding quickly. "Yeah, just more tired than I thought I'd be. Went to the gym last night when I began to feel better and didn't sleep well," he replied, avoiding her eyes.

Olivia frowned slightly, her warm eyes narrowing as if trying to read deeper into his expression. "You know, you don't always have to push through when feeling under the weather. You should give yourself a chance to heal."

"I appreciate it, Olivia. But as I said, I'm good."

She nodded but remained unconvinced. "Alright. Just remember, we're all here for you." She gave him a gentle smile before leaving.

The door shut behind her, and Parker slumped into his chair, burying his face in his hands. His meticulously constructed life was cracking at the edges, splintering into pieces he could barely hold together.

As the day continued, Parker struggled through his remaining sessions. His clients' voices blurred together, their problems sounding distant and inconsequential compared to the turmoil churning within him. The box in his drawer was like a weight dragging his attention under, and his head ached with the effort of trying to stay composed.

When his last client left, Parker was barely holding it together. He moved to his desk, opened the drawer, and pulled the box out. Parker needed to get rid of it. He couldn't let it stay here, a reminder of everything he couldn't explain.

He slid the box into his satchel. He would figure out what to do with it later—somewhere far away from here. But for now, he needed to get the box out of this building and away from his office. The office needed to be sanitized and restored to normal, just like his condo was. But just as he grabbed his keys, he heard another knock on his office door.

God, what now, he thought, every nerve in his body screaming for release while someone else wanted to delay his freedom. His grip on the satchel tightened, its contents gnawing at him as much as this new interruption. Parker didn't want to deal with anyone else right now, not when the weight of what the box represented already overwhelmed him.

"Parker?" Alyce's voice carried through the door, followed by another gentle tap.

His heart lurched, and he drew a deep breath, forcing his expression to relax before responding. "Come in."

Alyce entered, her presence commanding but kind. She glanced at him, her eyes narrowing with concern. "I wanted to check in on you," she said, calm but edging with curiosity. Her sharp eyes scanned his face, lingering long enough to quicken Parker's pulse. Alyce's presence was always steady, disarmingly so. Parker hated how exposed he felt under her quiet scrutiny.

He stiffened, trying to cover the anxious flutter of his heartbeat. "Better, yes." He didn't need Alyce's concern right now, though he acknowledged the care in her eyes and appreciated her effort to reach out to him. Parker forced a nod, adding, "Thanks, Alyce. It's just personal stuff. Nothing to worry about."

Alyce's expression softened, her gaze lingering on his face before she acknowledged his dismissal and left the room.

He let out a breath he hadn't realized he was holding. Refocusing, Parker slung his satchel strap over his shoulder and headed for the door.

As Parker walked through the hallway, the box's weight in his bag grew heavier with every step, like a dark secret refusing denial. The polished floors creaked under his feet, echoing the dread within him. Whoever sent him the package knew his vulnerabilities, and Parker knew he would have to fight to protect himself. He wondered if it was a fight he could win.

19

THE ART OF DEFLECTION

(Wednesday the 11th)

Parker glanced at the wall clock, tapping his foot rhythmically against the polished floor. Every tick sounded louder than the last. He'd never been this distracted before a session as he struggled to shake off the lingering anxiety from the package, the twisted reminder of his life unraveling. Its heavy emotional weight refused to leave him, clinging to him, casting a pall over his mind as he went through the motions. Parker instinctively lifted his cuff to glance at his watch but only saw his bare wrist, reminded again of the timepiece buried in the box at home. But as he heard footsteps approach, followed by a knock, he braced himself, forcing his mind back to its practiced composure.

"Come," he called out.

The door creaked open, and Parker straightened his back, taking a steadying breath as Mark stepped inside alone, his presence weighted and palpable. His eyes carried exhaustion, like the newly carved fatigue in his face, lines deeper and heavier with worry and sleepless nights. Mark closed the door behind him but didn't sit immediately, lingering instead as though measuring Parker with quiet intensity, waiting for a signal or a shift. The absence of Devin at his side sent a cold shiver through Parker, a discomfort tough to shake.

"Parker," Mark nodded and greeted, his voice thick with uncertainty. His posture seemed guarded, his eyes scanning the room as if searching for answers within its boundaries.

"Mark," Parker replied, gesturing toward the chair across from him. He noted Mark's cautiousness, hinting at unease. "Is Devin not coming today?" The question stuck in Parker's throat, but he managed to keep his tone casual.

"Not here," Mark answered, sounding both like a bold statement born out of frustration and a question. He exhaled heavily, rubbing a hand over his face as though trying to wipe away a bitter truth as he sank into the sofa. He didn't meet Parker's gaze—his eyes focused somewhere distant instead. "I don't know. That's the thing." He paused, the silence heavy between them.

"Devin's gone," Mark said, his voice taut, tinged with frustration and an undercurrent of hurt. His gaze dropped to the floor, his jaw tightening as though he was restraining an emotion threatening to surface. "You'd think I'd know him better after all this time. But he still knows how to disappear, doesn't he?" The words hung heavily in the air, reluctant and burdened, as though saying them out loud cemented their reality.

Parker's heart thudded heavily in his chest. "Gone?" He repeated his client's words, and his voice was carefully measured.

Resting his forearms on his knees and leaning forward, Mark's hands clasped tightly, his eyes finally meeting Parker's, searching, probing. "He's just gone. I slept in late Saturday, and when I woke up, he wasn't there. Figured he needed some space—sometimes Devin can be like that, you know?"

Mark admitted he and Devin argued late Friday night at Cityside after Parker left the bar. He spoke with a mix of defensiveness and worry, a tone layered with conflicting emotions. "But it's been days, and there's no sign of him. No calls, no texts. Nothing." Mark trailed off, his gaze drifting toward the floor as though some unspoken consideration held him captive.

Parker's stomach tightened. He forced himself to respond calmly as a cold dread seeped into his bones. "Have you contacted anyone? Friends who might have seen him?" The questions came out evenly, though his fingers fidgeted in his lap, twisting and untwisting themselves.

"I called his phone, but nothing," Mark replied, shaking his head. "I reached out to a couple of his friends, but no one's heard from him. It's just—" He hesitated, glancing at Parker with a furrowed brow. "I don't know, Parker. Something feels wrong about this."

Parker watched as Mark's face twisted in confusion, his shoulders drooping under the weight of his worry. Parker sensed the question before it formed, hovering unspoken between them.

"Do you think something might've happened to him?" Mark asked. His eyes were wide and searching, his voice betraying the vulnerability beneath his guarded exterior.

Parker controlled his breathing and fought the urge to look away. "What do you mean by something?" he asked, careful to keep his steady.

"I don't know," Mark said, his voice cracking slightly. He glanced down at his hands. "I mean, what if someone did something to him? Or what if he's just gone for good? He's always been reckless," Mark continued, "but this isn't like him." He leaned forward, his face close enough for Parker to see every fine line etched around his eyes. "I'm starting to wonder if maybe he was seeing someone else. Someone who, I don't know, wanted to take him away?"

Parker leaned back in his chair, willing his body to relax, though his nerves frayed beneath the surface.

"Mark," he began, choosing his words with care. "It's possible Devin just needed some space. He's been through a lot lately—your relationship has taken a toll on both of you." He paused, forcing himself to keep eye contact. "I think it might be best to give him a little more time before assuming the worst."

The silence in the room was oppressive, breached only by the faint hum of the air vent. Parker's palms were damp against the smooth leather of his chair, and the faint scent of Mark's aftershave—a sharp, earthy scent—hung in the air as Parker fought the creeping tension knotting at the back of his neck. He needed to stay calm; this was still his domain.

"Mark, I understand this is difficult," Parker added. "Have you considered the possibility that Devin might have just needed some space?"

"Space?" Mark's voice carried a quiet intensity but grew louder. "Is that what you think he needs? More space? From Me?"

Mark's question landed hard, piercing Parker's defenses. The implication was there—unspoken but impossible to ignore. He shifted his weight, arms crossing in a measured attempt to stay in command of the session. "Sometimes, people step away to reevaluate. It doesn't necessarily mean something bad is happening."

Mark stared at him, unblinking. The room grew colder, like some invisible force drained the air's warmth. "You know, Parker, sometimes I wonder about you," he responded, his voice barely a whisper. "The way you talk about Devin. It's like you understand him better than I do. Strange, isn't it?"

Parker swallowed, feeling the weight of the box back at his apartment, like a heartbeat, like a dark secret tethered to him. He leaned forward, holding Mark's gaze. "Mark, I'm here to support you. That's all."

Mark's expression softened briefly, only to harden again, his lips tightening into a thin line. "Support *me?*" he repeated, the words laced with sharp disdain. "And how exactly do you intend to do that?"

The question caught Parker off guard. He searched for an answer, a way to ease the intensity between them, but his mind raced, coming up empty. "By helping you make sense of things. By giving you the tools to process whatever happens next."

Mark leaned back, exhaling slowly, his fingers loosening slightly. For a moment, his shoulders relaxed, and Parker allowed himself to believe the tension was easing. But Mark's eyes narrowed, his gaze sharp and cutting. "You know, Parker," he said, his tone deceptively calm, "you always seem to know just what to say. It's almost uncanny."

Mark's words struck with an unexpected force, reverberating through the room's stillness. It was more than just a dismissal—it was a deliberate severing, a door closing firmly between them. The sting lingered as Parker grappled with the unspoken message beneath Mark's tone: *What did you expect, Parker? You're not the first man to get caught in Devin's whirlwind. But unlike the others, you thought you could tame it, didn't you? How's that working out for you?*

"Listen," Parker continued, trying to convey reassurance. "It's clear you care a lot about Devin, and that's important. You're doing everything you can, but don't let this consume you until you have more information. I think it's best not to panic or be rash."

Mark stood slowly, his gaze lingering on Parker, who was holding his breath, wondering if Mark could see through the façade. They stared at each other for a long moment, a silent exchange loaded with unspoken words, suspicions unvoiced. The lines on Mark's face seemed more profound now, carved from years of restraint and control. Parker's mind raced, but Mark was still unmovable—a man who mastered the art of patience and now stood as the embodiment of everything Parker feared.

Then Mark nodded, subtly shifting his chin, and turned to leave. He paused, his hand on the door handle, his gaze flickering back to Parker one last time. "If anything's happened to him," Mark said, his voice dropping to a chilling calm, "I'll make sure I know every detail. And I'll know who to hold responsible."

Parker remained seated, Mark's steely gray eyes holding him in place like a force of nature finally turning its attention toward him. Parker swallowed the lump in his throat as the guilt threatened to claw its way out of him. He watched Mark leave his office, the door closing behind him. He exhaled slowly and pushed the bridge of his glasses back into place. The session was tense—too tense—the words lingering heavy and unsettling, an ominous threat disguised as a promise.

The feeling of dread returned, heavy and inescapable, as Parker replayed another version of Mark's words in his mind. They sounded clinical: *People like you don't do well with chaos. You've always been terrified of losing control. But now? You've crossed the line. The question is, what are you going to do next?* The imagined words plagued Parker, feeding his paranoia and self-doubt.

Devin was missing, and Mark was worried. Parker felt as though he was standing on the edge of a precipice, his sanity teetering on the brink. He suggested Devin may have left of his own accord, but the reality of what happened—and the threat of discovery—hung over him like a dark cloud, a reminder the chaos was far from over.

The clock on the wall read 11:45 a.m.. Three more sessions stood between Parker and the end of the day, but the weight of his conversation with Mark—and the box waiting on his desk at home—pressed down on him, heavy and relentless. He leaned forward, pressing his forehead against his clasped hands, forcing down the rising tide of fear. Get rid of the box. Keep Mark from asking too many questions. If either slipped, everything he had built would come crashing down.

20

SELF-DIAGNOSIS

(Thursday the 12ᵗʰ)

Parker awoke with a jolt, the shrill alarm tearing him from a dream. The remnants of the nightmare clung to him, heavy and suffocating, as the morning light filtered through his windows.

He reached over and grabbed his phone—7:00 a.m., less than twenty-four hours since his unsettling session with Mark—two days since the unnerving delivery of the box and its shocking contents. A mere week ago, Parker was beginning couples counseling with new clients—a blur of unanticipated pleasures and unimaginable pain.

He sat up, the cool air of the condo prickling against his bare skin. His thoughts were thick and clouded by the fragmented images of his dreams—Devin's face, pale and ghostly, his eyes wide with fear and accusation. Parker shook his head, trying to dispel the memory, but it clung to him like a persistent fog. He swung his legs over the side of the bed, his feet meeting the floor to ground him. Today was another day demanding his focus and control.

Parker had spent years studying the human mind, peeling back its layers and guiding his clients through their darkest corners. Yet his own felt like a locked room—shuttered, unreadable, and immune to his practiced analysis.

The symptoms were apparent: auditory hallucinations, fleeting visual distortions, and a creeping sense of paranoia that seemed to grow with each passing day. Clinically speaking, Parker recognized the hallmarks of psychosis—the disconnection from reality, the delusions twisting his perception of the world around him. Yet, with his knowledge, the distinction between what was real and what wasn't blurred dangerously, leaving him uncertain and anxious. He found himself questioning his thoughts, unable to trust his mind.

The paranoia fed on every shadow he saw and every whisper he heard. Parker knew the human brain could turn on itself under severe stress, conjuring images and sounds as a coping mechanism. He had seen it happen in others, in clients who walked through his door seeking refuge from their unraveling sanity. Now, he was the one staring into the abyss, watching as his mind distorted the familiar into terror. The irony of it all was not lost on him. He spent his young career guiding others through their darkest moments, yet here he was, unable to pull himself back from the edge.

Parker heard Devin's voice more than once, a whisper calling his name in the dead of night. He knew, logically, it could not be him. Devin was gone—disappeared, conceivably dead. And yet, he heard him. Sometimes, it was just a word, other times a complete sentence, but each time, it was a chilling reminder. It was as if the guilt he carried took on a life of its own, manifesting in the form of the one person he couldn't get out of his head. It was psychosis—plain and simple, and Parker knew it. But knowing didn't make it any easier to endure. It made it worse.

He knew he was slipping, bit by bit, into a world where shadows had voices and ghosts refused to rest.

Parker's paranoia was taking on a life of its own, weaving its way through every corner of his mind like a vine, twisting, tightening, suffocating. He tried to convince himself everything was under control. Devin's absence was just a complication he could handle. But no matter how often he repeated that lie to himself, the truth clung to him like a persistent specter—Devin appeared gone, and the weight of what might have happened between them became mentally unbearable.

On his drive to work, for a brief moment, Parker thought he saw Devin walking along Piedmont Street. The figure vanished into the crowd before Parker could tell if it was real or just another trick of his strained mind. He steadied himself, muttering, "You're in control, Parker." His mind had been working against him lately, whispering doubts, playing tricks—visions of Devin in the corner of his eye, the echo of his voice in his dreams. Whether it was guilt or something more insidious—a warped repercussion of his choices—Parker couldn't tell.

The office was once a stronghold for Parker—a fortress of control, where every word and movement had purpose and precision. Today, it felt like a prison. He moved through his sessions on autopilot, his sharp mind dulled by the weight of his paranoia. He made small mistakes large enough for his clients to catch: a misplaced note, an offbeat comment or a suggestion that sounded wrong, an uncomfortable silence that stretched a beat too long.

His fingers quivered as he adjusted his glasses, watching the woman sitting across from him as she talked about her struggles with anxiety. Parker nodded, trying to focus, but her words slipped past him, lost beneath the roar of his own thoughts.

Devin's face flashed in his mind, his eyes wide, his mouth twisted in fear, anger, or both. Parker blinked, trying to shake the image, but it lingered, a ghost refusing to leave.

"Parker?" The client's voice pulled him back, sharp with concern. Her brows knitted together as she studied him. "Did you hear what I said? You seem distracted."

Parker forced a tight smile. "Yes. Sorry. I did hear," he said too quickly. "I'm just—" He cleared his throat, but her skeptical gaze lingered, making his stomach twist. "Please, go on," he added, his voice firmer this time, though he doubted she believed him.

He ended the session early, offering some excuse about an emergency, and watched her leave. Parker slumped back in his chair, rubbing his temples, trying to push back the pounding headache nestling behind his eyes.

The dreams were the worst part. Every night for the past three nights, Devin was there, his face hovering just out of reach, his voice echoing in the dark. "Parker," he'd whisper, the sound curling around Parker's mind like smoke. "Parker, you can't hide from this. You can't hide from me." Parker would wake up drenched in sweat, his heart racing, the echo of Devin's voice still in his ears.

He'd lie there, staring at the ceiling, the shadows shifting in the dim light. He'd tell himself it was just his mind playing tricks, the guilt and fear manifesting in his dreams. But it seemed real, too real, and the line between dream and reality was beginning to blur.

Parker avoided Olivia, Alyce, and Dr. Warren as much as possible, slipping in and out of his office with his head down and shoulders hunched. He didn't want to see the questions in their eyes or hear the concern in their voices.

He spent time between appointments thinking about the box containing the watch and the photographs sitting on his desk back at home. He considered getting rid of it, burning it, burying it, anything to make it disappear. But he couldn't bring himself to do it. It was a link to Devin, a twisted connection he couldn't sever, no matter how much he wanted to.

His watch had been on Devin's wrist, the leather band stained with his blood. He didn't know why Devin was wearing it. Perhaps to feel closer to him, like a girlfriend wears her boyfriend's worn and oversized college jersey. The only thing Parker was sure of was it was on Devin's wrist when he went into the ground, only to reappear three days later in the box delivered to his office.

He needed answers—a sensible explanation of what was happening. Why was he seeing Devin? Why did he hear his voice? Parker refused to accept the idea that he was losing his grip on reality and that his mind was coming apart at the seams. There had to be a reason, a piece of the equation he hadn't yet solved.

Parker's mind raced, grasping at straws, trying to find a way out of the darkness closing in around him. He couldn't keep going like this. He couldn't keep pretending everything was fine. He needed help—but from who? Who could he trust? Who would believe him?

That was when Parker thought of Nick. Nick knew Devin and had seen them together. Perhaps he could help him make sense of all this. He hoped the answers he sought were not more terrifying than those he imagined.

21

THE DETECTIVES

With each tick of the clock, a heavy drumbeat synced with Parker's pounding pulse. Each minute that dragged by pulled him deeper into the void of uncertainty that had settled over him since the start of the week. Olivia had rescheduled many of his missed appointments from Monday to today, but he was barely present, his mind more focused on his own turmoil than the needs of his clients.

Reassurance washed over Parker at the sound of the reception door opening, followed by firm footsteps echoing in the hallway. He forced himself to take a slow, measured breath, trying to project a professional demeanor for his last appointment of the day, even as his inner tension coiled and refused to ease.

The knock on the door was sharp and purposeful. Before Parker could respond, it opened, and two men stepped in, the badges clipped to their belts catching the light as they moved.

"Mr. Grant?" The taller of the two men asked. His partner remained silent, eyes scanning the room and lingering on Parker's desk.

"Yes. Can I help you?"

"I'm Detective Jacobs, and this is my partner, Detective Miller. Pardon the intrusion, sir," he stated, though the friendly tone didn't reach his eyes. "We're investigating the disappearance of one of your clients, Devin Marchand. We hoped to ask you a few questions."

Parker's heart dropped into his stomach as he carefully set the pen in his hand down on his desk, rising to shake the detective's hands. "Of course," he replied, gesturing to the seating area in front of him. "Please, have a seat."

The detectives exchanged glances before settling on the sofa, each taking an arm at opposite ends. Parker followed with his journal in hand, its familiar weight providing a sense of grounding. As he opened it, the neatly written observations and thoughts gave the appearance of composure—a fragile shield to conceal the faint tremble in his hands.

"I'm sorry, detectives, you said 'disappearance'?" Parker felt violated by their presence in this space—his office—a place he controlled.

"That's right," Jacobs answered. "His boyfriend, Mark Sutherland, reported him missing," he continued, his gaze unwavering. "How long have you known Mr. Marchand?" Jacobs asked, his tone conversational but his eyes sharp, watching Parker closely.

"Devin? Not long, just over a week. I had the first session with them on the Monday before last. His fingers trembled slightly, and he folded his hands on the journal to still them.

"Can you tell us about their relationship? Did Devin ever mention any concerns or problems?"

Parker hesitated. "I'm sorry, detectives, but I'm sure you know therapist-client confidentiality is protected under HIPPA laws. Those would be privileged communication between me and my clients."

The two detectives glanced at one another as Miller pulled a document from his folder and handed it to Parker.

"Yes, of course," replied Jacobs. "That's why we have a client waiver signed by Mr. Sutherland. He's allowing you to speak freely regarding your counseling sessions with them."

Parker took his time to study the form.

"Detective Jacobs, this form gives Mark's consent for me to disclose information but says nothing about Devin. Your question was about Devin and any concerns or problems he may have expressed. As his partner, Mark can't waive Devin's client confidentiality rights."

Miller sat up straight and spoke for the first time. "Mr. Grant, you understand we are investigating concerns over Devin's disappearance, don't you? Devin's not around to sign a waiver, and if he was, he wouldn't be missing, would he."

Detective Jacobs gave Miller a brief, knowing look—just enough to ease the tension in his posture.

"Mr. Grant," Jacobs continued, "I'm sure you are as surprised to hear about Devin's disappearance as much as anyone else and would like to help us look into the matter. So, if you don't mind, speaking from Mark's perspective, can you tell us about their relationship and if Mark ever mentioned concerns or problems?"

Parker hesitated again. He had to tread carefully here. The last session with Mark was tense, the unspoken accusations lingering like smoke. Parker had never seen Mark so charged—his eyes barely restraining his anger, his words clipped and barbed. He swallowed hard, his mind flitting through their last conversation, searching for safe territory. One wrong word could unravel everything.

"Couples who come in for counseling have challenges," Parker said slowly, choosing his words and speaking generically. "They sometimes struggle with each other's behaviors, straining the relationship. But both seem committed to working on it."

Detective Miller leaned forward and rested his elbows on his knees. His eyes bore into Parker, scrutinizing every detail of his expression. "When was the last time you saw Devin, Mr. Grant?"

Parker shifted slightly in his seat, trying to ignore his growing nervousness. "Last week. We all had a session on Friday."

"Did you have sessions with each individually?" Jacobs asked.

"No. Always as a couple."

"You said, 'We *all* had a session on Friday,'" Jacobs stated. "I thought that might mean you see them individually as well."

"No," Parker clarified, "Only as a couple. "Well, except for yesterday," Parker added. "Mark was alone yesterday."

"And why was that," introjected Miller, "if you only see them as a couple?"

"Well," Parker began to answer, shifting his gaze between the two men. "Only Mark showed up for the appointment. That's when he told me he hadn't seen Devin for a few days."

"Was he concerned? Did he act strangely in any way? Act out of sorts?" Jacobs asked.

"Well, yes. Mark was agitated."

"Agitated?" Miller repeated.

"Well, not agitated. You know, concerned. Mark thought it out of character for Devin to take off like that for so long. Moreso, the whole situation of not knowing troubled Mark. He was emotional, as would be expected."

"Is Mark typically an emotional person," asked Jacobs. "In your limited exposure to him, of course."

"No, not particularly," Parker answered. "Mark seems to be more reserved and measured."

"Yet yesterday, he was emotional, or agitated, as you say."

The detectives glanced at one another, communicating without words in a silent language like many people who work together as a team learn to do over the years.

Miller's eyes narrowed. "And you haven't had any contact with Devin since your session with them both last Friday? No calls, no messages?"

"No," Parker replied, his voice quieter than he intended. He cleared his throat, trying to keep his composure. "I haven't heard from him. I wish I had."

Jacobs jotted notes, the pen's scratching against the flip-pad filling the otherwise silent room, amplifying Parker's unease. The tension was palpable, and Parker couldn't escape the feeling these men weren't merely seeking answers—they were digging for more, withholding intentions yet unrevealed.

"Mark mentioned Devin being under a lot of stress," Jacobs said, his eyes flicking up from his notepad. "Did Devin ever express feeling threatened or afraid of anyone?"

Parker hesitated, his mind racing. Was this a trap? He reflected on past conversations with the couple, then on Devin's expression as he swung the heavy bowl with all his might.

Parker's unexpected movement surprised Devin, but the crystal bowl's impact on the side of his head shocked them both. A giant fear of losing control rose within Parker, previously and again now. Parker shook his head slowly.

"Detective Jacobs, as I stated earlier, I can't speak to you regarding what Devin has or has not expressed in this office."

Miller's expression stayed neutral, but a flicker of what appeared to be disappointment crossed his eyes, tightening Parker's stomach. Sweat formed at the back of Parker's neck as the weight of each question intensified the growing tension.

Jacobs closed his notebook, leaning back slightly, his gaze never leaving Parker's face. "Routine questions, Mr. Grant. We're just trying to get a sense of Devin's state of mind before his disappearance. We appreciate your cooperation."

Parker nodded, forcing a tight smile. "Of course. Anything I can do to help." But inside, his thoughts churned. Routine questions, they said, yet Parker caught Jacob's pen hovering over the paper, ready to capture the slightest misstep. He noted the way Miller's eyes never wavered from his face as if searching for a crack in the veneer. *Had Mark implicated him?* It didn't feel routine—it felt more like a hunt.

Miller spoke up again, breaking Parker's thoughts. "One last thing, Mr. Grant. Are you concerned about Devin's disappearance?"

Parker's frown deepened as he searched for possible responses, each feeling like a potential landmine. "No," he finally said, his tone cautious. "It's been my experience that sometimes a person just needs a little space to figure things out—at least what's right for them. Perhaps that's what is happening here."

Miller exchanged another glance with Jacobs. Parker hated the way they silently communicated with one another. It made him feel like they knew something he didn't, closing in on him, waiting for him to slip.

"Oh, sorry, Mr. Grant," Jacob stated this time. "You said you last saw Devin on Friday in your session with them. Is that correct?"

"Yes."

"Mr. Sutherland stated he and Devin saw you at a bar late last Friday night," he referenced notes jotted in his pad, "a place called Cityside. Do you recall being there and seeing them, Mr. Grant."

Parker's gut tightened with panic. He sensed the trap but struggled to maintain control of his wits. "Yes, I met a friend and ran into them briefly. I don't socialize with clients and left soon afterward."

"Mr. Sutherland said he saw you dance with Devin that night. Isn't dancing socializing?"

Parker's pulse quickened, and he fought to keep his voice steady. "The place was crowded, detective," Parker answered. "It's one of the reasons I left. I don't normally go out to bars at night. I dislike smoke and loud music and don't enjoy crowded spaces. As I said, that's why I left."

Jacobs stood first, Miller following a beat later. "Thank you for your time, Mr. Grant," Jacobs said, his smile sharp but devoid of warmth. He paused in the doorway, his hand resting on the frame. "We'll be in touch if we have more questions." His partner lingered a step behind, his gaze trailing over Parker's desk one last time before they left.

Parker also stood, moving to shake their hands, his hand

clammy and weak. "Of course," he said, his voice barely above a whisper. He opened the door and watched them leave, the stiff soles of their footsteps echoing down the hallway. Parker inhaled deeply when the door closed behind them and rubbed away the sweat from the back of his neck.

Returning to his desk, he sank into his chair and replayed the conversation repeatedly in his head. He dissected the discussion with the detectives over and over—Jacob's persistent questioning about Devin's mental state and their pointed reference to the bar. Had he said anything incriminating? Was it his hesitation when they brought up Mark? Or was it how his voice cracked when denying contact with Devin?

What were they after? Was this genuinely routine, or had Mark shared details casting him in a suspicious light, leading the detectives to dig deeper?

Parker let his head fall back against the chair, staring at the ceiling, his thoughts dancing on it in the afternoon light. He needed to find some way to get ahead of whatever was happening. Parker couldn't let himself become the target of their suspicions. He couldn't let this spiral further. Not again. He saw what happened when control slipped—Devin's lifeless eyes flashed before him. It was like a noose tightening, and Parker knew he had to act before it choked him entirely.

He glanced at his phone, a message from Nick still unopened. He needed answers, and he needed them tonight.

Relief swept Parker when Olivia informed him his last client just canceled her appointment, but the relief was fleeting. Olivia's next words made his stomach drop. Dr. Warren wanted to see him in his office before he left for the day.

His footsteps echoed in the short hallway as he walked toward the request. He anticipated the conversation's topic, pausing to inhale deeply before softly tapping his knuckles on the doorframe. "Dr. Warren?"

"Parker, come in."

He stepped inside, his gaze immediately meeting Dr. Warren's, giving him the quiet respect his presence commanded. The owner sat behind his polished oak desk, dressed impeccably as always, wearing his tie and vest, the plaid tweed jacket hanging on his coat rack. He gave Parker a slight nod of acknowledgment as he entered, a balance of kindness and wisdom sometimes softening his rigid expectations.

"Parker, take a seat," Dr. Warren instructed.

Parker nodded, moving slowly to the chair opposite the desk. He eased into it, careful not to let the day's tension show. He placed his hands on his lap, fingers tightening as he waited. He faced police officers less than an hour earlier, but this was worse. Dr. Warren's quiet authority was far more unnerving.

Dr. Warren removed his glasses and set aside the file he was writing in. His gaze was analytical, assessing. He had no immediate judgment, just a piercing curiosity, as though he was trying to understand what Parker wasn't saying.

"Parker, we need to have an honest conversation about what's happened recently," his voice steady but not without a hint of concern.

Parker nodded, his throat dry. He forced himself to speak. "Of course, Dr. Warren. I'm aware things have been unusual lately."

Dr. Warren leaned back in his chair, folding his hands in his lap. "Unusual is putting it mildly. You took Monday off without warning, sending Olivia scrambling to call your appointments. We've received comments from a few clients who have expressed, let's just say, some discontent. And now, a visit by the police here at our office to question you about a client's disappearance." He paused, letting the words settle.

Parker couldn't deny any of it; his focus was fractured. Since Devin's disappearance, he had been balancing on a knife's edge. He tried to find words that wouldn't sound like excuses. "I've been under some stress—a family matter, Dr. Warren. I know that's not an excuse, but I'm doing everything possible to resolve it."

Dr. Warren's gaze softened, though his expression remained firm. "Parker, I understand the nature of our work can sometimes be overwhelming. We all deal with stress, but it's how we manage that stress that matters. The concerns we're seeing aren't just about stress. They're about disruption, which we can't afford, nor will I tolerate here." His tone was gentle but stern; his words made it clear just how serious the situation was.

Parker was always the dependable one, maintaining a relaxed demeanor no matter what his clients threw at him. But that composure was slipping through his fingers. "I understand, Dr. Warren. I truly do. I don't want my situation to affect the practice. That's not who I am."

Dr. Warren sighed, leaning forward and resting his elbows on his desk. His expression was one of a mentor trying to guide instead of reprimand. "Look, Parker. You're a talented therapist, but police visits and client complaints negatively affect the firm. And it's not just about you. It's about the people who come in for help, the reputation we've built, and others who work alongside you."

Parker nodded, feeling the gravity of each word. "I want to make this right, Dr. Warren. I'll do whatever it takes."

Dr. Warren studied him for a moment longer before nodding. "Parker, I know you're going through something, but this is where others depend on us to be steady. Whatever's happening outside these walls—it can't follow you in here. Do you understand?"

The implications were clear—his future at the practice was on the line. Parker nodded slowly. "I understand. I won't let you down."

Dr. Warren nodded, a small, weary smile tugging at the corner of his lips. "I hope so, Parker. You're capable of great things. I don't want to lose a promising therapist. But this is on you now. Do you understand?" His voice was soft but carried an unmistakable gravity, a plea for Parker to take the reins and stop whatever was happening.

Parker nodded again. "Yes, sir. I understand."

Dr. Warren studied him a moment longer, his gaze probing for a hint of assurance—or perhaps a trace of honesty. Finally, he nodded and leaned back, a subtle signal of dismissal. "Good. That will be all for now."

Parker stood and left the office, closing the door softly behind him. He walked back through the now-empty hallway; Alyce and Olivia had left for the day. The usual warmth of the place seemed absent now, its walls mocking the support and security they had offered him.

When Parker reached his office, he shut the door and walked to his desk. His vision blurred, and for a moment, he thought he saw Devin sitting on the sofa, his pale face illuminated by the dim light filtering through the blinds. Parker could swear he smelled Devin's cologne—a faint, musky sweetness that twisted his stomach. Devin's mouth moved as if to speak, but no sound came. Parker's breath caught as the vision dissolved into empty air, leaving only the echo of what could have been a whisper behind.

Parker closed his eyes, but the darkness behind his eyelids offered no relief. There, the vivid imagery returned—Devin, alive, smiling at him, the soft warmth of his touch. And now, cold, his eyes lifeless, body collapsed upon itself. Parker shook his head and opened his eyes wide, desperate to dispel the dreamlike images. The fear, the panic, the pressure—they all mounted, a relentless tide pulling him under. The line between reality and delusion blurred further, and the more he fought it, the more it slipped from his grasp.

Reaching for his phone, Parker opened Nick's message and typed a quick response, his thumb hovering over the send button. It was time to retake control, of finally acting instead of reacting. It was the only thing left to do. He pressed send and would soon have his answers, one way or another.

22

Shadows and Whispers

Parker sat on the edge of his bed, his phone resting in his hand, its screen glowing in the darkening room. He hesitated, his thumb hovering over Nick's name before finally tapping it. He wasn't sure how Nick would take this—how far he could push without giving himself away.

"Parker? Hey, what's up?" Nick's voice came through slightly winded as if interrupted mid-task. Parker closed his eyes, drawing a steadying breath to center himself before continuing.

"Hey, Nick," he said, his tone unsettling enough to make it sound believable. "Sorry to bother you, but I need to tell you something. It's important."

"What's going on, Parker?"

He could hear the shift in Nick's tone, the concern edging in. "It's about Devin. The police were at my office earlier today. They're investigating his disappearance." He let the words hang, waiting for Nick's reaction.

"Devin is missing?"

"Yeah," Parker replied. "Since Saturday."

"Wait, the police? They came to you?" Nick's voice sharpened; all hints of casualness were gone now. "Why would they come to you? Do they think you know something?"

"I don't know," Parker lied, injecting a note of frustration into his voice. "They asked about his state of mind, about Mark, about their relationship. I think Mark might have said something—maybe about me seeing them at Cityside. I don't know, Nick. It's all really confusing." He let his voice crack slightly, painting himself as lost in confusion.

Nick's tone softened. "Hey, don't freak out. It's probably just routine questioning since you're their therapist."

Parker focused on Nick's words. He shouldn't have told Nick they were his clients when he ran into them Friday night at Cityside. He wondered what else he may have said to Nick, given the way he was drinking and his growing lapse of self-restraint as the night progressed.

"There's more, and this is the weird part," Parker continued. "I got a text from one of those weird five-digit phone numbers telling me where I could find Devin."

"What!" Nick exclaimed. "What did it say?"

"It just said, 'Devin's here' with a location pin-drop."

"Who's it from? You think Devin sent it?"

"I have no idea," Parker answered.

"Where is it?" Nick asked, the enthusiastic curiosity in his tone underscoring his effort to draw the words out of Parker with questions faster than Parker could fabricate answers to.

"It's off the lake north of here, near a campground and boat ramp. I've been there before with Tim." A pause followed, and Parker could almost hear the thoughts running through Nick's mind. "Maybe he's camping or just trying to put some distance from Mark for a while." Parker let out a shaky sigh as if the idea was too overwhelming.

"Devin out in the woods camping?" Nick finally responded with disbelief in his voice. He hesitated before continuing, his tone sharpening. "Parker, this doesn't add up. Who would even text you that? And why?"

"I don't know," Parker reiterated, the lie slipping off his tongue with less effort. "It was just a text message. Anonymous, you know? I'm concerned, Nick. What if this is real, and he's having some sort of crisis? What if it's from him?"

"What are you going to do?" Nick asked.

"I'm not sure if I should do anything. I thought about just telling the police, but," Parker paused, "I don't want to get him in trouble for just disappearing for a while if that's what he's doing."

Silence hung in the air while Parker waited for Nick to offer, and Nick anticipated the ask.

"I was thinking of going out there to see if I could find anything, but I don't know. What if it's nothing?

"Or what if someone's fucking with you or setting you up?" Nick added."

Parker hesitated before adding, "I probably *should* report it."

"Yeah, maybe you should check it out. I mean, if there's even a chance Devin's there and needs help, wouldn't it be worth it? Don't get me wrong, I don't care for the guy, but that doesn't mean I wish him harm. You could see if he's okay, talk to him if he's there, and decide what to do next. It's not like you'd have to involve the cops immediately."

Parker paused as if considering the idea. "You think I should?" he asked, his tone uncertain but his motivation sure. "I don't know. I'm not sure I should go alone. I mean, what if something's wrong and I need help?"

Nick exhaled, the sound of his breath crackling over the connection. It was inconvenient, and he had only known Parker briefly. Still, he had grown emotionally attracted to Parker since that first night they met him at Cityside. He was undoubtedly physically attracted to him since Parker's shower in his apartment. Nick had several motivators: empathy, lust, and ever-increasing guilt.

"You won't be alone. I'll come with you if you want to check it out. If Devin's there, I'll hang back and let you do your counseling thing. If not, at least you'll know. It's better than sitting around wondering, right?" Nick thought it best to keep his friends close—and his interests closer.

Parker allowed a few seconds for the illusion of hesitancy to settle before responding. He bit his lip and tried to sound small and vulnerable, desperate for someone to lean on. "You'll come with me?"

"Yeah, of course," Nick replied with conviction. "You don't have to do this alone, Parker. Do you know where it is, exactly?"

"Yeah," Parker replied. "Right next to a boat ramp on Lanier that Tim and I have used." Parker knew Nick didn't know who Tim was, but it didn't matter, and Nick didn't bother to ask.

Parker let out a slow breath, letting the relief show in his voice, though the emotion was as false as the rest of the story. "Thanks, I appreciate it. You mind picking me up?" He let the request hang in the air, allowing Nick to fill in the gaps.

"Yeah, sure." Nick agreed before thinking. Driving gave him

control—a smart move if things went sideways. "I'll pick you up in half an hour?"

"That works," Parker replied, his voice steadying as he believed the pieces were finally falling into place. "Meet you downstairs in thirty minutes. I'll owe you one."

Parker didn't think to give Nick the name of his building or address, and Nick hadn't asked for it. He didn't need to.

Parker let the phone drop onto the bed beside him, his eyes fixed on the floor. The truth was still out there, perhaps buried under the weight of lies. He needed to confirm it for himself, and if Nick went with him, it might make what came next easier.

A darker thought slipped in—one that had surfaced once before, unbidden yet impossible to dismiss. Nick wasn't just company. He was a shield. Parker hated the calculation behind it, but survival had always demanded a little cruelty.

He took a deep breath, reserving the thought for later if needed. Right now, he needed to focus—one step at a time to get through tonight.

The forest was dark and unwelcoming as Nick parked his car on the side of the road at the edge of the woods, near one of the hiking trailheads. It was near where Parker had parked his Bronco four nights earlier. Darkness draped a cloak of silence over everything; the wind silenced as they stepped out, the gravel crunching under their shoes the only sound. Parker tightened his grip on the flashlight, looking around as his breath blew visible plumes of anxiety into the cold air.

Nothing looked familiar, just trees and darkness mixed with

a few distant sounds skimming across the lake's surface from the campground. Parker saw the distant glow of a few campfires and lanterns but nothing near them. He knew they were close, though. He could feel it on the back of his neck and his forearm hair.

Nick exited his car and joined Parker, standing in the middle of the gravel road with a second flashlight Parker had brought him. They cast separate beams of light as they scanned their surroundings.

"Are you sure this is the right spot?" Nick asked, his voice low as if frightened to break the heavy quiet of the woods. "Devin? Out here?" Nick's voice was thin, almost swallowed by the dark. "He's more likely to be in the camping section at REI."

"I'm sure," Parker replied, barely glancing at Nick. He kept his focus ahead, his heartbeat pulsing in his ears, pounding alongside the rhythm of his thoughts, an incessant drumbeat of nervousness and doubt. The need to know what was real became an annoying obsession. Still, Parker knew he couldn't afford to let Nick see too much—not his panic, not his desperation, and not a shallow grave.

Branches clawed at their jackets as they veered off the path, their flashlight beams carving shifting shapes in the dark, each movement amplifying Parker's unease. The night was turning colder, and each step forward seemed to echo back at him like an accusation. Nick was beside him, but Parker still felt alone, burdened with memories he couldn't share.

Nick and Parker took turns calling Devin's name, first in a whisper and then progressively louder, cautious not to yell too loudly. They only wanted to attract Devin, not others who may be nearby and hear their voices.

The path was overgrown with thorny brambles snagging at

their pants, roots twisting upward like skeletal hands trying to pull them down beneath the undergrowth. Parker led them in sweeping circles through the dense woods, with Nick following close behind. Nick's flashlight swept over the ground, revealing nothing but newly fallen dead leaves, pine needles, and twisted roots.

"Are you sure about this?" Nick asked again, frustration starting to edge into his voice. "I mean, why would he be in this mess unless—?"

Parker didn't answer immediately, his eyes darting around, the beam of his flashlight jittering over the landscape. He could feel the pressure mounting, the fear that they stumble across something terrible or find nothing. He didn't know which he preferred or which would be worse.

"Why don't you head that way," Parker instructed, sending Nick off in a direction he felt confident would reveal nothing. At the same time, he paid closer attention to the area he was in—one that began to look more familiar and tug at his memory. Parker didn't need Nick to see anything he shouldn't, but he did need Nick close—not for comfort, but to ensure his flashlight stayed within reach if Nick saw something he shouldn't.

Nick called out to Parker when he illuminated an area of earth that appeared disturbed. "Parker, over here!" Parker approached and stopped beside him, training his light on the freshly turned soil.

"Is that anything?" Nick asked, stepping closer, his voice mixed with surprise and curiosity.

The ground was uneven, and the dirt was looser and darker than the surrounding area, suggesting recent movement. Clumps of weeds lay uprooted and scattered, bare patches disrupting the dense undergrowth.

Parker stared at the earth as an ominous chill shot through his body. He had already decided he'd prefer not to find anything out there—living with the question was better than discovering a buried truth. In either case, having Nick see something was the worst-case scenario. It would force his hand to act, regretting the thought of bringing Nick with him on that dark and cold night.

"Could it have been where someone was camping?" Nick asked. The concept of camping, or the outdoors in general, was as foreign to Nick as he had proclaimed it for Devin earlier.

Parker's grip tightened around the handle. He swallowed, trying to keep his breathing steady, but it was hard to breathe with his throat constricting. He could feel Nick's eyes on him, waiting for an answer, for some explanation. But what could Parker say? The truth was too heavy, too dangerous.

"Nah," Nick added, dismissing his previous question. "It's probably where a deer or some other animal rested or maybe was digging for grubs or something to eat."

It was difficult for Parker to focus, cycling through the various variables and ramifications, all while Nick asked questions and commented. *It feels all wrong*, Parker thought to himself. He shouldn't have come out here, or at least should have planned it better. How could hard and irrefutable evidence linking Devin to Nick be left in this exact spot if needed?

Earlier, when that dark, suggestive thought returned and spoke to Parker, just like it had done when he was in the back of Nick's apartment about to shower, he should have tamped it down, just as he did then. He had listened to it this time, however, and here they were. Parker's grip grew tighter around the flashlight handle as he mentally judged the distance between himself and the figure standing just behind him on his right.

"Parker?"

Nick's voice broke through his focus.

Nick stepped closer, his light flickering across the ground. "Hey, there's nothing out here, but at least you tried, right?"

Parker took a deep breath that centered him, bringing him clarity. He turned and stared at Nick, his grip on the flashlight loosening as the moment stretched, the urgency unraveling into something weightless, almost inconsequential.

"It's cold as shit, man. Let's get out of here," Nick added.

"Yeah, you're right. This was stupid. Someone's just fucking with me."

"Hey, on the bright side, you didn't send the cops out on some wild goose chase. That would've pissed them off."

Parker's flashlight beam bounced across the path as they returned to the car. "Sorry I drug you out here for nothing, Nick."

Nick followed behind him, his own beam of light weaving through the darkness. "We're good, Doc. No worries."

Just then, the wind picked up, rustling the leaves around them. Parker pulled his jacket tighter, his jaw set in determination. It had been almost a week since anyone called him 'Doc.'

Nick drove them back to Atlanta, the silence between them heavy, charged with everything left unsaid. The road stretched ahead, and Parker stared through the window at the blackness surrounding them as he thought, his hands folded in his lap. In the shadows and whispers of that darkened forest, Parker learned he could do whatever it took—if he chose to.

After Nick dropped him off at his condo, Parker sat with his legs folded beneath him and his back propped against the bed. He recounted his choices and the moments leading to this point. How had he ended up here? For a moment, Parker considered disappearing—letting go of his career, his routines, the order. The idea curled around him, seductive and terrifying, a quiet promise of freedom from the crumbling life he was clinging to.

Falling asleep was difficult. As Parker lay in bed and stared at the ceiling, he heard a noise—a soft creak, like a footstep. He sat up, his eyes scanning the darkness. "Devin?" he whispered, the word barely more than a breath. A faint creak answered him, like the sound of a floorboard in an old farmhouse under the weight of a cautious step. His heartbeat thudded in his ears as he strained to listen, his eyes darting to each shadow and every corner. The silence was more oppressive than the noise, as though the room held its breath.

He walked through the condo. "Devin?" he called again, his voice shaky. But he heard no answer—just the suffocating silence around him. Parker's eyes landed on the box on his desk in the living room. The lid was slightly askew, the contents partially visible in the dim light of the city shining in. Knowing the contents of the box sent a chill down his spine. How was the watch removed from Devin's wrist? Who removed it and sent it to him? Who took the pictures of him and Devin consumed in one another's embrace? Had his mind finally slipped? Was control just an illusion all along?

He stepped closer to the box of mysteries and reached out, tapping the lid back into place, once again concealing its contents from his thoughts.

Parker moved to the glass windows. His gaze scanned the streets below. It was the middle of the night, the city quiet, and the streets mostly empty. But there, just for a moment, he thought he saw a figure—just a shadow, maybe—standing in the darkness below, staring up at him. But as quickly as it appeared, it was swallowed by the night.

Parker jerked away from the window. Whether it was a shadow or a ghost, real or imagined, he couldn't trust his eyes—or himself.

23

What Does He Know?

(Friday the 13th)

Parker awoke in his condo, his body aching and his emotions drained from the previous night. The morning light streaming through the bedroom glass was harsh and intrusive, and Parker squinted against it as he sat up. His mind was a tangled mess—emotions and fractured memories refusing to align. He rubbed his eyes, and despite the exhaustion and turmoil churning inside, he awoke with clarity and resolve on one matter. He now understood what it was like when his world slipped into chaos, and he couldn't allow it to continue.

Parker went through his morning routine on autopilot. As he washed his face, he listened to the coffee maker hum in the kitchen and smelled the sharp aroma filling the air. The cold water shocked his senses, grounding him for a moment. His reflection looked foreign—dark hollows beneath his eyes, stubble casting shadows along his jaw, the haunted look of a man slipping further from himself.

The harsh light overhead revealed every line, every trace of anxiety etched into his skin. Parker splashed cold water on his face again, the chill snapping him into focus. He needed to stitch himself back together, every frayed edge tucked beneath a mask of composure. Today was another opportunity to keep his secrets buried and save his old way of life. That meant playing his role—and silencing anything, or anyone, that threatened his fragile order.

Parker sat at his desk, his fingers tracing the edge of his notebook. The sunlight slashed through the blinds, too bright, too honest. He wasn't ready for this. Part of him wanted to cancel the appointment, to hide, but he knew it was pointless. Sooner or later, Parker would have to face him. It was better he did it here than somewhere he couldn't control.

A knock echoed from the door, sharp and deliberate. Parker's heart jumped, and he took a deep breath. "It's open," he called out, his voice steadier than he felt.

The door opened, and Mark stepped inside, his expression unreadable. Parker noted a distinct shift in his demeanor, the set of his jaw, and how his eyes scanned the room before meeting his gaze. Mark usually was composed, but that composure carried a resolute and unyielding edge today.

"Hello, Parker," Mark said, his voice smooth and polite. Closing the door behind him, Mark bypassed the client sofa, choosing the hard-backed chair across from Parker's desk. His movements were precise, every step claiming space Parker struggled to hold. He leaned back, his eyes never leaving Parker's face.

"Good afternoon, Mark." Parker tried to mirror the calm in his voice, though his stomach churned. He picked up his pen, a habitual gesture to occupy his restless hands. "How have you been?"

Mark smiled, but the display of emotion was cold. "I'm doing well. Better, to be honest. Devin and I, well, we're no longer together."

Parker's fingers tightened around the pen. He forced a smile. "So, Devin's no longer missing? You've spoken to him?"

Mark nodded. "We haven't spoken, but he's left town. I agree it's for the best."

Parker blinked, trying to process the words while a cold chill moved through him. "Devin's left town?" The words were heavy and nearly impossible to say. The image of the disturbed dirt flashed in his mind, vivid and raw. He could still feel the irritation of the dirt under his fingers, the earthy smell of the soil swirling in his nose.

"Yes," Mark said, his voice casual yet calculated. "He's gone. Decided it was time to move on, I suppose." Mark's gaze remained steady, his eyes locked on Parker's as though probing for a reaction or hidden truth.

Parker's breath caught. Mark was lying. He had to be. Devin didn't just 'leave.' Yet Mark's steady, unblinking gaze betrayed nothing, while a cold sweat crept down Parker's neck. Was this a test? Did Mark know? Parker forced a nod, the movement stiff and detached from his racing thoughts. Every instinct screamed something was off, with Mark's words hiding layers of unspoken intent.

Parker swallowed and tried to keep his expression neutral, but the confusion and disbelief must have shown. "That's— sudden. Isn't it? When we spoke on Wednesday, you sounded concerned. You thought something happened to him."

Mark shrugged, a small smile tugging at the corner of his mouth. "Things change. Devin changes. You know how he is—always impulsive, always unpredictable."

Parker didn't know what to say—how to respond. The words swirled within him, nonsensical. Devin couldn't be gone in the way Mark was suggesting.

"I see," Parker managed, his voice barely above a whisper. His focus fell on his notebook, the words blurring on the page. He needed to stay in control, to keep the truth—whatever it was—buried.

Mark watched him, his eyes narrowing. "You seem tense, Parker. You look tired and confused—a little rough, to be honest. Are you alright?"

Parker forced a smile, though brittle. "I'm fine. It's just," he paused, "the shift, it's just a lot to process."

Mark leaned forward, resting his elbows on Parker's desk—his unwavering gaze locking onto Parker's, slicing through his defenses. "You've been helpful, Parker. More helpful than you know." The tone in Mark's voice carried an undercurrent that sent a chill down Parker's spine. It wasn't just the words, but the darkness threaded through them.

The floor seemed to tilt beneath Parker. What did Mark know? Could he see through the cracks he fought to conceal?

"What do you mean?" he asked, the authority in his voice collapsing. Parker tried to steady himself and maintain his composure, but Mark's gaze was piercing, as if he could see right through him.

Mark relaxed and smiled, the type of smile making Parker's skin crawl. "Just that. I couldn't have done it without you, Parker." Mark stood and glanced at his watch, the movement slow and deliberate. His lips curled into a half-smile as if privy to a secret. "Time's a funny thing, isn't it?" he said, his thumb tapping the watch face as if he had just rewound it. "I guess there's no need to continue now, right? No need for couple's therapy when there's no couple."

Parker absorbed Mark's words as they sank in. It was as if Mark twisted a knife into him, the insinuation cutting deep. He could only sit and stare at Mark's movement toward the door, his heart pounding, the words echoing in his mind. *'I couldn't have done it without you.'* What did that mean? What was Mark implying?

Stopping short of the door, Mark adjusted the framed diploma on Parker's wall. The frame was already straight, but Mark's hand lingered on the glass, his reflection overlapping Parker's behind him. He turned back to Parker one last time, his eyes cold and his expression unreadable. "Take care, Parker. I have a feeling things are about to get interesting for you."

The door clicked shut, and the silence swallowed Parker whole. Only the faint echo of Mark's fingers on the glass frame remained, like fingerprints smudged atop his reality.

The weight of Mark's words was heavy and suffocating. Parker's mind spun, each thought possibility darker than the last. The memory of disturbed earth clawed at him while Mark's words echoed like a taunt. Had Mark pieced everything together, or was this another layer of the game? It had to have been Mark who left the box with the note, pictures, and bloodied watch at the doorstep. But how?

Parker needed to prove he wasn't the one to blame. Somehow, this wasn't his fault. But deep down, he knew he was already too far in. Whatever the truth was, it would destroy everything he created and fought to maintain.

As Mark's words lingered and swirled like smoke from a fire, Parker's gaze drifted to the harsh and uncompromising sunlight across the desk. The pen slipped from his fingers, rolling to the floor with a quiet plunk. He didn't bother to pick it up. Instead, he sat frozen, only whispering, "What does he know... and how?"

24

LOOKING FOR ALLIES

Parker's eyes affixed on the words he scribed in his notebook: *Find out what Mark knows.* He stared at the letters as if they offered him an answer—as if they could unravel the twisted knot of events and memory. Time was running short. He couldn't do this alone. He needed help.

The journal closed, its cover snapping shut with a muted finality. Parker knew what he had to do. He stood and walked out of his office toward Olivia, his determined footsteps announcing his approach. She was shutting down her computer and gathering her things to leave for the day but paused as he approached her desk.

"Hey, Parker," Olivia greeted, her smile fading as she detected the tension on his face. Her fingers traced the rim of her coffee mug as she spoke, slow and deliberate, a gesture of her measured thoughtfulness.

Parker, meanwhile, clenched his fists at his sides, his nails digging into his palms as if trying to anchor himself. "Olivia, listen, I need your help. It's about Mark. Mark Sutherland."

She nodded in acknowledgment. "Yeah, poor guy. I've already canceled their standing appointments, as he requested."

The faint scent of lavender lotion clung to the air around Olivia's desk, a reminder of her nurturing presence.

Parker felt out of place here, his growing panic sharply contrasting Olivia's warmth and calm. He stepped closer to her desk and lowered his voice. "Yes, well, I think there's something off about him."

"How do you mean?" Olivia asked, her eyebrows knitting together in confusion.

Parker squatted beside her desk, eye level with her, to induce a sense of seriousness and confidentiality in their exchange.

"I think he's involved with Devin Marchand's disappearance," he whispered, his tone carrying urgency. "He just told me the wildest story about them breaking up—about Devin leaving town. I could tell it was a complete lie."

Her eyes widened, and she leaned back, her expression wary as he spoke.

"Listen, Olivia, I need some information on him. You remember mentioning that friend of yours, someone in one of your college classes who can look up background information on people?"

"Parker, what's going on?" she asked, quietly scanning the room and lowering her voice to ensure Alyce did not hear anything from her office. "Are you in some type of trouble?"

Parker steadied his voice though desperation clawed at his insides. "No, it's not like that. I just," he paused to scan the office himself. "I just need to be sure of something. Please, Olivia. I wouldn't ask if it wasn't important."

"To make sure of what, Parker? You shouldn't even be discussing details of your clients with me. If you have concerns or information, you should call the detectives who were here yesterday."

"No, Olivia," Parker responded, his tone impatient and growing louder. "I just want to know if there's anything in his past to suggest a pattern of violence or abuse. A criminal record, or maybe just charges dropped later. Anything that…" Parker's words trailed off as he processed her expression of increasing disbelief and discomfort as he spoke. He was beginning to sound irrational, even to himself.

There was a long pause, Olivia's gaze searching Parker's face as if trying to read his intentions. "Parker, I don't know. It doesn't sound right. My friend—he could lose his job for doing that. We could lose our jobs, too. I'm raising two boys. I can't jeopardize my job."

Parker's eyes flicked to the framed photo on Olivia's desk— her boys, their matching grins wide and unburdened by the responsibility their mother carried. Beside it sat a coffee mug with a chip on the rim, the words 'World's Best Mom' faded but legible.

"I can't explain everything right now, but I need to protect myself. I have reason to believe Mark might be dangerous, and I need to know what I'm dealing with. Please, Olivia."

"Parker," she replied, the motherly rational rising in her tone. "We're not investigators. He's not a client anymore. To be honest, the whole thing feels off. Come on, Parker. No."

Olivia shook her head, the concern apparent in her eyes. "Parker, I care about you but can't risk getting involved. I don't know what's going on, but it sounds serious. I'm sorry, but I can't help you."

Parker clenched his jaw and forced a tight smile as he rose. "I understand. I just thought—never mind. Thanks anyway."

To Olivia, it sounded like manipulation, like the tactics her children sometimes used to guilt her into doing or buying things she had already refused. "Parker," Olivia added, her voice gentle yet pleading, "please be careful. If you need help—genuine help—you should call the police."

Parker's nod was a sharp jerk, his jaw tight enough to ache. "I will." As he walked down the hallway, a single thought motivated him. He needed help, and he knew who to ask next.

If Olivia wouldn't help, maybe Alyce would. She had always been pragmatic—more willing to blur lines if the situation called for it."

Alyce was in her office, her door slightly ajar. Parker knocked lightly before pushing it open, his eyes meeting Alyce's as she turned her attention to him.

"Parker, it's Friday, shouldn't you be starting your weekend?" Her expression softened when she spotted the strain on his face. "Come in here. What's going on?"

He stepped inside and closed the door behind him. "Have a minute?"

"Of course," she replied, gesturing toward the chair in front of her desk. Alyce's office was as methodical as the woman herself. Stacks of books lined the shelves, their spines perfectly aligned, and a single plant—a small fiddle-leaf fig—sat in the corner, its leaves catching the soft afternoon light. The serenity of the space seemed a cruel mockery of the desperation in Parker's mind.

"Alyce, I need your help," he began, the urgency evident in his tone. "It's about one of my clients, Mark Sutherland. I think he might be dangerous, and I need to know if there's anything in his past, anything to help me understand what's going on."

Alyce looked puzzled, her gaze turning wary. "Dangerous?"

"I'm trying to understand if there's anything in his medical history—any signs of psychosis or any record of mental health issues. You're a licensed doctor. You have access to that, but I don't. I know it's a lot to ask, but I need to understand what I'm dealing with."

Alyce leaned back in her chair, her eyes narrowing as if she could see through Parker's words to the desperation hidden beneath. The silence stretched between them, the rhythmic ticking of a clock on her desk filling the room like an unspoken reprimand. "What do you mean by 'what you're dealing with?'"

Parker leaned forward, placing his forearms on the edge of her desk, closing the distance between them much like Mark had done with him earlier that afternoon. "It's just he's said some things that," he paused, searching for the right words, "things that don't add up, that's all."

"Parker, his boyfriend is missing, or so he says. It's natural for anyone to act strangely under those circumstances."

"That's just it," Parker rebutted. "Today, he has an entirely different story. Today, he said they broke up amicably, and Devin left him, just up and moved somewhere, just like that."

"And what's unusual or *dangerous* about Devin leaving their relationship?"

"I don't know," he hesitated, "it's how he said it. Mark told me things were about to get interesting for me. Don't you think that's odd?"

"It sounds to me like they decided to break up, and he's accepted it and is moving on. That's what I hear you saying."

Parker ran a hand through his hair and stood, pacing back and forth in front of her desk. "Alyce, I know he's done something or is about to do something. I'm certain he's dangerous."

"Parker, you know I can't do that. It's unethical. We have rules for a reason. And right now, it feels like you're asking me to do something more than bend them. What aren't you telling me?"

Alyce remained still, reclining in her chair, her fingers intertwined and her hands in her lap, listening, responding, evaluating, and judging. "You keep using that word, Parker. If Mark indicated he harmed someone or signaled he might be a threat to someone or himself, you need to notify the police. Detectives were just here yesterday asking questions, right?"

Parker's tone intensified, "Alyce, I can't go to the police. They wouldn't understand, and I can't afford the implication of something I didn't do. I need to protect myself. And Mark—there's something about him that doesn't add up. I need to know what he's capable of by understanding what he's done in the past. I need you to trust me, Alyce."

"Parker, I get you're under a lot of stress. But asking me to break confidentiality? That's a line I can't cross—for you, for anyone. You know better."

Parker stopped pacing, turning to face her. "Alyce, I wouldn't ask if I wasn't desperate. I'm not asking just as a colleague but as a friend. You're the only one I can trust."

The office grew colder as Parker spoke, the air thick with unspoken judgment. Alyce's brow furrowed, her hands resting on her lap. At the same time, Parker's anxiety cast shadows on the walls—dark shapes echoing his spiraling thoughts.

Alyce's head shook slowly, her voice a soft wall of resistance. "No, Parker. I won't cross that line. You need to take care of yourself, but this isn't how to do it."

Alyce's rejection cut through him. He knew what he was asking from her wasn't fair, but the desperation was relentless, festering within him. "I understand," he said quietly, his voice hollow. "Thanks anyway."

She stood, moving toward him, her hand resting lightly on his shoulder. "Parker, it isn't easy when our counseling doesn't positively affect our clients. People are complicated. You know that. They are going to do what they decide to do. We can try to influence positive results, but we cannot control people's decisions. Please, don't do anything reckless."

Parker nodded, though he was frustrated. "I'll be careful," he said, shaking his head in agreement.

He left her office, the door clicking shut behind him, leaving him alone in the hallway. Olivia and Alyce's refusals settled heavily on his shoulders. No one would help him. No one would take a risk for his sake. And why should they? They didn't understand the truth. They didn't understand how far Mark had gone or would go to destroy him.

One person, though, stayed by his side each time things became dark. Parker hesitated before finally grabbing his phone from his desk.

"Parker?" Nick's voice came through, his tone cautious. "What's up?"

"Nick, I need your help. I think Mark's fucking with me. He's trying to set me up, and I need to prove it, but I can't do it alone."

There was a silence before Nick's response, his voice filled with concern. "Setting you up for what?"

"Devin's disappearance. I think Mark's behind all of it. He's trying to make it look like I'm responsible. I can't explain everything over the phone, but I need you to trust me. Please, Nick."

"Parker," Nick began slowly, his tone cautious, "this sounds... I don't know, man, like it's way over both our heads. Are you sure about this?"

He could sense the hesitation through Nick's pause but waited.

"Parker," Nick said, breaking the silence first. "We drove out to the lake last night to look for Devin, wasting our time on some crazy text message. Now, you say Mark's setting you up? I'm sorry, but I can't—"

"I know," Parker cut in. "But Mark came in today, saying things that don't add up. He said Devin's gone—up and left town—no big deal. It was a complete one-eighty from his concern on Wednesday."

"Devin's gone, for sure? Not missing, but left?"

Nick's mind raced with this new information, though he kept his tone level. *Devin left town? Without a word?* The thought was unsettling. There had to be more to it. Devin always had a plan. Nick forced himself to breathe. His mind raced as the truth threaded through his thoughts like a virus. *Devin left without a word.* No—there had to be a reason, a twist they hadn't planned. *Stay calm*, he reminded himself. *Act natural.*

"Nick, I need your help. Please."

Nick conceded. "What do you have in mind?"

Relief flooded Parker, chasing away the shadows of guilt. He knew he was dragging Nick into a dangerous game, but wasn't that what Nick was there for? After all, if the choice was between his survival and Nick's innocence, the decision was easy.

"Oh God, thanks," Parker replied, feeling the tension ease from his shoulders. "I need you to help me find evidence to prove Mark's setting me up. I know it sounds weird, but we can turn this around." Parker's voice wavered, the desperation unmistakable.

Nick was quiet for a moment before he responded, his voice steady. "I'll help, but you need to promise me one thing—we're not doing anything reckless. We have to be careful, okay?"

Parker nodded, though Nick couldn't see it. "I promise. We'll be careful."

"I'll call you in a while from home. Thanks, Nick."

"Sounds good, bye."

When Parker hung up the phone, relief washed over him. For the first time in days, he had a plan—a purpose. He wasn't alone. Nick was willing to help him, which meant everything.

Parker scanned the notebook on his desk, his eyes lingering on the words he had written: _Find out what Mark knows._ He picked up his pen and added another line beneath it: _Make sure he can't destroy me._ Again, Parker underlined the words, a promise to himself. Mark was shifting pieces on a board Parker couldn't see, but it was time for Parker to make his move. When he did, Mark wouldn't know the game was about to end.

25

THE BREAK-IN

(Saturday the 14th)

Parker woke with a sense of restlessness. The sunlight streaming through the windows was a cruel contrast to the turmoil simmering beneath the surface. Everything seemed normal—his apartment was tidy, and the coffee brewing smelled rich and familiar—but he sensed something wrong in the air, like the drop in pressure accompanying the calm before the storm. Still, today was the day they would execute the plan and prove Mark was behind it all. The anticipation was like a hook in his chest, yanking and urging him forward, though his heart pounded uncertainly.

Parker moved through the motions of his morning. He spread butter on his toast, the knife scraping too hard against the bread, tearing it. He stared at the ragged edge, his mind elsewhere, before tossing it into the trash. He made his bed, showered, and dressed. His mind repeatedly circled back to yesterday's appointment, to Mark's words, to the spot of disturbed dirt in the woods. Each second spent thinking about it strengthened Parker's conviction he needed to prove Mark orchestrated this entire nightmare.

Parker buzzed Nick up when he arrived late in the morning, right on time. Nick knocked on 2606 with a brisk rhythm, momentarily startling Parker though he knew Nick was on his way up. He opened the door and took in Nick's upbeat expression.

"Morning," Nick said enthusiastically, stepping inside and glancing around. His gaze took in the furnishings and the view. "Very nice place," he commented, his eyes lingering on the minimalist décor. "A little too perfect, maybe," he commented.

Parker closed the door behind him, the latch clicking into place with an audible decisiveness. "Yeah, well, it's home. Thanks for coming. We need to finalize the plan."

Nick nodded, moving to the living room, scanning the space as if trying to understand Parker's life—his world. Parker gestured to the couch, and they both sat.

"Okay, here's what I was thinking," Parker offered, getting right to it. "I'll head to the office to find Mark's address. Most of the files are electronic, which Olivia has access to, but there's a paper intake form patients fill out before their first session. That will have his address. Once I have it, I'll text it to you." He tried to gauge Nick's reaction. "You're sure you're okay with this?"

Nick met his gaze, his expression unwavering. "Yeah, I'm in." After hearing Devin had left town, Nick needed some answers of his own.

"We just need to find proof Mark is behind all of this. Anything to expose him."

"And you're sure Mark's the one pulling the strings? So we're going to his house?"

"Yes," Parker replied. "I'll go from the office, and you'll meet me there. But first, I need you to confirm he's gone to the gym so we know the house is empty."

Nick nodded slowly, his eyes narrowing as he studied Parker. "Alright. So, you'll send me the address when I confirm Mark is at the gym, and then we meet at his house?"

"Yeah. He goes to The Athletic Club in Ponce City Market every Saturday morning. He talked about it during a session. He's pretty consistent—every Saturday morning. Once you're sure he's there, I'll head to his place, and you meet me there."

"Well, how do I get into the club? I don't know what car he drives. How will I spot him?"

"Just go to the gym and tell them you're interested in joining," Parker suggested. "Ask them for a tour; they do it all day long. You know who he is. Just take your time and look around until you spot him."

Nick watched Parker with a strange intensity, his gaze fixed but not intrusive. Though Nick's expression remained calm, his eyes carried a hint of unease—a mix of curiosity and a subtle wariness. It wasn't entirely concern nor judgment but rather quiet anticipation, as if he were waiting for Parker to reveal more than he intended. Nick tried to push the feeling aside, focusing on their plan. Yet, the unease lingered, a quiet tension he couldn't entirely dismiss.

"Parker, I'm not breaking into someone's house."

"Yeah, of course not," he assured Nick. "I wouldn't ask you to do that. I just need you to park on the street and keep an eye out while I'm inside looking for anything that might help us."

"And if you don't find anything?"

"Then we'll figure out what to do next. We have to find something, Nick. I can't let him get away with this."

After Parker detailed the plan, Nick's gaze shifted from the window back to him, his expression unreadable. He leaned back slightly, crossing his arms. "You've really thought this through, huh?" he said, his tone light but carrying an undertone Parker couldn't quite place.

Parker nodded. "I've had to. I can't let him keep pushing me into a corner."

Nick tilted his head, studying him. "You sure this is just about Mark setting you up? It seems like there's more to it."

Parker stiffened, forcing a tight smile. "What else would it be about?"

Nick shrugged, holding Parker's gaze a beat too long before breaking it. "Just saying. People don't usually go this far unless there's a bigger reason."

Parker nodded, acknowledging Nick's concerns. His mind also buzzed with unease. He wanted to believe this plan would work—that they could prove Mark's guilt and end this nightmare—but a pang of doubt resounded within Parker each time Nick voiced a concern. Could he trust Nick? Did Nick genuinely understand how far this had already gone? He forced a smile, trying to mask the inner conflict.

Parker's mind looped through the plan repeatedly, but shadows clung to the edges no matter how he turned it. What if they found nothing? What if Nick realized Parker needed him as a pawn, not a partner? What if the gym tour didn't buy Nick enough time? What if Mark left early? What if the neighbors saw him? Every 'what if' tightened Parker's chest until breathing felt like stepping on thin ice.

"Alright, let's head out. I'll text you with the address, but we need to get going." Parker stood and walked through the kitchen into the foyer to grab his keys.

"Hey, Parker," Nick called to him. "Mind if I use your restroom first? Morning coffee, you know."

"Yeah, sure," Parker replied. As Nick disappeared down the hall, Parker's thoughts raced. He forced himself not to follow, not to double-check the rooms. Trust was a fragile, dangerous thing.

"Just push the lock on the knob on your way out," Parker called out. "You don't need a key fob for the elevator. Text me when you spot him at the gym. I'll send the address."

Parker's heart pounded as he pulled into the empty parking lot, relieved Dr. Warren wasn't there like last Saturday—no one to question why he was rifling through client files on a weekend. Once inside, he quickly located the filing cabinet key and unlocked the drawers behind Olivia's desk. She kept the key in the bottom of her World's Best Mom coffee mug filled with pens and pencils on her desktop. She showed him where she kept it once before going on vacation, just in case.

His fingers trembled as he fumbled with the cabinet lock, every slight clink of metal against metal a threat. He half expected Olivia to walk in, her face a mirror of disbelief and betrayal.

Devin and Mark's file was right where he expected to find it. Parker flipped through the pages, his eyes scanning the

handwritten information until he found what he needed—
Mark's address and phone number.

He pulled out his phone and typed a quick message to Nick.

[17483 Buckner St. Let me know when you spot him.] he
typed.

Parker hesitated momentarily before hitting send, a sense of
finality settling over him as the message disappeared into the
ether. There was no turning back now.

After returning the file and securing the cabinet, Parker drove
to the coffee shop around the corner. He sat in the parking lot,
waiting for Nick's confirmation. It only took a few minutes
before his phone buzzed, the screen glowing with Nick's
message.

[He's here. On my way.]

Parker exhaled, but the relief felt thin, like a sheet of ice
underfoot. There was no turning back now.

Mark's tree-lined neighborhood in the historic Highland Park
district was quiet, filled with bungalows and cottages built in the
early 1900s. It was a picture of suburban normalcy. Parker drove
past the house and parked his Bronco three homes down the
street in the first space he found. It was all street parking and
shaded by large old oaks, a good place to remain inconspicuous.

[Here] he texted Nick.

Parker waited a few minutes without a reply, keeping an eye
on the sidewalk in front of Mark's house in his rear-view mirror.
He waited a few more minutes before his second text.

[Where R U?]

The silence felt deliberate, a yawning absence where Nick's reply should have been. Parker's mind chewed on the possibilities—traffic, a dead phone battery, or something else? Something worse. A thread of doubt pulled tight in his gut, but he pushed it aside. Nick wouldn't abandon him. Not now.

In the five minutes that followed, a single car passed him on the quiet residential street. He saw no one walking, riding their bike, or doing yardwork in their front yards despite it being a Saturday and good weather. He grew impatient as he stayed vigilant for signs of Nick, exposed to pedestrians or neighbors who might spot him. He was wasting valuable time sitting there, and after a few more minutes, he decided to wait no longer.

Parker's heart rate rose as he stepped out of his truck. He moved quickly as his eyes scanned the street for any movement but saw no one to witness his approach to Mark's house. When he reached the rolling trash can at the end of the driveway, just emptied by the morning collection and still by the curb like most of his neighbor's cans, Parker instinctively grabbed the handle and pulled it behind himself, up the driveway and path leading to the side of the house. He acted like just another resident bringing his can in after pickup.

Parker hesitated at the back door, his fingers hovering over the handle. He could hear his pulse in his ears and feel it in his throat. The neighborhood's stillness was worrisome, the calm that only existed in the gaps between ordinary moments. He had to act before he lost his nerve. His fingers tightened on the door handle, one more step, and there would be no turning back. This was the line between desperation and disaster, and he was about to cross it.

The lock on the back door was old and easily manipulated if you knew what you were doing. The door had no deadbolt. Still, Parker was no expert, and when he grabbed the knob and tried to turn it, it wouldn't open. With his hand lingering on the unyielding knob, a new concern crept in. *Did Mark have a dog?* Parker hadn't factored this in. He paused, ears straining for any sound of movement inside while jiggling the knob and trying to recall if there had been any mention of a pet during the couple's sessions. None came to mind.

Parker scanned his surroundings. A six-foot wooden privacy fence ran along the back and sides of the yard, with bordering shrubs and trees for additional shade and privacy. No cameras hung from the eaves. A pair of French doors connected the patio to the living room, and he reached for the latch on them, but the lever stuck, refusing to budge. He jiggled it again, glancing nervously over his shoulder at the empty yard. His pulse thudded in his ears as he tugged harder, the latch finally clicking open and reverberating like a gunshot in the silence.

He slipped inside, freezing as the wooden floor beneath him creaked loudly. Parker held his breath, listening for any sign of movement. A dog barked faintly in the distance, but the house remained still. He took a cautious step forward, the floor groaning under his weight. *Just keep moving*, he told himself as he closed the door behind him, the latch clicking impossibly loud in the house's silence.

Parker hesitated, straining to hear any sound—a dog barking, footsteps, the creak of a door—but the house remained deathly still. Every creak of the floor beneath his feet echoed, his heartbeat thudding in his ears. He swallowed hard, his mouth dry as he forced himself to move through Mark's home.

His eyes probed the rooms as he walked. The furniture, the walls, everything seemed ordinary. The house was neat and orderly, nothing out of the ordinary, though not as organized or efficient as his place. The house was over eighty years old, a Craftsman style like the office where he worked, filled with furnishings more traditional than his own. He imagined what Mark and Devin might have looked like as they cooked together in the kitchen, shared dinners at the dining room table, or watched television embraced in the living room. Frustration grew with each step, though Parker wasn't sure what he expected to find. There had to be evidence confirming Mark was orchestrating all of this.

Parker stepped into the bedroom. This was the room where they had made love—and likely fought, too. He could almost see the rumpled sheets, the shadows of bodies intertwined, the echo of laughter bleeding into whispers. The room felt alive with ghosts, the air thick with secrets he imagined, jealousy tangling with grief in his chest.

Parker pulled open the nightstand drawers, sifting through the expected clutter—reading glasses, a few pieces of jewelry, and various items used by two people in the throes of intimacy. Lust and resentment tangled inside him as he tightened his grip on the drawer's edge. Still, there was no sign of Devin or evidence of Mark's wrongdoing. Parker had come for proof, yet he found nothing. He couldn't leave empty-handed, however.

Parker reached into his pocket, his fingers brushing against the object. He had removed it from the box and wrapped it in a handkerchief at the last minute—an impulsive decision sparked by Nick's question earlier at the condo. 'And if you don't find anything?' Nick had asked. Parker wasn't sure how to respond then, but an idea struck him in those final moments before leaving his home.

Sure, the watch belonged to him, but it had Devin's blood on it, its crystal broken from Devin's last-minute reflex to protect himself. Parker didn't see Devin raise his hand before the blow, but here it was now—the watch returned to Parker as a threat he could now use as a defense. He just needed to plant it somewhere. The police would find it, the DNA would show it was Devin's blood, and Mark couldn't prove the watch didn't belong to them. It wasn't much, but it was all he had.

His hand quivered as he pulled the watch out and unwrapped it, his eyes scanning the bedroom for a good place to hide it. But he hesitated, the weight of what he was about to do folding in on him. Could he do this? Could he plant evidence and cross that line?

Parker's hands trembled, the weight of the watch far heavier in his hands now. If he left it, Mark would take the fall. It would all end. *Mark takes the blame, and I walk free.* But the thought twisted his stomach into knots. It wasn't just survival. It was betrayal, a final leap into the dark. Was this who he was now— a man willing to bury his sins in another man's home?

He'd already done so much—hurt so many people. Could he live with himself if he crossed this line, too? He wanted to leave it behind, to hide it, but a voice deep within whispered doing so would make him just like Mark—cold, calculated, unfeeling. Parker wrapped the watch back in the handkerchief as a deep shudder wracked his body. He couldn't do it, not like this.

A low, insistent beeping pierced the silence, sending a jolt through Parker. He spun toward the sound, his eyes locking onto the small red light blinking on the alarm panel. Panic surged through him as the wail of distant sirens began to rise, faint but unmistakable.

Parker's vision narrowed, the edges of his sight darkening as panic gripped him. He sprinted before it registered what he was doing, his body slamming into the back door. His fingers fumbled with the latch on the French doors, slipping twice before he finally twisted it open. He stumbled into the yard, the cool air slapping his face as he sprinted toward the fence. A neighbor's dog barking erupted to his left, sharp and guttural, echoing through the stillness. Parker froze. He scanned the surroundings, his mind racing. *Keep moving*, he thought, forcing his legs to carry him forward.

The fence loomed ahead, and he launched over it, the rough wood scraping against his palms. He hit the ground hard, pain jolting up his legs. He pushed through it, the sharp scent of cut grass and damp earth filling his nose as he ran. The sirens were closer now, their wail chasing him through the narrow alley behind the houses.

Parker sprinted and exited the alley a few houses down, slowing to a brisk walk. He kept his eyes trained on his car, walking purposefully until reaching his Bronco. Parker yanked the door open and threw himself inside. He started the engine, his hands trembling as he shifted into gear and pulled away from the curb. Glancing in the rear-view mirror, Parker watched as the patrol car's flashing lights turned onto Buckner Street behind him.

Parker's mind raced as he drove, his hands gripping the wheel so tightly that his knuckles became white. He had gotten out of the house, gotten away. He couldn't afford to be caught now, not when he was so close to proving Mark's guilt. He turned down a side street, relief washing over him as he saw they were not chasing him. Parker slowed the car and steadied his breathing, his hands still shaking on the wheel as he turned into a shopping center parking lot. He slotted the Bronco between two larger SUVs and switched the ignition off.

Parker slumped back in the driver's seat, his chest rising and falling in ragged bursts. His fingers ached from gripping the steering wheel so tightly, his knuckles white against the black leather. He stared at his reflection in the rearview mirror—a pale, wide-eyed version of himself he barely recognized. A man who had crossed the line and who knew, deep down, there was no way back.

"You're losing it," he whispered, the words rasping in his throat. He pressed the heels of his palms against his eyes, trying to erase the blinking red light, the watch in his hand, the way the bedroom seemed to breathe with the weight of his guilt. But they lingered, etched into the backs of his eyelids, waiting for him to slip back into the dark.

Mark knows. He knows what I did. The thought burrowed into him, gnawing at the thin walls of his sanity. He reached for the handkerchief-wrapped watch in his pocket, his fingers brushing against the bundle but stopping short. He couldn't bring himself to pull it out, to face it. Instead, he gripped the edge of the seat, his jaw clenching as a single tear rolled down his cheek.

In the distance, the wail of sirens faded. But Parker knew— this was far from over. The real danger was the silence wrapping around him, whispering the truths he didn't dare acknowledge.

26

THE CONFRONTATION

Parker sat quietly in his living room for several hours, allowing his anxiety to settle and the adrenaline to slowly drain away. The disappointment in his failed mission pressed on him, and for a moment, he wasn't sure if he could keep going. But the image of Mark's sneer when he last left his office cut through his fear like a sharp blade. He needed to regroup, to find another way forward. As the sun continued its slow descent, casting long shadows across the floor, Parker decided. He and Nick needed to replan.

He pulled his phone from his pocket, the screen glowing in the dim room as he typed a message.

[Meet tonight? Need to figure out the next steps.]

Nick's reply came immediately.

[Can't. Working tonight.]

Parker hesitated for a moment, staring at the response. He knew they couldn't wait after what happened at Mark's house.

[I'll stop by. Okay?] Parker texted back.

A few minutes passed before a thumbs-up emoji flashed on his screen.

Parker exhaled, setting the phone down on the coffee table. He wasn't sure what their next move might be and considered the possibilities. Different options cycled through his mind during his shower. He knew what he wanted and was getting a pretty good idea of his limits to securing his innocence by implicating Mark. But a nagging question echoed in his mind—if he was willing to go further, how much of himself would he lose in the process? He clenched his jaw. It didn't matter anymore. This was about survival.

The realization didn't shock him like it might have before. Instead, it settled into him, a grim acceptance of the lines he was prepared to cross, the boundaries he was ready to obliterate. In the end, survival was all that mattered. Mark had pushed him to this edge, and he wouldn't back down now.

As Parker walked toward the entrance, the idea of walking into Cityside on a Saturday night hurt his head. The bar would be bustling, crowded with young guys and older men, a mixture of out-of-town weekenders coming from Alabama and Tennessee to the big city of the South filled with gay men and good times. Parker expected it to be noisy and full of second-hand smoke and distractions. Still, he needed to talk with Nick. He needed answers, and they needed a new direction.

By the time Parker walked in, the bar was already filling up for the night. The low thrum of music reverberated beneath the hum of chatter, creating a layered symphony of sound. He spotted Nick behind the bar, shirtless, wearing only tight black pants hugging his lower frame, accentuating his confidence as much as his smile. He watched Nick pour drinks, his beaming personality lighting up the room, making the patrons feel as comfortable and welcomed as Nick had made him feel the first time he walked into Cityside.

For a moment, Parker felt an odd sense of tranquility as he watched Nick move behind the bar with the grace of a dancer. Thin but muscularly defined, Nick's body spoke of precision and fluid strength, his expressive face framed by golden strands of blond hair bouncing with each movement, catching the light like fleeting sparks. Nick seemed untroubled, unaware of the storm raging in Parker's head. How could he be so at ease when everything was coming apart?

The scent of cologne wafted through the air—a sharp, musky blend tugging at Parker's memory—Devin's cologne. He clenched his fists, forcing the image of Devin's crooked smile out of his mind. But it wouldn't leave. He thought about the grave, about Mark's smug face.

I didn't mean for this to happen, Parker thought, the words echoing with the rhythm of his racing heart. *But I'll be damned if I let Mark ruin me now.*

Nick caught sight of Parker approaching and gave him a nod, gesturing toward the end of the bar where it was quieter. Parker squeezed through the crowd and waited until Nick was free to step away from the other customers. Parker's thoughts swirled, disjointed and frantic. He tried to focus on regaining the composure he knew he needed.

"Hey," Nick said, his voice loud over the noise. He leaned in, his grin unfaltering. But beneath the smile was a flicker of something else—hesitation, maybe—a break in Nick's easygoing facade, like a mask slipping for just a breath. His eyes darted to the side, just for a second, as if he expected someone else to be watching. The smile returned, but now it felt like a placeholder—something he wore rather than felt.

"How did it go?" Nick added.

"Didn't go as planned," he muttered, running a hand through his hair. "Why didn't you show up at Mark's place? I needed you. What happened?"

Nick's gaze shifted, his expression unreadable. He reached beneath the bar for a rag and wiped down the countertop, buying himself a moment. "Parker, I'm sorry," he said, his voice calm. "I got spooked. Besides, it seemed like you had it handled."

Parker narrowed his eyes, irritation bubbling just beneath the surface. He leaned over the bar top and into Nick, speaking above the music and chatter around him. "Handled? I was nearly caught. There was a silent alarm. I barely got out of there before the cops showed up."

Nick met Parker's gaze with concern and an unreadable flicker in his expression—was it dismissal or annoyance? "But you did get out. You're here, aren't you?" he said, his tone measured. Nick continued wiping the bar top and rearranging glasses, his movements deliberate, as though justifying his lingering presence at the end of the counter where Parker sat.

Parker's mind raced, every delay a thread unraveling. Was Nick choosing his words too carefully? Calculating the safest response? A fresh wave of doubt crawled up his spine.

"That's not the point," snapping back in contradiction. Parker lowered his voice, conscious of the people around them. "We were supposed to do this together. I can't do this alone."

Nick frowned, his gaze darting to Parker's trembling hands before meeting his eyes. "You're sure about this, Parker? You're sure Mark's the one pulling the strings?" His tone was cautious and measured—too measured.

Parker hesitated, his throat tightening. "What are you saying, Nick? You think I'm making this up?"

Nick held his gaze for a beat too long before shrugging. "I'm saying, be sure. That's all." His face softened, and he touched Parker's forearm. "Look, I get it. I'm sorry. I should have shown up or at least texted you. I can't afford to get caught, either." He glanced down the bar at the waiting customers before returning to Parker. "Let me find someone to relieve me for a break, and we'll figure this out, okay?"

Parker nodded, a heaviness settling into his chest as Nick walked away. He hated the feeling of vulnerability—needing someone else to help him hold the pieces together. It wasn't supposed to be like this. He watched Nick speak with the other bartender before coming from behind the bar, gesturing for Parker to follow him toward the back exit.

They pushed through to the rear of the club and the darkened hallway connecting the main space with the back rooms where dancers gave patrons private performances. The bar's lights barely reached into the narrow space, leaving them cloaked in near darkness. Nick lit a cigarette, the orange glow illuminating his face for a moment before he offered it to Parker.

Parker shook his head. He hated cigarettes and hated the smell, but he let Nick have his vice. "We need a new plan," Parker said, his voice quieter now. "Mark knows something. I swear, he's trying to set me up."

Nick took a long drag from his cigarette, the smoke curling around his head like a halo before he exhaled. "What exactly did you find in his house?"

Parker shook his head, the disappointment still raw. "Nothing. No pictures of the two. Nothing resembling Devin's sized clothes. It's like he knew I was coming—like he'd already cleared everything out."

Nick frowned, his gaze studying Parker's face. "Maybe he did. Maybe he's one step ahead of you. Or maybe what he said was true, and Devin did leave town."

Parker clenched his fists, the frustration surging. "How do we stop him, then? He's making me look guilty while keeping his hands clean."

Nick was silent for a moment, his eyes narrowing thoughtfully. "We need leverage," he finally said. "Something we can use against him. Something he can't deny."

Parker nodded. "But what?"

"Listen, I need to get back. Follow me," Nick instructed.

Maneuvering through the crowd toward the bar, Nick turned around to speak to Parker, his voice attempting to rise above the pounding music and bursts of laughter from clustered groups of men. That's when Parker saw the figure ahead of Nick moving directly toward them.

Mark moved with purpose, his face illuminated intermittently by the flashing lights of the dancefloor and bar area behind him. The crowd seemed to part around him, a ripple in the bar's chaos. His movements were slow, deliberate—like a predator pacing toward wounded prey, and Parker's skin prickled as if the temperature had dropped.

"Well, well," Mark said, his voice carrying easily above their immediate surroundings. "Isn't this convenient? Parker Grant, right where I'd expect him to be." He glanced at Nick and back to Parker, a small, amused smile curling on his lips.

Parker's pulse quickened, his mouth going dry. "What are you doing here?"

Mark stopped a few feet away, his eyes glinting with an inscrutable emotion—mockery, perhaps. "Oh, just taking a walk. Thought I might run into you." His head tilted slightly as his gaze flicked between Nick and Parker. "Imagine my surprise when I discovered my house was broken into today. I couldn't help but wonder who might have been behind it."

Parker's heart pounded while his stomach twisted painfully. He tried to keep his voice steady. "I don't know what you're talking about."

Mark stepped closer, his eyes never leaving Parker's. "No? I think you do." He ran a hand over his beard—slow, deliberate, unnervingly calm. His stare held steady, the intensity tightening around Parker's throat. Mark's presence was impenetrable—like a mirror where only one reflection held the truth.

"You see," Mark continued, his voice measured and sharp, "Devin wasn't the only one I knew about. I know about you, too, Parker. I know what you did."

Parker's breath hitched as the room shrank to only Mark's words, each a blade cutting deep. "You don't know anything," Parker managed to say, though his voice betrayed him.

Mark smiled. It was a cold, empty smile. "Don't I?" He leaned in, his voice dropping to a near whisper. "Devin always did like his secrets, didn't he? And you—you couldn't resist, could you? You wanted him, wanted what I had. But you've always had a taste for forbidden things, haven't you? I bet you always wanted what wasn't yours." Each syllable Mark spoke was a knife meant to cut deep into Parker's psyche. "What were you hoping to find in my house—proof or permission? Well, congratulations, Parker. You can have him."

Mark spoke of Devin in a detached and clinical way; his lack of visible grief or emotion was unsettling. Parker's face flushed with anger for it, his fists clenching at his sides. "What are you talking about?" he snapped. "You're the one who pushed him, manipulated him. You wanted him out of your life, didn't you?"

Mark chuckled, a dark, humorless sound. "You think you know me, Parker? You think you know what I wanted?" He shook his head, his eyes cold and distant. "I was simply watching a story unfold. A tragic story, but a fascinating one nonetheless."

Mark's unsympathetic demeanor pushed Parker closer to his breaking point. He found reconciling Mark's coldness with his own spiraling guilt difficult. Mark embodied everything Parker feared in himself—emotional detachment, indifference, and the ability to suppress all feelings in the face of tragedy.

The room shrank, Mark's voice the only sound. Parker's vision tunneled, the colors around him bleeding to gray. His body felt disconnected—like watching someone else's fist clench, someone else's pulse thrum with fury. But when Mark's lips curled into that mocking smirk, the thread of Parker's restraint snapped. He lunged at Mark, his hand reaching out to grab him by the collar. He could hear Nick shouting out his name. Parker felt the jolt as Mark shoved him back, laughter ringing in his ears.

"You think you can fight me?" Mark said, his voice calm even as Parker struggled against him and Nick tried to hold him back.

"You're out of your depth, Parker. You have no idea what you're dealing with."

The realization hit Parker like a punch to the gut—he *had* lost control. He was falling right into Mark's hands, doing what Mark wanted. But it was too late. The sound of people yelling reached his ears as the bright flashes of cell phone cameras captured the scene—proof of his aggression.

Parker's world fractured into sharp, unbearable fragments. He could already see the fallout—the cell phones immortalizing his outburst, the whispers spreading like poison through the crowd. His body felt weightless, as if the floor had given way, suspending him in freefall, the ground a distant promise of pain.

Nick and two guys nearby pulled Parker back, forcing him away from Mark as the crowd gathered around them. Parker's breath came in harsh gasps, his heart hammering as the weight of what he just did hit him, all to the backdrop of Mark's laughs and heckles.

Mark straightened his collar, brushing off the front of his shirt as he smiled—a cold and calculated smile. "You're finished, Grant," he yelled loud enough for everyone around them to hear. "I couldn't have planned this better if I tried."

Parker could only stare, his throat too tight to speak, the reality of what just occurred sinking in. He had lost. He had played straight into Mark's game.

Nick tugged at Parker's arm, pulling him toward the back room behind the bar reserved for employees, away from the onlookers and their cellphone cameras. "Come on," Nick muttered, his voice urgent. "You need to get out of here."

Parker's phone vibrated as Nick led him toward the back room. He ignored it, his pulse still roaring in his ears from the confrontation. Once inside, Parker pulled his phone out. It was a text from a number he recognized.

[We need to talk ASAP. Call me.]

It wasn't just Mark he needed to deal with now. The fallout was already beginning.

27

THE WARRANT

(Sunday the 15ᵗʰ)

The pounding on the door shattered the stillness, pulling Parker from sleep with the violent clarity of a fire alarm. Each thud reverberated inside his skull, demanding action and commanding his attention. Parker's eyes shot open, his pulse surging as the haze of sleep suffocated his thoughts. The world around him was a smear of shadows and sharp edges. He couldn't tell if he was still dreaming or if the nightmare had bled into his waking life. His feet moved before his mind could catch up, a marionette pulled by strings of instinct and dread.

"Police! Open up!" The words sliced through the fog, each syllable a slash, leaving no room for confusion. *The police?* Parker jolted upright, adrenaline rocketing through his veins, leaving him dizzy and light-headed. He scanned the room wildly, his thoughts a scrambled mess. Panic hit him hard—like ice cracking in his chest.

He threw himself out of bed, stumbling as he shot his legs into the sweatpants draped over the chair near the bed—the same chair Parker found Devin's jumper seven days ago before grabbing it to wrap around the cold body. Parker scrambled to the front door, fueled by surprise and confusion.

The fisheye view through the peephole revealed two uniformed officers outside his door. Two other men stood behind them. Parker recognized them as Jacobs and Miller, the two detectives who visited him at his office on Thursday. He swallowed, his throat dry as he reached for the deadbolt.

"Mr. Grant, we have a search warrant. Open the door immediately, or we will force entry."

Parker fumbled with the lock, his fingers trembling. He barely had time to register the officers—two in dark uniforms, the other two familiar faces—before they surged past him like a flood through a broken levee. Their movements were swift, their presence undeniable.

"What's this about?" Parker asked, his voice cracking as he tried to sound composed. He already knew what they were searching for, but the helplessness of the situation twisted his insides. His home was abruptly filled with strangers, dismantling it piece by piece.

"Please step aside, Mr. Grant," Detective Jacobs said, his voice cold, the words as impersonal as the warrant he held aloft. "We have a warrant to search the premises," handing the document to Parker to scan before snatching it back.

Parker stepped back and watched them spread out. Each drawer they opened and each cushion they upturned was a piece of him exposed, dissected, and discarded. The police were reducing the perfect order of his sanctuary into a crime scene. Every object they touched screamed at him, accusing him of sins he may or may not have committed.

Detective Miller motioned to the sofa, gesturing for him to sit. Parker lowered himself onto the edge of the couch, his breath shaky as he tried to focus on the detectives who now stood before him.

"Mr. Grant, I'm Detective Jacobs, and this is Detective Miller. We met a few days ago at your office—"

"Yes, I remember," Parker interrupted. "Why is everyone here tearing through my home?"

"We have reason to believe you may be connected to Devin Marchand's disappearance," Jacobs said, his tone like a judge delivering a verdict.

Parker's gut twisted as the words echoed in his mind—*connected to Devin's disappearance*. The absurdity of it, the terrifying precision, transformed his fear into an icy knot. His mouth opened and closed—he couldn't find his voice to respond.

"We'll need you to answer a few questions," Jacobs added. His gaze bore into Parker, waiting for a crack, a flicker of guilt.

'Connected,' Parker thought. It sounded hollow and pathetic. The word was heavy and damning, like a noose tightening around his neck. He forced himself to meet Jacobs' eyes, a void ready to consume him. "I haven't seen Devin since his appointment the week before last. Mark said he left town," he stated. The words faltered, the lies too close to the truth, the truth too close to the lies.

Jacobs raised an eyebrow, his expression unreadable. "Mark Sutherland claims you and Devin have been romantically involved for some time." His tone was flat but purposeful. The words hit Parker like a physical blow, each sharpened by Mark's calculated cruelty. He could practically hear Mark's voice weaving the lies, each designed to tighten the net around him.

"He also claims you argued with Devin not long before he disappeared."

Parker's stomach twisted. Naturally, Mark would say that. He could feel the pieces shifting around him, the story Mark was weaving—a narrative painting Parker as the culprit to frame him neatly in the crosshairs. He took a deep breath, willing himself to stay calm.

"Argued? Mark is lying," Parker said, his voice firmer now. "Is that your 'reason to believe'? Mark's been trying to make me look guilty from the start. He's manipulating everything. Devin made overt advances towards me, and Mark didn't like it. I didn't like it either."

Jacobs studied him for a moment, his eyes narrowed, his silence stretching on as the sound of officers searching the condo filled the space around them.

Parker could feel the sweat gathering at his temples, the pressure building behind his eyes. He needed to stay focused to keep his story straight. Words clumped together at the back of his throat, sticky with half-formed lies and fragmented truths. His brain was an engine choking on oil—too many thoughts, too little clarity. He forced himself to remember the script he'd rehearsed in the quiet of his mind, but the lines blurred.

"You're telling us Mark has a motive to lie about Devin's apparent disappearance, although he is the one reporting him missing?" Jacobs said slowly. "Mr. Sutherland has stated Devin is missing, not that he left. There's no evidence to suggest Mr. Sutherland is involved in any false claims or reports. You, on the other hand, have been seen with Devin on multiple occasions, including the night of his disappearance."

Parker shook his head, his frustration mounting. "That's not true," he stated, his voice rising despite his efforts to keep it level. "Devin was here uninvited. He was," Parker paused, "confused, acting like we were together—like we were a couple. I didn't know what to do. He just appeared."

Detective Miller's eyes flicked up from the notepad he was writing in, studying Parker's words and posture, his scrutiny unwavering. "So, Devin was in your home, uninvited. Do you have any proof of that, Mr. Grant??"

Parker opened his mouth to respond, but before he could speak, a voice called out from the bedroom, cutting through the air like a dart of suspicion.

"Detective! You're going to want to see this!"

Parker's ears perked up as a cold sweat broke across his skin. He watched, frozen, as Jacobs walked toward the voice, disappearing down the hallway for what seemed like an eternity. He strained to hear the muffled voices in the other room as they blended into an indistinguishable hum. He prayed for the next sounds to be mundane—footsteps, muffled conversation, nothing more. But when Jacobs' voice called out, sharp and commanding, Parker felt the air thin around him. He didn't need to see it. He knew. His world began to tilt, reality a tightrope snapping beneath him.

Jacobs returned, holding something small wrapped in white cloth, and Parker knew what it was before Jacobs spoke. How had he forgotten? The chaos of yesterday—the rush to escape, the confrontation with Mark. It all happened too quickly. His breath caught, his mouth dry. He could feel everything slipping further, the control he clung to dissipating.

"Care to explain this?" Jacobs asked, his voice cutting through the anxiety in Parker's mind.

Parker stared at the watch, his vision narrowing until it was the only thing he could see. His mind raced, trying to piece together the fractured timeline of the last twenty-four hours. He meant to get rid of it, deciding against planting it in Mark's house. Still, between the silent alarm, the cops, and the confrontation at Cityside, he hadn't remembered putting it back in the handkerchief and his pocket. It was a careless mistake that could now cost him everything.

"I…, I don't…" The words stuck in his throat, his voice barely a whisper. His mind raced, the reality of what was happening sinking in. He could feel the air around him growing thinner. He was trapped.

"Mr. Grant, you're going to have to come with us down to the station," Jacobs said, his voice steady and unyielding.

"What!" Parker yelled. "No, I didn't do anything. That's my watch." He instinctively moved backward, away from the appearances and accusations, until Detective Miller's hands caught Parker's arm to stop him. "Are you arresting me?" he asked in disbelief of what was happening to him in his own home.

"No, Mr. Grant. For the moment, we're simply detaining you for questioning."

"You can't do that," Parker protested, though he knew they probably could, and he wouldn't talk his way out of a trip downtown. His world was collapsing, the gravity of his words pulling him down into the abyss he was fighting so desperately to avoid.

While Detectives Jacobs and Miller remained in the living room examining Parker's desktop, carefully lifting papers and moving objects with the tips of their pens, the two patrolmen escorted Parker to his bedroom and stood nearby as he changed.

They watched Parker peel his tee shirt and slide his pajama bottoms off. It was humiliating—he felt flayed open, his skin too thin to protect him from the quiet judgment in their eyes. Still, Parker imagined how much worse it would be if it occurred at the police station—if they strip-searched him and inspected him in the most private of ways. This was bad enough, though, violated in his own home again.

After putting on some briefs, jeans, and a fresh button-down shirt, the officers moved closer and grabbed his wrists, twisting them behind him as they secured the cuffs. The cold metal cuffs weren't just a restraint but a declaration. A boundary crossed. Parker's career, reputation, and carefully constructed identity— all were on the brink of collapse. He spent his life trying to control the narrative, but now he was at the mercy of others, his story slipping through his fingers like dirt filling a grave.

"Is this necessary?" Parker asked.

"I'm afraid so, Mr. Grant," one of them replied. "It's required for transport."

Parker had too many questions, thoughts, and concerns to process. He needed his wallet. What else would they find in the condo? What did Mark tell them? He needed to call someone, but would they allow him to do so, and who would he call? How was he going to explain the blood on his watch? Should he ask to take his car keys? Would the detectives lock his condo before leaving? His journal; he needed his journal. Parker's mind flooded with worry and concern, overwhelmed by fear.

As the patrolmen led him out, the bright morning light seeping in from the open sides of the darkened parking garage blinded Parker. He couldn't process or wrap his mind around what was happening, the sound of his heartbeat drowning out everything else. He saw his Bronco parked in its usual space.

They would search it, too, no doubt, relieved he left the blanket in the shallow hole to keep Devin's decomposing body warm.

Parker's thoughts tumbled in a chaotic spiral as the officers guided his head into the back seat, his body folding awkwardly with his wrists cuffed behind him. He needed a plan—anything to fight back, to save himself. *This isn't real. It isn't happening*, he told himself, but the heavy silence of the police officers beside him said otherwise. He was losing. No, he had already lost.

As Parker sat in the back of the squad car, the cold metal cuffs biting into his wrists, the realization settled in—he could no longer trust himself. He could no longer trust his own mind. The car pulled away from the garage, the city rushing past in a blur outside the window, the boundaries between reality and illusion blurring beyond recognition.

28

The Interrogation

The fluorescent light overhead flickered intermittently, each pulse slicing through Parker's fogged mind like a jarring reminder of his reality. The cold metal of the chair pressed into his back, and the lingering sting of the handcuffs carved ghostly impressions on his wrists—faint but enough to remind him of his vulnerability.

Parker's mouth was dry, and his shoulders ached from having his hands restrained behind his back during the uncomfortable ride in the patrol car. Still, none of it compared to the crushing sense of dread filling the space. He was detained for hours but wasn't sure how many. The world outside was a distant reality now, isolated from the box of concrete and anxiety he found himself in.

The interrogation room was cramped and featureless, barely large enough for a metal table and two chairs. The walls stood windowless, painted a dull gray that seemed to absorb light rather than reflect it, casting the room in a perpetual gloom. A single fluorescent fixture buzzed overhead, flickering intermittently as though it, too, found this place unbearable. The scuffed linoleum floor bore the weight of countless restless feet.

One corner of the room held a mounted camera, its black lens coldly observing everything. It was a silent and unnerving reminder someone was likely watching from the other side. The cinder block walls carried a heavy presence—like they soaked up the weight of all the voices over the years—lies, confessions, desperate bargains, and sobs of regret. They were the indifferent witnesses to the unraveling of people's nerves, absorbing every whispered plea and empty promise. It was a place designed to wear you down, to remind you how utterly small and powerless you could be.

When the door opened, Parker jerked upright. Detective Jacobs carried a thin folder tucked beneath his arm. He glanced at Parker while taking his seat across the table. His gaze was steady and dispassionate as if Parker were just another suspect, nothing more. Parker's throat was painfully tight as Jacobs opened the folder, flipping through the pages with deliberate slowness.

"For the record, Mr. Grant, you have the right to remain silent, and you can ask for a lawyer at any time," Jacobs recited, his voice mechanical, disinterested. "But that's not what we're here for, right?"

Parker opened his mouth, about to say it. "I think I want—"

Jacobs sighed dramatically, shaking his head. "Look, Parker, I've seen this before. You call for a lawyer, and it's over. No more explaining, no more clearing things up. We stop talking, we stop listening, and next time you see us, we're filing charges. Is that what you want?"

"Wait," Parker retorted. He didn't make eye contact with Jacobs but studied his thumb as he ran it across the tabletop from one side to the other. His voice cracked when he finally spoke.

"I already told you everything I know. I don't know where Devin is."

Jacobs studied Parker's face, his eyes narrowing slightly. "And yet," he said, his tone calm, "we found a watch covered in blood in your possession. That's quite an inconvenient piece of evidence for a man who knows nothing, wouldn't you say?"

Parker's stomach churned, and bile rose in his throat. He gripped the edges of the chair, trying to steady himself. "I didn't do anything to him," he managed. "It's my watch and my blood."

Jacobs leaned back, his gaze never wavering from Parker's face. He tapped the folder. "A little unusual to have blood on a cracked crystal like that, Parker. May I call you Parker?"

"It's not unusual when you take a hard fall on your mountain bike riding trails," Parker responded. He raised his left arm, the cuff already folded over several times due to the uncomfortable temperature of the room, to reveal an old scar on his forearm, hardly noticeable now, covered by a coat of arm hair. It was an old injury from an actual fall, making the words rolling off his tongue true and legitimate.

"That's a nice dress watch for mountain biking, right?"

Parker glanced at Jacobs' watch. He wanted to ask the detective how many watches he owned and how many times he switched them based on whether he was working or doing whatever else he did in his personal life. He wanted to turn his nose up at the detective's cheap-looking digital watch and ask him if it was all he could afford on a cop's salary. Parker didn't, of course. Instead, he stared at the detective like he had just asked a stupid question undeserving of an answer.

After an uncomfortable pause, Jacobs spoke. "We have statements from Mark Sutherland and your neighbors stating they saw Devin coming and going after he was reported missing. We know you were involved with him. We also know things got, let's say, tense." Jacobs leaned forward, his eyes hardening. "So, let's cut the bullshit, Parker. Where is Devin?"

Parker's defiance faltered for a second, a tremor of doubt rattling him. His pulse quickened, and he fought the urge to lower his gaze. He needed to stay strong. He straightened his shoulders, forcing the fear down. "They're wrong," he snapped, but the seed of uncertainty had already sprouted. The truth and lies blurred; he couldn't remember what happened anymore. He blinked nervously, trying to focus and bring clarity to the chaos in his mind.

Jacobs's voice cut through the fog, sharp and unrelenting. "You want to protect yourself, Parker? Then tell us what happened. Tell us where Devin is. Did you kill him? Is that his blood on your watch?"

Parker shook his head violently, his eyes snapping open. "No! I didn't kill him!" The words burst from him louder than he intended, desperation breaking through his attempt to act composed and convincing.

Jacobs stared at him for a long moment, sighing as if pitying him. "You're not doing yourself any favors here, Parker. The evidence is mounting against you, and your story doesn't add up. The longer you keep this up, the worse it will get for you."

Parker slumped back in his chair. He could feel the tears threatening to well up in his eyes, but he blinked them back. Parker couldn't afford to break down—not here, not now. He needed to stay strong and think clearly.

The door opened again, and Detective Miller stepped inside with a cup of water. He placed it on the table in front of Parker and leaned against the wall, crossing his arms. "You look tired, Mr. Grant," Miller said, his voice softer and sympathetic. "This can end if you just tell us what happened. It doesn't have to be this hard."

Parker stared at the water, his throat aching with thirst, but he didn't reach for it. He stared up at Miller with pleading eyes. "I didn't kill Devin. I don't know where he is. You have to believe me."

Jacobs tapped the table in rhythm, his fingers drumming as if he waited for Parker to break in time with the beats. Meanwhile, Miller watched silently. His eyes softened as if he genuinely wanted to help. It was the standard good-cop, bad-cop routine Parker had seen in movies and television a hundred times before. But recognizing it didn't make it any less terrifying.

Miller sighed, shaking his head. "It's not about what we believe, Parker. It's about the facts. And right now, the facts don't stack in your favor."

Parker closed his eyes, his mind spinning. He thought of Mark and the smug satisfaction in his eyes, how he twisted everything to make Parker appear the villain. He had to convince them Mark was behind this. But how? He had no proof, nothing to back up his claims. All he had were his words, crumbling under the evidence against him.

"Parker, if this goes to trial, you know how this looks, right? People like Mark—yeah, they're talking. The jury's going to see the blood, the missing client, the witness testimony, and the lies stacking up. That's what we're trying to stop. Help us before this gets out of hand."

The hours dragged on, the questioning relentless. The detectives took turns, their voices blurring together, the words blending into a constant assault. They asked him the same questions over and over, trying to catch him in a lie, trying to break him. Parker's head throbbed, his vision blurring as exhaustion and hunger set in. He lost track of time as minutes stretched into hours without reference to the time of day.

At one point, Jacobs leaned in, his voice dropping to a near whisper. "Look, we're not the bad guys here. Help us understand, Parker. Make this easier—for you."

His sudden change in tenor threw Parker off balance, the unexpected tone in Jacobs's voice sending a shiver of suspicion through him. It was as if the detective could sense Parker's mental exhaustion and was trying to push him over the edge.

Parker's mind drifted back to Devin and how his laughter filled his condo. This easy, genuine sound seemed impossible to imagine in this cold, ugly place. The memory of Devin's scent, his skin still damp from the shower, tugged at Parker's senses like a cruel reminder of what had once felt real. But was Mark right—had Parker wanted Devin and, in desperation, done something terrible?

No. Parker shook his head. He removed his glasses and rubbed his eyes, stinging with unshed tears and fatigue. Parker couldn't let himself believe that. He knew what he saw, what he touched, and how he felt. Devin and Parker had bonded in an intimate passion together in a way impossible for Parker to have anticipated or imagined. Mark was manipulating everything, twisting the truth to suit his ends. Parker had to hold onto that—to believe in his innocence and Mark's guilt.

The door opened once more, and Jacobs returned, his expression weary. He sat across from Parker, folding his hands on the table. "We've got enough to hold you for forty-eight hours, Parker," he said. "But we don't want to keep you here. Help us out, and we can end this."

Parker's pale face framed his bloodshot eyes. He was exhausted and drained, every ounce of fight slowly seeping out of him. He wanted to go home, to leave this nightmare behind. But he couldn't until he found a way to prove Mark was guilty.

"I can't tell you what I don't know," Parker stated, his voice barely audible. "I know you don't believe me now, but what if I could prove it? What if I could find something to prove Mark's involvement in Devin's disappearance?"

Jacobs stared at him for a long moment, shaking his head. "You're not helping yourself, Parker. If you keep this up, you'll end up facing charges."

Parker's heart sank, despair closing in on him without allies or anyone to turn to. He was alone, trapped in a web of lies and manipulation, and no matter how hard he struggled, he couldn't break free. The realization settled over him, heavy and suffocating—he *had* lost control, and there was nothing he could do about it.

Even in the solitary quiet of the interrogation room, Mark was an omnipresent manipulator, deepening Parker's paranoia. He sensed Mark's presence. He imagined Mark sitting in his condo, his infuriating, detached smile, watching Parker's life unravel precisely as he'd planned. Mark was everywhere, pulling strings, controlling the narrative—and Parker was the puppet.

Time lost its meaning in isolation. The hours stretched endlessly, the fluorescent light above a constant reminder of where he was—trapped in an unyielding loop of questions. The walls pressed in closer, the light's buzz tormenting his senses. Parker blinked, trying to shake the haze, but it clung to him like a second skin. His world was shrinking to the size of this small gray room. He fell asleep several times, sitting upright on the hard metal chair and, on one occasion, sitting on the floor with his back propped up against the hard cement wall. When Parker saw Jacobs and Miller return to the room, each holding a cup of coffee and wearing different clothes, he knew he had just spent Sunday night there.

Jacobs leaned forward, his voice dropping an octave, firm and unrelenting. "We're not here to play games, Parker. Every minute you waste, the evidence piles higher against you."

Miller, standing in the corner, shifted slightly, his voice softening. "Come on, Parker. You're a smart guy. We just need the truth. Help us so we can help you." The contrast between their tones made Parker's head spin, their words a relentless pendulum swinging closer to his breaking point.

After several new rounds of questioning, threatening, and negotiating for the truth, followed by hours at a time of isolation throughout the day, Parker considered telling them what they wanted to hear. If he gave in to them, they might finally listen to him—hear what he was saying about Mark and take his warnings of Mark's involvement seriously.

The image of Devin's lifeless body flashed before Parker's eyes again, unbidden. It seemed so real—his blood pooling on the floor, the heavy silence that followed. Was it a memory or a nightmare? Parker couldn't tell anymore. The lines between what he did and what he feared he could do blurred until they were indistinguishable.

Parker opened his mouth, the words 'I did it' forming on his lips. He considered giving them what they wanted to end this nightmare. But as he glanced at Jacobs's eyes—cold and indifferent—a wave of stubbornness surged within him. No. He couldn't let Mark win. Not like this. Not while there was still a chance of proving his innocence.

The detectives finally released Parker just as he was close to giving up. They told him not to leave town. They sent his watch to the lab for blood testing, and they would talk to him again when they received the results. They also impounded his car and cell phone under evidence retention laws. If the blood on his watch turned out to be Devin's, they could move to classify his vehicle as evidence of a crime scene. His phone, too, might hold incriminating texts or location data. If he were arrested and charged, they wouldn't just retain his things but seize them.

It was late evening, and the sky was dark. The Monday air was sharp and cold. Parker stepped out of the station, his body aching, his mind hollow. Nearly forty hours in that room had stripped him down to nothing. The world felt distant, surreal—the city lights smearing as he descended the steps, his breath visible in the crisp night air, his clothes no match for the cold.

Parker scanned the empty streets as he walked from the station to the waiting cab. No one was there for him: not Nick, not Alyce, not Olivia. He was always the one people leaned on, the one who had it all together. Now, he was adrift, untethered, like the world already decided he was guilty.

As he rode in the back of the cab on his way home, his arms folded and head leaning against the window, Parker made a stubborn, silent vow—he would not let Mark win. But deep down, a small voice whispered, taunting him, reminding him of the blood on his watch, the memories not adding up. Could he trust himself? Could he trust his mind? Parker pushed the thoughts away, forcing himself to focus on one thing—survival. He couldn't let the darkness consume him. He needed to fight, which might mean fighting against himself.

The cab wound through the darkened streets as Parker stared at his ghostly reflection in the window. He couldn't trust anyone—not even himself. But if Mark wanted him to break, he'd have to push harder.

29

THE EVIDENCE

(Monday evening the 16th)

Parker clicked the door shut behind him, the sound reverberating through the emptiness of his condo. He leaned back against the door, eyes closed, his breath ragged. He had never been so defeated, lost in a maze of uncertainty, trapped by every wrong turn he made. The echoes of the interrogation room's flickering lights and the detectives' unyielding questions were still fresh in his mind, an unshakable reminder of his vulnerability. He felt like a fallen beast, once strong but now weak, its corpse picked apart by scavengers.

Pushing himself away from the door, Parker moved through the kitchen to the living room. His body ached from sitting in that damned metal chair for hours. His mind was heavy from exhaustion, the aftereffects of adrenaline leaving him drained. He was hungry but too tired to think about food. He scanned the apartment, taking in the aftermath of the police search. It wasn't as bad as he expected; the police put things back where they belonged, or at least as well as they could to their standards. Still, his home was ransacked and violated, and his sense of order shattered.

Parker shed his clothes in the laundry room, tossing what he wore at the station straight into the washer. He considered throwing them into the trash to rid himself of the evidence of the ordeal. Standing there, naked and exposed, he grasped the washer's top for support, staring down into the deep, hollow tub. The clothes twisted into tangled layers, each fold and crease like his fragmented thoughts—unresolved, without purpose. As a tear slipped down his nose and fell into the chasm of the washer's tub below, an image flashed in his mind—Devin's body, lying twisted and folded in the shallow grave, each crease in the fabric a memory he couldn't erase or wash away.

Parker walked into the bathroom, the soft echo of his bare feet on the tiles swallowed by the dim quiet of his condo. He paused and faced his reflection; the lights above the vanity mirror highlighted every detail he wanted to ignore. Parker forced himself to face the image before him—stripped down to the core of what he had become.

Dark circles hung beneath his eyes, deepened by two weeks of restless nights and his mind's constant worry. His cheeks hollowed, and his skin pale and drawn as if life was slowly seeping out of him. Once firm and defined, his muscles had softened, fatigue carving shadows into his frame. His chest and arms, solid from gym sessions and playing sports, had weakened. Parker's ribs were faintly visible beneath his skin, each one a testament to skipping meals and chaos taking root within him.

His eyes fell to his reflection—green eyes yet dimmed and clouded. The fire once fueling him, the relentless hunger for control and perfection, faded, leaving behind a hollow visage of uncertainty. He hardly recognized himself, a stranger staring back—a man who lost his way. For a fleeting moment, grief pierced him—not for Devin, nor anyone else, but for himself.

The Parker he meticulously built, the man who shaped his destiny precisely, was slipping away, leaving behind this fragile, unmoored version in his place.

Parker tore his gaze away, unable to stand the sight any longer. He exhaled shakily, stepping away from the mirror and toward the shower. He let the steam fill the room, hoping it might wash away the doubts and the fear that clung to him like a dirty second skin. The hot water scalded his back, but he embraced the pain. It grounded him and reminded him he was still here, still alive, still capable of fighting.

After drying off and putting on a fresh pair of sweatpants, Parker poured himself a glass of wine. The urge for food passed. Instead, he craved a drink to dull the edge and give him just a moment of peace.

Sitting on the sofa, he took a sip, his gaze unfocused on the darkened sky outside. His thoughts churned, desperately trying to make sense of everything that happened. The police impounded his truck to search for clues. They confiscated his laptop from his desk. They seized his cell phone to comb through his picture gallery, emails, text messages, and anything else that could incriminate him. The text messages worried Parker the most—the messages to Nick, in particular. He thought about the text with Mark's address sent to Nick just before his botched attempt to find evidence in his home.

He stood and began pacing around the living room and kitchen. Perhaps the police would link soil samples from the Bronco to the site. Parker's ball cap undoubtedly contained Devin's DNA evidence. The clear packing tape he used to secure chunks of Devin's skin and flesh back to his head likely held Parker's fingerprints.

There were so many things Parker had done wrong, missteps he took, evidence he left. There was also Nick. He had taken Nick out into the woods to the site, though they were searching for Devin, trying to find him to help him. That was the reason Parker gave him, at least. Did Nick suspect the real reason they were there? There was an immediate urgency to contact Nick. Parker needed to talk to him before the police did.

Parker set the wine glass aside as he sank into the chair at his desk. "Think, Parker, think," he murmured, his mind spinning with fragments of plans, fears, and possibilities. He stared at the satchel he'd tossed onto the floor, the sight of it stirring fragments of half-formed images. His satchel—the practice—his clients—his journal—his old cell phone!

Parker tore into the satchel, his hands a blur, the phone his last lifeline. There it was. The police had confiscated his journal but left the bag containing his old cell phone concealed inside one of the organizing pockets. A spark of hope ignited within him.

It only took Parker forty-five minutes to throw on clothes, run two blocks to the cell phone store before it closed, purchase a new SIM card, and sprint back to his condo.

Parker hated waste. When he bought his current phone, he debated trading in the old one or selling it for a few extra dollars. In the end, convenience and practicality won out. He used the old device when connected to Wi-Fi to listen to music, watch videos, or dictate session notes before transcribing them into his journal. It was just a spare, a backup for convenience, or if he were to lose his phone or drop it and shatter the screen. Now, the old phone was his lifeline.

Sitting back at his desk, Parker opened the older model's card slot and slid the new SIM card in. He powered it on, and the faint blue screen displayed the familiar logo as it did. Parker released a sigh of relief when he logged in and noted his data updating from the cloud—his contacts, calendar, messages—all his lifelines to the world he missed over the past two days while detained. Parker leaned back, the old phone in his hand a reminder he wasn't entirely cut off. He still had a way to communicate and a means to continue the fight.

The phone buzzed as the data synced, his email alerts, text messages, and voicemail notifications appearing one after another on the screen. Parker felt a pang of both relief and dread. He scrolled through his contacts, pausing at Nick's name, his finger hovering over the screen. He needed to warn and prepare Nick before the police reached him.

Still, he hesitated before finally withdrawing his thumb from the urge to press the screen.

Parker stood and paused. He walked to the sofa and sat down, leaning back to calm himself and regain his composure before doing anything rushed. No, he would review what he missed—catch up on messages, and reassess before proceeding. He needed to be careful.

Phone voicemails were first on Parker's list. His mother had called for her usual Sunday afternoon check-in, the second Sunday in a row he missed. The second voicemail was from Dr. Warren earlier that afternoon when Parker was still in custody.

"Parker, this is Dr. Warren. You weren't in the office today, and we haven't heard from you. I hope everything is all right, but—" There was a short pause, Dr. Warren's frustration dripping off of every word. "Well, Parker," he continued, "To be honest, I'm taken aback by your absence and lack of communication today, especially after our discussion last week."

He paused the recording and considered what he might say when returning the call. Parker would have to face him, but he couldn't tell Dr. Warren the truth. Taken into custody and questioned? That would mean the end of his employment and apprenticeship at the practice. It would likely mean the end of his license, as well. Parker could think of no good reason for his absence or reasonable justification for not informing them of it in advance. Parker hit play and continued Dr. Warren's message.

"Do you have any idea how unacceptable this is? Parker, this behavior is simply untenable. Once is tolerable, but twice—twice is unprofessional. This isn't just about you—it's about the clients who are counting on you. Please give me a call as soon as possible."

Parker's heart sank as he listened to the click. He wondered what Olivia and Alyce might have said about his absence throughout the day. Since neither had called nor left messages, he wondered if they were as disappointed in him as Dr. Warren was.

The new emails were inconsequential; nothing but the usual advertisements, bank confirmation of bills paid, or new credit card charges posted. The senders were familiar: LinkedIn, Amazon, American Express, and links to online articles or YouTube videos Parker sometimes sent to himself for viewing later but rarely made time to revisit.

Parker reviewed his text messages, which, as a practice, he rarely deleted. He scanned his text thread with Nick first, and there was nothing new—not since their meeting Saturday night at Cityside. There was one text, however, from that familiar number received when Nick pulled him away from onlookers and their cellphone cameras following the public altercation with Mark.

[We need to talk ASAP. Call me.] The text had been from Tim. With the police banging at his door early Sunday morning, followed by the interrogation, the text had slipped Parker's mind.

Parker exhaled and rubbed his temples before pressing Tim's contact. The phone barely rang twice before Tim picked up.

"Holy shit, Park," Tim's voice crackled over the line. "Where the hell have you been?"

In the background, Parker heard the faint clink of silverware against plates and the murmur of conversations in the distance.

"It's late there," Parker muttered, almost regretting calling.

"Yeah, but it's fine, we're still up. You know how it is—one more glass of wine turns into three. These people don't even start dinner until ten," Tim chuckled. "Besides, when I saw it was you, I wasn't about to let it go to voicemail."

Parker swallowed. "Yeah. I should've called sooner. It's been a rough couple of weeks."

"Damn right, you should've. I saw the video." Tim's voice carried a sharp edge, something Parker wasn't used to hearing from his friend.

Parker stiffened. "What video?"

"Don't play dumb, man. A buddy of mine was at Cityside and live-streamed the whole damn thing. I had to watch it three times to believe it."

Parker squeezed his eyes shut, the memory of the altercation flashing back—the music pounding, Mark's mockery of him, and his lunging at Mark to grab him by the collar—the way everything spiraled so quickly.

"Yeah, that was—" He stopped, unsure how much to say. "It got out of hand."

Tim scoffed. "Out of hand? Parker, that was a full-blown shitshow. The comments were brutal. People were saying all kinds of stuff—calling you a jealous homewrecker, saying you lost it over the dude's boyfriend. A few even suggested—" He hesitated.

Parker's chest tightened. "Suggested what?"

Tim sighed. "That you might have done something to the guy's boyfriend."

A chill ran down Parker's spine. He turned his gaze to the dark window, his reflection staring back, warped by the night. "That's insane."

"Is it?" Tim's voice softened, losing its edge. "I mean, I know you, Parker. But the way you looked in that video—you weren't yourself."

Parker clenched his jaw, trying to steady his breathing. "I was trying to help them. That's all."

Tim was silent for a moment. Then, in a quieter but more deliberate voice, he asked, "You sure?"

"What's that supposed to mean?"

Tim sighed again as if choosing his words carefully. "Look, you're always the guy looking at the big picture, analyzing everything, searching for hidden meanings. But sometimes, the answer is right in front of you. Sometimes, the truth isn't buried—it's sitting in plain sight, waiting for you to see it."

The words rippled through Parker, shifting inside him like a puzzle piece snapping into place.

Tim continued, "Things are never what they seem, Parker. And when you're stuck, you don't dig deeper—you step back and look at what's been staring at you all along."

Tim's voice cut through the silence. "By the way," Tim added, "what the hell were you doing in a gay bar?"

"What?"

"Cityside. Not exactly your scene." Tim's voice was not judgmental; it was only curiosity. "I mean, you always said it wasn't your thing. Guess things change?"

Parker's mouth was suddenly dry. "I—" His mind scrambled for an answer. Something casual. Something dismissive. "I was meeting someone. It wasn't planned."

"Okay."

The pause that followed was just a little too long.

Tim exhaled. "Look, we'll be home in a week. Just hang in there, alright?"

A week. It might as well have been a year.

"Yeah," Parker murmured. "I will."

"Good. Whatever is going on, be careful, man." Tim's voice was lighter, but the warning beneath it was unmistakable. "You never know who's fooling who."

Parker swallowed hard. No. You never do.

The call ended, and Parker set the phone on the coffee table. He stared at it. Hearing Tim's voice should have been comforting, but it wasn't. The distance between them had never felt wider. Tim would return in a week, but would he ever be able to tell Tim the truth? If he did, would Tim still see him the same way?

Parker let out a slow breath and poured another glass of wine, the bitterness of the liquid matching the bitterness inside him. There were so many things Tim didn't know. And maybe, Parker realized, he might never be able to tell him.

Tim's words swirled in his head. 'Sometimes the answer is right in front of you.' Parker sipped his wine and stared at his phone. 'Sometimes it's sitting in plain sight, waiting for you to see it.'

He was losing everything: his career, relationships, and sense of self. Parker had no one left to turn to. Tim was still overseas, and they had new questions and confessions that might redefine their friendship. Olivia and Alyce were avoiding him. He would never regain Dr. Warren's trust and respect. Nick was—Parker paused.

Thoughts of Nick began to unsettle Parker. Minor inconsistencies once seeming insignificant now demanded attention. The timing of his appearances, how he steered their conversations, and his pointed questions about Devin and Mark all began to feel deliberate, even calculated.

Parker's eyes narrowed, his thoughts turning to the small, inexplicable things that happened recently. Little details hadn't made sense, the strange way Nick would show up at just the right moment, the way he seemed to know things Parker hadn't told him. Parker's gut twisted as the possibilities settled in.

Desperate for answers, Parker picked up his phone. He repeatedly searched his text messages and call logs to piece together timelines. There had to be something here to explain everything.

That's when Parker spotted it—the little red dot in the bottom right-hand corner of the Recorder application. He occasionally used the application to record notations about client sessions or research he was doing—they were reminders to himself, thoughts, and comments he would later transcribe into his journal.

Parker tried to remember the last time he used the application. *It must have been Friday night*, he thought. It was the evening after his third session with Mark and Devin, the night he was reading his entries about them and had difficulty falling asleep. It was the night he decided to venture out and ran into Mark and Devin at Cityside. It was the night Nick poured him so many drinks, and Devin pulled him out to the dance floor. It was the night before he awoke to find Devin in his shower.

His pulse quickened as his eyes scanned the list of recordings, each timestamp a breadcrumb leading to revelations he wasn't sure he was ready to face. What if they contained incriminating evidence? What if they unveiled secrets about him—or someone else? The device's screen glowed like a doorway to his crumbling sense of reality.

There were recordings from each day over the past twelve, some timestamped during the day and some at night. There were multiple recordings from each day. Parker glanced at the top of the screen and saw the auto-record feature switched to voice-activated recording—the phone had been listening, recording. But what had it heard?

He studied the screen's dates and time stamps on the list of recordings. He sat back, letting the sofa engulf his tired body while his finger hovered over the screen. When Parker listened to the first recording on the list, it changed everything.

30

Unmasking the Enemy

(Tuesday the 17th)

Parker arrived at Clover & Thorn an hour early, around 4:00 p.m., giving himself time to settle in before the others showed up. The popular café near Piedmont Park off 10th Street and Monroe Drive bustled with energy. Its open-air feel provided the perfect backdrop for the meeting. Parker chose a booth in the corner to keep an eye on the entrance and watch the people strolling along the promenade outside.

He cradled a cup of hot tea, taking in the mingling scents of roasted beans, fragrant teas, and freshly baked pastries. Time dragged while his leg jittered beneath the table. This Tuesday afternoon, Parker couldn't afford any mistakes.

As Parker sipped the tea, his phone buzzed with a message from Detective Jacobs. He stared at the screen, his thumb hovering over the reply button. The weight of this moment pressed down on him. Parker had made the call that morning, giving Detective Jacobs the details—the place, the time, the evidence he would present. Now, all he needed was for the truth to reveal itself. If this gamble didn't work, everything would fall apart. Parker exhaled slowly, typed a few words, and slipped the phone back into his pocket.

The door swung open, and Nick walked in, his eyes scanning the half-empty café before they locked on Parker. A quick, well-practiced smile spread across his face as he approached.

"Hey, Parker," Nick greeted, his voice warm and too casual. He slid into the seat across from Parker, feigning concern as he reached across the table, placing his palm on Parker's forearm. "How have you been holding up, man?"

Parker tensed, the touch intrusive and unwelcome, and withdrew from Nick's hand. He leaned back, eyes narrowing as he studied Nick's expression. He tried to see beyond the warmth in those bright blue eyes—eyes that conveyed charm and warmth but seemed veiled now.

"I've been better," Parker replied. "I found something."

He called Nick that morning after discovering the recordings the previous night. The unintentional revelations brought clarity to Parker, allowing him to formulate his plan. He asked Nick to meet him on the promise of new evidence—a vital game-changer Nick needed to hear.

Surprise filled Nick's face, his eyebrows lifting, giving him the appearance of curiosity. But Parker caught a brief flicker of unease—just a flash before the mask of composure returned. "Oh? What's that?"

Before Parker could reply, his attention shifted over Nick's shoulder. Mark had just entered the cafe, and Parker's pulse surged. Mark spotted them and tentatively made his way over, his expression quickly shifting from confusion to suspicion.

"What the hell are you two doing together?" Mark said, his tone harsh as he arrived at the table.

Parker's body was a wire ready to snap. "Have a seat, Mark."

Mark's eyes narrowed, his jaw tightening as he slid into the booth beside Nick, effectively boxing him in. "What's this about?"

Nick's reaction was immediate. His eyes widened, a flicker of alarm flashing across his face. He shifted, his body instinctively tensing as Mark's uncomfortable closeness made his casual demeanor nervous. Nick's forced smile wavered as he glanced uneasily between the two men. He cleared his throat, his discomfort palpable as he tried to adjust himself in the cramped space, one hand sliding off the table and disappearing beneath it, as if trying to make himself smaller. Nick's carefree mask quickly cracked under Mark's presence, revealing apprehension beneath.

Parker leaned forward, his voice loud enough to hear but quiet enough to stay between them. It quivered for a second, not from fear but from the effort to keep his rage contained.

"It's about what's going on. I know how both of you tried to set me up," Parker said, his eyes boring into Nick's before shifting to Mark. "You manipulated me, you planted evidence, and you tried to make me believe I was losing my mind. But it's not going to work anymore."

Parker's pulse raced as he watched Mark's face twist with realization. For the first time in weeks, he sensed a flicker of control, a hope he could reclaim his life. But beneath satisfaction, a dull ache reminded him of everything he'd lost— his reputation, friendships, and carefully constructed life—all shattered by this betrayal. Even now, the bitterness of loss lingered, threatening to overshadow his resolve.

Mark laughed. It was a spontaneous laugh, the type of response one sometimes can't entirely control. It sounded jagged, raw, and mocking, as if forced from his chest. "You're crazy, Parker. You're not well, man."

"Oh, I'm not?" Parker's eyes burned into Mark's. The edge in his voice sharpened, cutting through the noise of the café. "What if I told you I have proof of what the two of you did?"

Mark shifted his expression, a mix of anger and disbelief. "This is ridiculous, shithead. You're trying to blame me for your delusions."

Nick just sat and listened, his gaze shifting between the two men as they squared off against one another. He abruptly changed his mind about being there; he had no interest in Parker's new information and wished he hadn't come. Nick's fingers drummed anxiously on his thigh under the table, betraying the confidence he tried to project.

"Am I?" Parker countered to Mark. Parker pulled his cell phone from his pocket, holding it up briefly before sliding it back beneath the table, his thumb hovering over the play button. He kept his voice low, but his gaze never wavered from Mark's. "Why don't we let this recording speak for itself?"

Nick's face tightened for just a split second—barely visible—before he plastered a nervous smile back on. "Why don't you two take this somewhere more private?"

"Why?" Parker asked. "You've got nothing to hide, so right here should be fine."

Nick's expression finally cracked. His eyes darted towards the door, the muscles in his jaw clenching. He moved to exit the booth, but Mark blocked him.

"Sit," Mark barked, his tone rigid. "Let's hear this supposed proof."

Nick swallowed hard, his breathing shallow as he sank back into the booth.

Parker pressed play, and the tinny sound of Devin's voice on speakerphone filled the small space between them.

Nick's voice was on the recording first, tinged with amusement.

"Look at him, Mr. Control, completely out of it."

A chuckle between them erupted, low and mocking.

Devin's voice joined in, the rustle of clothing audible as he moved closer to the phone lying under the journal on the nightstand. It was where Parker had placed it before his impromptu Friday night outing to Cityside.

"It's kinda sad. All his discipline and restraint, and now here lay Doc—naked, helpless, and exposed in his own bed."

Devin's voice on the recording was dripping with ridicule, cruel glee lacing every word.

"Honestly, it makes you wonder if he ever really had it together."

Nick laughed softly in the audio.

"Not so perfect after all, huh?"

Devin's tone became more affectionate.

"Shame, I was growing to like him. He's going to be okay, right?"

There was a pause, followed by a sigh that sounded like pity, then Nick's voice.

"Yeah, of course. It was just a roofie. Dumbshit is a lightweight, I guess."

Mark's eyes narrowed as the realization set in. The betrayal cut deeper than he anticipated from his conversation with Parker earlier that morning. Mark had directed his anger at Parker for weeks, convinced he was the culprit. But now, the narrative unraveled in his mind, each thread leading back to Nick and Devin. Mark's jaw tightened as humiliation mingled with fury. They played him, and he hated the taste of it. He clenched his fists, the veins in his forearms bulging as he processed the truth. This wasn't just manipulation; it was a calculated, cruel betrayal.

They both turned to Nick, who reeled as if struck by a heavy blow. His face went pale, his eyes wide with panic. His lips parted, but no words came out. He swallowed hard, his gaze darting between Parker and Mark. The tension in his body was apparent as he tried to force an uncomfortable smile. Finally, he shifted, his voice trembling as he spoke.

"Parker, listen, it was just a stupid prank. We didn't mean to—I think this is all a big misunderstanding."

As Nick scrambled to explain himself, Parker felt the power of the recording in his hand. "Before we go further," he said, his voice cutting through the tension, "let's hear what you have to say, Nick. And I mean everything." He placed the phone on the table, its screen dark but loaded with evidence, a silent threat hanging over them. "Because once I press play, there's no going back."

Nick moved to stand, his body already angling towards the edge of the booth, but Mark's hand shot out, gripping Nick's thigh and shoving him back down to the seat forcefully. The thud of Nick hitting the seat reverberated through the booth, and Mark leaned in close, his voice low and threatening.

"You're not going anywhere. Sit down. I want to hear more," Mark growled, his eyes locked onto Nick's with a dangerous intensity. Mark's fingers dug into Nick's shoulder with his other hand, his knuckles whitening as the grip tightened. The threat was unspoken but crystal clear. Mark glanced at Parker. "Play it," he commanded.

Parker hit play, and it was Devin's voice again.

"Hey, we should have some fun with this. Go get your phone."

Chuckling could be heard, followed by the distinct sound of a hand brushing across fabric and the creak of the bed as bodies shifted about. Nick gave directions to Devin, followed by unmistakable kissing sounds in the background. The sounds were close and intimate.

Nick's face crumpled, his eyes filling with desperate fear. His lips trembled as if words could somehow undo what they were hearing.

"It wasn't just about Devin," Nick admitted, his voice cracking. "You don't know what it's like to feel invisible—always to be the guy in the background, serving others. Devin promised—he said we'd have something better. We could leave all this behind and start fresh. I believed him. God, I wanted to believe him."

Parker wanted to leap over the table in a rage despite the number of times he had listened to the recording the night before. He memorized the cruelty and knew what to expect. He didn't, though. Too many questions remained unanswered.

The recording crackled momentarily, followed by Nick's voice.

"You know, once we're out of here, we'll have nothing to worry about. Just you and me."

They could hear Devin sigh contentedly.

"Yeah, you and me, away from all these assholes."

Nick laughed in the recording, the sound both tender and wicked. There was another short period of silence, just the faint sound of their breathing before Devin whispered.

"Come on, let's go."

There was movement again, followed by Devin's final words.

"Hey, grab his watch."

But only one of them left the condo that night.

The recording clicked off automatically after a period of silence. Parker's eyes locked on Nick's expressionless face, but the icy water in his eyes said everything.

Mark's face twisted as he processed the words. Parker watched the confusion give way to understanding, followed by anger. He had believed Parker was guilty, yet here it was—the truth.

Nick, now visibly panicking, tried to push past Mark again.

But this time, it was Parker who leaned forward, voice cold. "You're not going anywhere." Parker's gaze bore into Nick, his voice trembling with anger and hurt.

Mark kept his left arm around Nick's shoulders and grabbed his arm with his right hand, squeezing it and leaning into him to hold him in place. Anyone looking in their direction might have thought the two men were a couple embracing. Nick tried to flinch, to shake loose, but Mark held firm.

Nick sagged, the fight draining from his limbs as Mark's grip held him in place. "I'm sorry, Parker," he said, on the verge of tears. "It was Devin's idea. It wasn't supposed to go as far as it did."

"Where's Devin, you little shit," Mark demanded to know. He balled his fist and appeared ready to gut-punch Nick in the ribs had Parker not interjected.

"You drugged me, Nick." Parker's voice was sharp, cutting through Nick's stammering. "You took pictures. You stole my watch. Why, Nick? I trusted you." Parker's voice cracked—the vulnerability in it betraying the fierce expression on his face.

"I'm sorry," Nick restated, choking up as his will yielded, a tear running down his cheek. "We took you home when you passed out that Friday night. Devin just wanted to have some fun. He wanted to hook up with you but knew you would never go for that. It was innocent at first, but then he—" Nick paused.

"He what?" snarled Mark.

"He wanted to hurt you," Nick replied with tear-filled blue eyes. The confession seemed to drain what little fight he had left. "He wanted to make you jealous, Mark."

"Where IS he?" Mark once again demanded.

"I don't know," Nick barked back, his voice cutting sharply through the café's hum before the surrounding noise swallowed it again. "We argued," he added, his tone dropping, the words hesitant. "Once things started getting out of hand, I got to know Parker better." Nick's eyes shifted to Parker, filled with a desperate plea for forgiveness mingled with a longing that was now painfully unreachable. Whatever hope he may have had of being with Parker was now and forever lost.

"Whose blood is on the watch, Nick." Parker's question was direct and rigid.

"No one's," Nick replied. "It's fake blood—actor's prop. Devin had it. It was his idea—"

Parker slammed his fist on the table, and Nick jumped back. It also surprised and jolted Mark. "You asshole," he shouted at Nick. "You had me arrested! You cost me my job!"

The outburst drew the attention of their immediate surroundings this time. Parker felt their stares, the scattered whispers prickling at the edges of his awareness. A barista paused mid-pour, the steady stream of coffee splashing onto the counter as her wide eyes locked on the scene. Chairs scraped against the floor as a few patrons shifted, caught between morbid curiosity and the instinct to retreat. The energy in the café changed, tense and expectant, like the air before a lightning strike.

Parker could barely contain his rage, all sense of control now exhausted. He lunged across the table at Nick. The charge caught Mark by surprise, and he instinctively released his grip on Nick to protect himself. When he did, Nick recoiled and pushed his hands against the tabletop and seatback, scrambling upward and out across the table and over Mark. Mark's hands flailed as he did, trying to grab Nick's legs, forcing him to trip and fall to the floor.

The abrupt outburst and commotion of movement caused tables and booths around them to jump and scramble from the sudden and confusing chaos.

Two men from the booth directly behind Mark and Nick swiftly stormed out of their seats and pounced on Nick, one of them flashing a badge and bellowing, "APD!" The men instructed the crowd to stand back. The second man, Detective Miller, held a knee against Nick's back and pulled his arm around his waist to place his cuffs around his thin wrists.

Nick's face went pale, pressed against the hard tile of the café floor—his bravado collapsing into raw, unguarded fear. His breath came in ragged gasps as he lay trembling beneath the pressure of Detective Miller's knee against his back. His mind raced, clawing for a way out, but the reality of his actions crashed over him like a tidal wave. He thought of Devin—how this started as a game, a reckless thrill—and how quickly it had spiraled beyond their control. Now, the one person he trusted had abandoned him. A tear slid down his cheek, born of fear and the sharp sting of regret.

"No, no, you don't understand." Nick sputtered, his voice breaking as Miller cuffed him. His eyes appealed to Parker, but Parker's reply was icy and unyielding.

The satisfaction of the moment didn't feel as sweet as Parker imagined it would—tinged with bitterness and regret for everything lost along the way.

"Nick Owens," Miller shouted above the noise of people shuffling out of the way as the detectives raised Nick to his feet and moved toward the door. "You're under arrest for conspiracy, administering a drug with intent to commit a crime, reckless endangerment, assault, unlawful restraint, and theft. You have the right to remain silent—"

The detectives led Nick out of the café. Parker and Mark followed, joined by two other plain-clothed officers posted outside. As the group left, the crowd inside slowly filled the space again, conversations resuming as the patrons strained to witness what was happening outside. Parker's gamble, his phone calls this morning, first to Nick, then to Mark, and finally to the detectives, paid off.

Parker stood next to Mark while the police led Nick away. He was the first to speak, his sturdy demeanor inside the café beginning to sink into exhaustion. "I'm sorry for breaking into your house, Mark. I didn't mean for all of this to happen."

Mark's eyes trained on Parker's. "No, I'm the one that should apologize. I believed it, you know. I thought you and Devin…" He trailed off, shaking his head. "Then I was sure you did something terrible. Everything pointed to you."

Parker nodded, a hollow feeling in his chest. "I know. And I understand why you did. I don't blame you."

Parker glanced at Mark, meeting his eyes. There was exhaustion there, mixed with softer, apologetic remorse.

"What now?" Mark asked.

Parker slid his hands into his pockets, exhaling deeply. "I don't know—talk to the detectives, get my truck and stuff back, sort out the details, I guess. There's a lot to unpack. There's a lot to fix. But at least it's over."

Mark nodded, his expression conflicted. He opened his mouth as if to say something but didn't. After a moment, he told Parker, "I'm sorry for what I believed and some of the things I said. I hated you. For weeks, I hated you. I thought you'd taken everything from me. But now—now I don't even know what to feel. Anger? Guilt?" He shook his head.

Parker nodded and gave Mark a weary but accepting smile. "So, what about Devin?" he asked.

"Devin's twisted games. He knows how to break people." Mark's expression darkened, his gaze turning inward as if wrestling with unvoiced thoughts. "Devin always knew how to vanish when things got messy," he muttered, his voice lowered. "But trust me, Parker—he's not finished with either of us yet."

His words lingered a grim warning, sending a chill crawling down Parker's spine. Was he?

"What he did was terrible," Mark added, "to us both."

The two men still had unanswered questions. They were led away, separately, Parker by Detective Jacobs and Mark by Detective Miller.

There were statements to take, reports to write, and the tangled threads of deception to unravel. As Parker walked away from the café, flanked by detectives, a cold clarity settled over him. Nick's revelations weren't the end—far from it. There were still pieces missing, questions unanswered, and the ghost of Devin looming over them all.

31

Regret and Remorse

(Wednesday the 18th)

The holding cell was dim. Nick sat with his back against the cold wall, knees drawn up, the scratchy blanket wrapped around his shoulders offering little comfort. The air was stale and heavy with the scent of bleach, sweat, and despair.

He hadn't slept. Every time he closed his eyes, Devin's face flashed behind his eyelids—smiling, charming, and cruel. Nick let his head fall against the wall, a hollow sigh escaping his lips. How had he been so stupid? It all started in the shadows of the dance floor at Cityside, where alcohol blurred judgment, Devin maneuvering like he owned the place—like he owned Nick. And maybe, for a while, he did.

~

(Two weeks earlier)

The neon glow pulsed over the crowded dance floor, bodies swaying, heat rising, the air thick with cologne and liquor. Devin leaned casually against the bar, watching Parker from across the room, his smirk growing as Parker quietly nurtured his cocktail.

Nick stood beside him, his arms crossed, watching Parker too—but for a different reason.

"He's pathetic," Devin murmured into his drink, taking a slow sip before setting the cup down.

Nick didn't respond.

Devin turned toward him, raising an eyebrow. "What?"

Nick shook his head. "Nothing."

Devin exhaled, eyes back on Parker, staring into his drink like it held the answers to all of life's mysteries. "It's kind of sad, don't you think?"

Nick glanced over. "What's sad?"

Devin gestured toward Parker. "Look at him. All wound up, all repressed. I'd bet money he doesn't even jerk off unless it's scheduled on his calendar." Grinning, Devin swirled the ice in his drink. "But I bet if you get a few drinks in him, he's just like the rest of us."

Nick frowned. "Maybe, but he's *not* like the rest of us."

Devin's smirk faded. "Yeah. That's exactly why we're doing this."

Nick turned toward Devin. "No, really. Why are you doing this?"

Devin's eyes gleamed with something Nick couldn't quite read—amusement? Spite? Hunger?

"Because I can."

Nick's stomach churned. It wasn't just the insult—it was the truth beneath it. While he poured drinks for strangers, Devin was already a step ahead, scheming, planning. Nick had always been good at reading people, but Devin had slipped past his defenses, wrapping him in a plan from which he wasn't sure he could escape.

"You're not just trying to screw over Mark, you want to mess with Parker too?"

Devin grinned. "Oh, babe. I can multitask." He leaned in closer, his voice dropping to a conspiratorial whisper. "That's why you're stuck bartending for tips while I'm about to walk away with enough money to disappear for good."

Nick looked at Devin, really looked at him, and he saw it all—the calculation, the cruelty, the sheer delight Devin took in wrecking things.

Nick turned his attention back toward the bar and the growing evening crowd. He needed a way out.

A couple of days later, the house smelled like clean linen and faint cologne, the artificial scent of curated imperfection. Technically, it was Mark's house—everything Devin loved about their arrangement and everything he despised.

Nick sat on the worn but comfortable leather couch, flipping an unlit cigarette between his fingers. At the same time, Devin paced in front of him, his expression taut with frustration.

"We need to move fast," Devin said abruptly. He was talking more to himself than Nick. "Mark's already halfway checked out. If I play this right, he'll be the one to end things."

Nick looked at Devin with mild amusement. "And you want that? I thought you liked this comfy little arrangement."

Devin shot him a look. "Please. I'm bored out of my fucking mind." He flopped into the chair across from Nick, propping an ankle over his knee. "You have no idea how exhausting it is—always being 'too much,' always having to tone it down." He mimicked Mark's deep, measured voice. "'Devin, do you have to be so loud?' 'Devin, do you always have to make a scene?'"

Nick smirked. "To be fair, you do love an audience."

Devin waved him off. "Mark just doesn't get it. I'm meant to be more than some aging attorney's afterthought." His gaze sharpened. "And so are you."

Nick stiffened, but before he could respond, Devin leaned forward. "Think about it. Parker's practically unraveling already. He thinks he's so untouchable—so in control." Devin's lips curled into a knowing smirk. "But he's already doubting himself, isn't he?"

Nick rolled his shoulders, feigning indifference. "I don't know. He's different than I expected."

Devin's expression darkened. He leaned in, close enough that Nick could smell the faint trace of cigarettes and gin clinging to his breath. "You're not getting soft on me, are you?"

Nick scoffed, but the breath caught in his throat. For a moment, he almost laughed—Devin played the part so well, like a gangster about to plant the kiss of death on him. But the gleam in his eyes wasn't an act. Devin wasn't laughing.

"He's not special, Nicky," Devin said, voice laced with something bitter. "You think he's different? He's just like Mark—another over-educated, self-righteous hypocrite who thinks he's better than us." Devin's fingers drummed against the armrest, his smirk fading. "You should've seen how he looked at me in that last session. Like he fucking pitied me. Like I was some reckless mess."

Nick didn't reply. He had seen how Parker looked at Devin but also something else—something Devin refused to understand. Devin didn't repulse Parker. If anything, Parker was attracted to him, but he'd rather suffocate himself than admit it.

Nick's mind raced, scrambling to find the thread that might unravel this whole plan. But Devin's confidence was like a fog, thick and overpowering. Nick told himself he was doing what he had to—surviving like always. But the lies didn't fit as neatly as they used to.

Devin exhaled, regaining his composure. "We'll push him a little further. If we do this right, we won't have to force it—he'll convince himself."

Nick frowned. "And if he doesn't?"

"Then we give him a little nudge."

"And what happens when Mark catches on? Or Parker? You think they're really that stupid?"

Devin's laugh was light and dismissive. "Oh, honey, Parker doesn't know which way is up. He's scrambling. Second-guessing everything. It's delicious to watch."

"If he's already spiraling, why push him?"

"Because it's fun," Devin said, stretching like a satisfied cat. "And because Mark's pissing me off."

Nick sighed, rubbing his temples. "So this is about Mark now?"

Devin rolled his eyes. "It's about both of them. Mark thinks he can fix me like I'm some broken little stray he picked off the street. And Parker—" he scoffed. "Parker has the nerve to take his side. Can you believe that? He looks at me like I'm some spoiled gold-digger who needs a sugar daddy. I'm going to make sure they both pay. And when it's done, I'll walk away with my hands clean."

Nick hesitated. "Devin, you shouldn't—"

Devin stood and stretched, already bored of the conversation. "Relax, babe. By the time Parker realizes what's happening, we'll be long gone."

Nick watched him disappear into the bedroom. He had played a lot of games in his life, but this time, he wasn't sure he wanted to play anymore.

~

Nick sat in the holding cell, his head against the cold cement wall, Devin's words still echoing in his mind. 'Because I can.' He rubbed his hands over his face, closing his eyes again as childhood recollections surged, unbidden.

He was eight again, crouched in the shadow of his mother's rage, her voice echoing off the grimy walls of the trailer. "You're both useless! Damn babies, both of ya," she screamed, slamming her palm against the filthy countertop. Her face was flushed, her words slurred from the vodka she'd been nursing since noon. His older brother stood rigid and defiant, absorbing her insults like a punching bag as she hurled dirty dishes filled with spent cigarette butts and ash at him.

Nick learned to stay quiet, shrinking into the corner with his tattered stuffed rabbit clutched to his chest. Silence was his shield, his way of disappearing to avoid becoming the target of her wrath. He would slip out of the trailer undetected when the storm passed, like a shadow—unseen and unscathed.

By the time Nick was a teenager, he'd figured out how to stay one step ahead—read people, charm them, and twist their expectations to his advantage. He told himself it was a skill, a gift, but deep down, he knew it was born from necessity. The polished charisma was the armor he built to survive the volatility of his childhood.

Cityside had been his sanctuary, a stage where he controlled his roles. Bartending and dancing were all performance art, a way to remain untouchable. His youthfulness, charm, and wit were tools sharpened to keep the world at a safe distance. What others saw as personality was his survival mechanism, perfected over years of slipping between shadows.

Devin saw that. He unraveled Nick—saw through the mask to the loneliness beneath. Devin's charm worked like a drug, numbing Nick to the warning signs, weaving lies and promises that felt real until they unraveled. "We'll get out of here, you and me," Devin had whispered, his voice smooth as silk. "We just need to finish this."

Nick believed him. He believed in Devin's plan, the idea of a fresh start. But then there was Parker.

Parker changed things. He wasn't pretending. Unlike Devin, who devoured people, or Mark, who held them at arm's length, Parker was vulnerable—he craved connection. Nick had spent years decoding masks, but he saw Parker wearing none—he saw only trust, uncomplicated and unguarded. That terrified Nick more than Devin's cruelty ever could.

Nick's fists clenched. He had wanted to stop it, to tell Parker the truth, but fear had kept him silent. Devin had a way of making sure you couldn't say no. His control was a subtle chokehold—you didn't realize he had you until you were already gasping for air. Devin twisted reality to make you believe you were in control when you were nothing more than a pawn. It was his gift—his poison.

The truth crashed over Nick, relentless as a wave. He had delivered the box—the watch, the photos, the police—all set in motion by his hands. Devin, wherever he was, wasn't coming back to save him.

Nick remembered Parker's green eyes, how they burned with anger and hurt during their final confrontation. Nick wanted to explain, to make Parker see he wasn't the monster he appeared to be. But what could he say? That he was weak, that he had let himself be used? That he had fallen for the man he was supposed to help destroy?

Nick leaned back against the wall, each press of bone against cement a reminder of where choices and circumstances had led him. He had been running his whole life—escaping the poverty, his mother's cruelty, his insecurities. But there was no escape now. Not from this cell. Not from what he did.

The small, fragile voice inside him whispered of longing, regret, and the faintest hope for redemption. He didn't know if he deserved forgiveness or could ever earn it. But as he sat in the cold silence of the holding cell, he knew one thing for sure— he and Parker were not so different.

I'm sorry," he whispered into the silence. But silence doesn't forgive, and what do apologies mean when you're the one who struck the match?

32

Postcard From the Edge

(Friday the 20ᵗʰ)

Dusk settled over the Midtown skyline, wrapping the city in muted grays and blues. Parker stood before the glass, his reflection barely discernible against the gathering night. Three days passed since his confrontation with Nick, yet the emptiness inside him remained. His once-pristine condo perched above the city no longer felt like a sanctuary. The space mirrored the hollow void within him—a testament to how far he'd fallen.

Parker believed he could walk the thin line between control and chaos. Structure, discipline, and routine were his armor, his defense against the unpredictable forces of life. But in the end, control was nothing more than a fragile illusion, shattered by the slightest tremor of truth. Chaos wasn't the enemy, he now understood. It was a part of him, an unrelenting shadow he could never escape.

Behind him, the condo reflected his unraveling. Papers cluttered the coffee table, books lay discarded on random pages, and dishes stacked in the sink—starkly contrasting the meticulous order he once maintained.

Parker turned from the window and walked to his desk,

sinking into his desk chair. The weight of exhaustion clung to him, heavy and unearned, as if even stillness demanded too much.

On his desk, the picture of Devin and him smiling at what seemed an unguarded and happy moment caught his eye. He hadn't remembered the occasion, but the image was painfully vivid. He picked it up and held it. Fragments of memories surfaced: Devin's laughter, the intensity of his gaze, the warmth of his presence.

Tears welled in Parker's eyes as he placed the photo back on the desk. Regret gnawed at him, not just for what he lost but for what he was too afraid to pursue. Devin's presence, real or imagined, awakened a longing within him—a yearning for connection he buried too deeply to confront.

His old cell phone ringing startled him, and he hesitated before answering. When he did, his voice was hoarse from days in isolated silence and not speaking. There had been no one to talk to and nothing to say.

"Parker," Detective Jacobs said on the other end, his tone measured. "We need to talk. There's been a development."

Detective Jacobs' call provided clarity but no comfort. During interrogation, Nick admitted to helping Devin orchestrate the fear and paranoia that consumed him. Devin and Nick's manipulation was a cruel game, and Parker had been their victim.

The blood on the watch wasn't real—it was, in fact, stage blood. The detective apologized and explained they would need to retain it as evidence regarding charges against Nick and Devin. Parker was free, however, to reclaim his car, phone, and laptop at the station. The detective failed to mention Parker's earlier story about the blood on his watch, damaged in a biking accident.

Nick would take a plea deal to conspiracy, theft, and drugging Parker but was unable to reveal Devin's location or endgame. The authorities were closing the case with Nick's confession, yet Parker knew there was still more truth to uncover.

"There's one more thing, Mr. Grant," Detective Jacobs added. "We've reviewed the video footage from your building."

"Yes?" Parker responded.

"It's clear Devin Marchand and Nick Owens accompanied you into your apartment in the early morning hours of Saturday, the 6th. It was only Nick Owens, however, who left your residence four hours later. It seems your client, Devin Marchand, was with you until Sunday evening."

"Devin?" Parker asked, connecting the true meaning of the detective's words.

"Yes, Mr. Grant. We have footage of Devin walking through your lobby and exiting the building at 10:04 p.m. on Sunday, the 7th. Can you recall that?"

Could it *all* have been just a game? Parker's heart pounded as he tried to piece together the fractured timelines, the truths buried beneath layers of lies.

"So Devin didn't leave until Sunday night? He walked out? By himself?" Parker asked for clarification.

"That's correct. The footage collaborates with the confession by Nick Ownes."

"No sir," answered Parker. "Sorry, I can't recall. The whole weekend is sort of a blur, to be honest. Everything after Friday night, I'm afraid."

"It's understandable, Mr. Grant, considering the dose of Rohypnol. The effects can be intense when combined with alcohol: cognitive fog, emotional instability, physical weakness, and especially memory gaps. As a precaution, you may want to check in with your physician to let him know."

Parker's grip on the phone tightened as he struggled to process Detective Jacob's words. Relief and confusion swirled together, a tempest of emotion crashing against the fragile walls of his composure.

Devin was alive. He had walked out of Parker's condo unscathed and very much alive. Parker's mind, always racing to fill the gaps with horror and self-doubt, stuttered against the truth and its implications. The blood wasn't real. Devin wasn't dead. Parker's hands were clean—but his mind remained stained with doubt and grief.

Anguish swelled, swallowing the brief whisper of relief. If Devin had been alive and walked out Sunday night alone, their weekend together must have happened. The touches, the whispers, the vulnerability—Parker hadn't imagined those. But they were tainted now, marred by manipulation and deceit. What he thought was a connection had been nothing more than another thread in Devin and Nick's twisted game.

"Mr. Grant?" Detective Jacobs' voice filtered through the phone, steady and grounding. "Are you still there?"

"Yes," Parker managed, his voice thin and fragile. "Thank you, Detective."

He hung up and let the phone slip from his fingers, the dull thud as it hit the floor echoing in the silence. Parker remained still, his body carved from stone, as the truth settled into him. He was free from the nightmare, yet the emotional chains remained.

Unable to return to the practice, Parker resigned. He knew Dr. Warren wasn't going to let him return. He also knew he couldn't sit in therapy sessions pretending to help others while feeling so damaged himself. Resigning was a small act of control in an otherwise unmoored life.

He gazed out the window again, his reflection in the glass nearly unrecognizable. The ball cap on his head, the same one he had imagined placing on Devin's head, felt oddly comforting. It was a stark reminder of how thoroughly his mind had unraveled.

The photograph on the desk drew his attention once more. He knew his time with Devin was real, but not in the way he had imagined. The moments they shared—laughter, touches—perhaps nothing more than his mind's way of coping with his unprofessional and taboo attraction to Devin and his inability to act on his suppressed desires. They were nothing more than fantasies, consistent with themes of self-deception and repression.

Yet, as Parker stared at the image, a quiet wish stirred within him. In another realm of reality somewhere, he hoped there was a version of him brave enough to embrace the authenticity he craved.

He sank deeper into the chair, his thoughts shifting. Maybe the answer wasn't in controlling every aspect of his life but in accepting the chaos. It wasn't the enemy—it was a mirror, reflecting the parts of himself he had been too terrified to confront.

Parker stood, and a glint of white drew his attention. His hand hesitated over the stack of mail, a prickling sensation spreading across his skin. When he finally pulled the slim object free, the postcard slipped from his fingers, fluttering to the floor like a severed leaf. It landed face up, the words sharp and taunting:

"Miss me yet?"

The phrase hit like a physical blow—his mind raced, the world narrowing to the thin rectangle of cardstock on the floor. The ache in Parker's chest flared, spreading like wildfire through his body. He reached down, picked up the postcard, and traced the letters with a shaking finger as though their touch might reveal answers. The letters seemed to shift, the ink almost wet. Parker rubbed his eyes, but the words remained steady and taunting.

Then came the scent—a faint trace of damp earth, the loamy richness of soil clinging to his memory. His fingers tingled with phantom sensations: the weight of loose dirt, the slick cold of it sliding through his hands. The room tilted, the air too thin, as fractured memories clawed at the edges of his mind.

Parker forced himself to focus, every nerve screaming for answers. He stood, his knees unsteady, and moved to the front door. His fingers tightened around the deadbolt, twisting it to lock. But as the click filled the silence of the space, he knew it wouldn't hold—not against the chaos—not against Devin.

END

Thank You!

I greatly appreciate the time you took to give my book a read. As a small indie publisher, it means a lot, and I hope you enjoyed the story. You are making a difference in my journey as a writer!

If you have a few minutes, **please consider leaving your honest feedback on Amazon.** Your review or rating means the world to me and helps other potential readers decide if this story is right for them. You can still leave reviews on Amazon even if you obtained the book elsewhere. Reader feedback does wonders for a book, and I would love to hear about your experiences reading it!

Thank you again for your support!

Acknowledgments

Completing this novel would not have been possible without the encouragement and support of the following people, all of whom I am deeply indebted.

To **Juan Delgado.** Thank you for your expert proofreading skills and input while developing the plot and characters.

To my beta readers, **Juan Delgado, Jo Ciccarello, David Singleton, Michael Casisi, Nanc Van Fleet, Pax Straub, and David Middleton**. Thank you for the hours spent reading those early drafts and your invaluable feedback.

To my cover designer and artist, **Juan Jose Padron**. Thank you for the countless tweaks and adjustments necessary throughout the production process. (https://jcovers.com/)

To **Paul Myrick**. Thank you for designing, building, and maintaining my website. (https://pmyrick.com/)

LET'S STAY CONNECTED

I have many stories in the works to offer you in the future. Please visit my website for a complete list of past and upcoming works. For exclusive updates and announcements, please use the QR code below to subscribe. Thank You!

https://www.djciccarello.com/

Thank you again for your support!